THE BROKEN KEY

A NOVEL

PAUL KILGORE

*All my best,
Paul*

MCP
BOOKS

MCP Books
2301 Lucien Way #415
Maitland, FL 32751
407·339·4217
www.MCPBooks.com

ISBN-13: 978-1-63505-559-7
LCCN: 2017900922

Distributed by Itasca Books

To those who have unfailingly graced my work with their support: my parents; Emily and Mara; Robert S. P. Gardner; and Becky, always Becky

HOME

L ife is lived entirely between the ears. I've believed this for a quarter of a century. The insight first arrived while watching Charlie Boyle.

Who, being Charlie, was focused on living between two very different appendages. "I know what you're thinking," he said while hovering over Marian Blake, a malevolent magnifying glass burning away a ladybug. "You could be my great granddaughter."

Marian responded with a small, exasperated smile. "It's not about me, it's not about you. Tonight of all nights. The story tonight"–nodding in my direction–"is Tom."

Charlie followed her gaze. The subtle mix of disappointment and resentment in his expression would on any other occasion have been amusing: he truly believed that with Marian he had a chance. "I suppose there's no point in anyone leaving tonight before Tom tells us just what in the hell he was thinking."

We had not known one another even four months ago. And then we had sat in the same classrooms day after day–obedient to, of all things, a seating chart–scratching our way through Socratic foolishness and tortuous pedantry, puzzling over eight-hundred-page tomes filled like fruit crates with rotting judicial opinions. A peculiarity of law school was the way it dispensed with the quizzes, papers, and periodic exams that constituted the flotsam and jetsam of undergraduate progress. Fifteen weeks of unvarying classes, the uneasiness–terror, for some–of moving into each new week without having grasped the fundamentals of the last. In that era legal education encouraged the conceit of baptism by fire. Maybe it still does today. There was some truth to this, probably because even the students were invested in the conceit. Competition was never far from the surface: no one was quite sure who was *getting* it. Was I? Only a three-hour test, the sole exam of that first year first semester, would tell. When the results bounced back at us–maybe over the holiday break, was the rumor; so much about law school was rumor–we would know our places. We would live the rest of three years, maybe much longer, in those places.

The examination had begun at three o'clock, ninety minutes before a mid-December Minnesota nightfall. Now, five hours later, two dozen of us had staked claim to the booths and tables of what had become our favorite Seven Corners house of solace. I had arrived first, and knew I would be the first to leave. But not yet: though leaving would be only the latest of the irreversible decisions I had been making my entire life, it seemed to me now, in that moment, the most consequential.

Marian gave a sigh and looked into a corner of the high, faux-tin ceiling. The dry air lifted strands of her dark hair off the shoulders of the thick, collared sweater she was wearing. "So exhausted," she said. Looking then at Charlie: "That third question, the one about anticipatory breach." She paused. "It *was* about anticipatory breach, wasn't it?"

"Not thinking about that anymore. What's done is done. We're released until January."

"Tom?" Marian asked. "Did you think that third question –" Her eyes widened in alarm. "I'm sorry," she said. "Oh my God."

I pushed a wave at her and shook my head slowly. It was funny, though, how only in the past few hours had the semester come into focus. All the parts indeed made a whole. Yes, that third demand for an explication had been asking about anticipatory breach of a contract, and I was fairly certain I could expound on the subject to the satisfaction of the most unreasonably demanding law professor. The idea of the exam had been daunting, but the exam itself had been straightforward. This discovery, though, had arrived late.

Now three others appeared. Jason and Clay had been in my study group; with Clay was his wife Tess, a day-care worker who had appeared at two or three social events through the fall.

"Clay's trying to make a fool of me," Tess said, looking my way.

"Hey, Tess." I smiled. "It's true. Not the fool part, of course. Never. But Clay wasn't lying to you."

"It's true? How? I mean, tell me about it step by step." Jason smiled at her audacity.

"Not so much to tell." For the past few hours I had been debating whether I *wanted* to tell, never mind what I might say. But I was still hanging out with the class, still at Seven Corners as the punishing night tightened its grip. So I must have decided that talking would be necessary.

"I'm trying to imagine the scene. All fifty of you in the lecture hall –"

"One hundred of us. They combined two sections for the final."

"One hundred. And Clay said there were eight questions."

"Yes."

"What question were you on?"

I paused. "I'm not sure, Tess. I'd have to think about that."

"It was right away, wasn't it?" said Jason.

"No," said Clay. "Me, I just thought you had finished early. Not confoundingly early."

"You're both off," said Marian, who had been observing the exchange with what seemed to me an unnecessary measure of the guilt you feel slowing down to gaze upon a wreck. My age—I was no pre-law lockstep; I had been around—had earned me a deference I wouldn't have received had I, like them, come to school a year or two from college. Then again, Charlie was even older than I and generally thought a buffoon. But that could be attributed to his absence of seriousness, his *randiness*—a trait that wasn't helpful to someone even a bit younger or older than his companions. "It wasn't at the beginning but it was way too early. No one thought you were finished, Tom."

"What did everyone think?" Tess demanded. "I mean, did you make a scene?"

"I hope not." And suddenly I was servant to an urge to tell the story so I would never have to tell it again, at least to anyone associated with the university. As though I would be likely to see any of these people again after walking out of the room.

"Contracts was a hard class," I said. "We all thought so. Which meant the examination would be hard. Look, classes ended last Friday. If they give you a whole empty week to study every waking hour, the exam damn well better be a killer.

"But it wasn't a killer. I looked it over. Counted eight questions. Didn't read any except the first."

"Which was the worst of the bunch," said Jason.

"Maybe," I smiled. "I'm not the one to ask." I paused to reach for a glass that turned out to be empty. "So I plowed through it, trying to recall what Priley had said way back in September, trying to picture in my mind's eye the page of my outline that might be germane. And also thinking about time, three hours divided by eight being . . . ."

"Twenty-two minutes, thirty seconds," Clay said. "We all wasted a minute making that computation."

"And by God, I got her done in twenty-five or so, close enough. I'd have to improve, and do it seven more times."

"Ugh," said Tess.

"And that's how it went. The second one, elements of contract formation, a bit easier, and then the third about anticipatory breach. But the fourth –"

"Harder?" Tess asked, being drawn in by my story. With the baby fat in her cheeks she struck me as little-sister young; incredibly, earlier in the year she had been sitting on a stage, wearing a college cap and gown, playing the part of the beaming graduate. "Really hard?"

"I have no idea." But the moment was returning. "I read it through, and the only thought I had was, 'You know, this is a slog. This is, you know, unpleasant.'"

"You could have done it," Charlie piped in from the shadows.

"Sure," I said gamely. "But I didn't want to do it. The thought occurred to me that there was an option." *Option*: saying the word proved to me how weak I was, the embodiment of a character defect I should have done everything in my power to fix back when fixing had mattered. "I could just say no. Walk away."

"Why would you do that, after going through all the late nights, all that work and anxiety? All that effort just to get *in?*"

7

"It was a release, Tess. I guess I saw more of it ahead. I don't know. Bottom line, the temptation was too strong."

"Did you think about consequences?" said Charlie. "I suppose I wouldn't have."

"I thought about *thinking* of consequences. But it was the wrong time to be doing *that*. Not with twenty minutes per question. My legs lifted me out of the chair and down the steps toward the front of the room, and by then it was too late." Recounting the action was reliving the action. I felt a wounding sadness.

Clay gave me a look of sympathy. "Like I said, it was possible you had legitimately finished. When I saw you I felt a bit of panic, because there I was not half done. But at least in theory you might have been done."

"A prodigy," I said.

"No way," said Marian. "I knew something was going on. But you looked pretty serene, Tom. You just set the blue book on the desk and turned around and walked out. I could tell you were trying not to disturb anyone."

"'Set the blue book on the desk,'" I repeated, laughing suddenly. "Yes I did. No abrupt walk-out for this fella. Obedient to convention to the last."

"You were *smiling*," said Charlie, but the others demurred.

"In a way it must have been a great feeling," Jason said.

"It was no kind of feeling at all. But when I got out of the room, into those empty commons, there was a powerful loneliness. A separation. I wanted the rest of you to be done. So I crossed the street, found a nice table, and here I've been. The cold helped, the blowing snow. Brought me back into the real world."

8

All was quiet. It was the quiet of accusation. How could people who had worked so hard to get into law school understand quitting? Already I sensed the distance between all of them and me. The empty chair come early January. "It's not like you wouldn't have done fine on that exam," Marian said, making things worse.

Others stopped by; I was a novelty. How fast those four months now seemed to have passed. Another chapter closed–I was building a collection, it seemed, and maybe this pattern would simply be the defining characteristic of my life. In disgust I pushed back against the self-pity. I won't deny there was a certain romance to the scene. The physical setting itself was unusually attractive, the Friday night crowd being populated by friends predisposed to liveliness and, the burden of the final exam now lifted, eager to wear the Yuletide cheer. Beyond the large streetfront window, corners frosted, paired headlights illuminated spurts of light snow. Those on the sidewalk moved rapidly, backs stiff and angled forward against the extreme cold. The tavern had a balcony that rimmed two sides of the room; when a classmate with a table near the railing waved down at me, I thought of the time Amy believed herself pregnant and, before learning otherwise, read everything she could about what the next nine months would bring us. She told me about dissociation, the idea of coping with delivery by floating above the room in dispassionate observation. Were I now in that balcony I would see Clay and Tess pulling each other closer, Jason chatting up the tender, a boisterous half-dozen cheering the hockey game on the elevated corner television, and Charlie Boyle still hoping to plumb the depths, as he would have said, of the Mariana Trench. I would hear the back-and-forth, the dissection of Professor Priley's diabolical examination, its place in an enterprise I was no longer part of. There would be no reason to believe the conversation I had been party to for four months now held nothing for me, no reason to know the words were melting into a *bar bar bar*. And from that perch I would see myself amiably entertaining the well-wishers who were stopping by now and then. It would take great perception to grasp that I was even a little subdued. Looking down, I would know nothing of the reality. Everything of consequence would be out of sight, hidden between the ears.

Without notice I slipped out the door, completing the transformation from classmate to archetype. Contributing to the myth of baptism by fire: there are roughly two hundred lawyers from the Class of 1992 who, over the last couple of decades, have undoubtedly attempted to enhance their standing by making great use of what I did in sixty or seventy seconds that winter afternoon. Not that I ever saw a single one of them ever again.

§

For all its cosmopolitan aspirations, Minneapolis darkened quickly in the rearview mirror of the driver pointed north. The freeway took me over the Mississippi and beyond the downtown towers' illumination. I wound past the car dealers' floodlights, which gave way to residential streetlights and then the yawning blackness of swamps and small lakes. The night was tremendously cold; only after twenty miles did the car's interior begin to feel tolerable. I had planned all along to make this late-night drive to Duluth and couldn't see why walking out on the final exam should change anything. Christmas was ten days away: of course I would be home for the holidays. It was my parents' home, not mine, but the household I had grown up in–all those long evenings, contentedly alone with my guitar and books about Leif Erikson and Cabot and Hudson and all the other New World explorers–awaited. Duluth was a second city to my parents, who had moved to town in the decade after the War, front and center to take in the decline. The mines to the north slowed but my father's law practice thrived. I was their only child, born between the dates Buddy Holly and John Kennedy passed through town.

Of course the day's events tormented me like a bad tooth. I worked anxiously to find an explanation that couldn't be found. Certainly my action represented a failing, but what kind of failing? Had I been motivated by fear? Laziness? An absence of will? Rebellion? Each option was attractive enough to be considered, but none struck me as true. The only truth was shame.

My thoughts weren't linear, but at one point I became conscious of reconstructing a life that had so clearly, so mysteriously, led me astray. On a spring day in the late sixties a Miss Peterman had called us one by one to the second floor window overlooking the Chester Park schoolyard. "Do you see it?" she asked me. I looked out into the branches but saw nothing. "Uh huh," I answered.

"Are you sure, Tommy? It's right there."

"I see it."

"Alright then," she answered doubtfully. And back to my desk I went, making way for Amy Tiedlow. At lunch everyone enthused about the wondrous blue eggs cradled by the nest that had clung to the window ledge, inches from our faces. I had denied myself the opportunity to see that nest, had *lied* about seeing it, to avoid admitting I *couldn't* see it. To avoid admitting I was different.

And the fantasy land I occupied as I grew! I'm not talking about general adolescent dunderheadedness, those years when the body outraces the mind–I once climbed on a bathroom scale to see if I weighed more with an erection–but instead a willful denial of reality. I recalled all those afternoons of basement hockey with the Norgaard brothers, slapping an orange plastic puck across the cement floor. I had fashioned a cardboard goalie mask that had the virtue of looking like the one worn by Jacques Plante and the handicap of effectively blinding me. And of course cardboard is no protection against even a plastic puck. Taking a shot to the cheek had the same wake-up call effect as sticking a finger into a light socket. But I wore the mask nonetheless, slave to the idea of portraying a goalie rather than actually being one.

Did this have anything to do with abandoning law school? By now I was deep into the countryside, snow-fields on each side stretching toward dark groves of trees. Security lights punctuated the night, making each farm a frontier outpost or a buoy floating in a sea of loneliness. I had also quit seminary, though in that case had summoned the wherewithal to make it through an entire academic year. That had occurred three years earlier, the Year of Amy. Whereas walking out of law school had been prompted by little more than a reflex–never in my over-active imagination had I entertained, even that morning, the possibility of not finishing Priley's exam–leaving seminary had been the culmination of relentless pondering, searching, justification. One gorgeous Chicago spring day, almost certainly *after* I had decided to leave, it occurred to me that the rock of faith could not, by its own terms, be anything other than imper-manent. Faith would of course come to an end if it turned out there had never been anything to be faithful to, but even if a faith were validated it would dissolve, necessarily replaced by certainty. I had nothing against certainty. Hooray for certainty. But certainty, I grasped, is a heavy price to pay for the evaporation of hope.

The towns to which the freeway was giving its cold shoulder were becoming progressively smaller. In my unhappiness the entire Midwest seemed doomed, especially these towns. Evolution would do it. It wasn't just that the brightest would leave and take their superior genetic material with them. That was the least of it. A semester with verbally gifted (albeit anxious) classmates had demonstrated for me the way in which words not only expressed, but also nurtured, intelligence. Opinions had circled like hornets using scraps of this and that to construct an enormous, elegant nest. I saw *Henriette* announced by the Department of Transportation's large, green, metal sign and thought it unlikely that such wordplay might exist in the smoky country bar or truck cemetery off the exit ramp.

Hornet's nest. Miss Peterman's nest. I passed Hinckley, the halfway marker, and the hardwoods began to give way to bushy, snow-dressed pines that narrowed the roadway. Even on a moonless evening the white ditches provided a dim illumination. And the massed snow now bubbled like boiling water; a boundary had been crossed. Few cars shared the road. Who, after all, would be out at this hour on such a night? An engine betrayal would have placed me in significant danger, but the Civic was warm (though frost was spreading across the windows) and as single-minded as a drill bit penetrating layer beneath layer. In ninety minutes I would be at home in the town I had left. I could only imagine what would then begin. Broadly, there were three issues: (a) what had happened? (b) what version of what had happened could

I make peace with? and (c) would a (d) be needed as my explanation to the world of what had happened? Failure on a cataclysmic scale was of course what had happened. From dust to dust implies both an ascent and a descent, and when I walked to the front of that intensely quiet lecture hall I had stepped over the apogee. My life was no longer a matter of prospects: no difference now existed between what I was and what, here on out, I would be. It seemed scarcely possible that such wreckage could occur in the space of a minute or two, but of course the fall had been years in the making. I could see that now.

Although I didn't recognize it then, I have been blessed with a tendency toward mental health. Even as I catalogued my failures and the bleak future that would be their consequence, I attempted to fashion from the evening a rescue line. This idea of life occurring inside one's head—wasn't there an element of control in that? An escape from events? A couple of years earlier, deep in turmoil, I had come up with the idea of ranking each day. A 1 would be the lowest (I never used this number; expecting that the worst was yet to come, I kept it in reserve). A 10 was for the best of all possible days, and obviously I didn't use that number either. But each night, accustoming myself to being alone again, I would assess the day and on a desk calendar write a 3, or maybe a 4 or, less commonly, a 2, 5, 6, or 7. The amount of sunlight would make a difference; also, my body—so many days I just *ached*. How well I had slept the previous night. And my plans for the weekend played a role as well. Life is lived in anticipation: that was a lesson I was learning. What I hoped to achieve is beyond me. I suppose I was pursuing a misguided obedience to Socrates. After a few months I discovered that by midmorning I was able to assign that day's number. My days weren't being affected by actual events. This struck me then as odd but now, closing in on midnight, it was an insight that might be turned to my advantage.

The freeway, like the end of a whip cracked days earlier on the Mexican border, hooked east. The car seemed to accelerate in response to a changing (though largely unseen) landscape. This was a drive I had made so many times before, the frenzied happiness of college finals week–hours among the books punctuated by makeshift parties and gifts, carols and farewells–abruptly metamorphosing into a luxuriant hometown Christmas, exams and dorm-mates and fall semester flirtations suddenly a fresh layer of history, *my* history. On Christmas Eve, nestled among cider and Handel, sweatered and warm–perfectly, in other words, happy–I would call back with nostalgia the world left behind, so foreign and fetching, the way Darwin in his late years must have called back the Galapagos. Those years had ended long before I recognized they had ended. My grip on the steering wheel tightened. As the road lifted toward the hill's crest I passed the orange neon glow of a small cross topping the steeple of Pine Hill Church. There was reassurance in the constancy of those two tubes of light: a stay, while the world slept, against the tumult ahead. I liked to imagine on this stretch the reaction of the new visitor grown familiar with Midwestern grain elevators and dairyland, now puzzling at this sign announcing the scenic overlook, that sign admonishing trucks to prepare for the long, steep descent. And then the city appeared in view. In daylight the eye would have taken in thirty miles, the hill rolling down to the expanse of an improbable inland sea. At this hour the scene resembled nothing so much as a toppled Christmas tree, the dark bulk of the hill sloping from its side while strings of lights–white, blue, gold, here and there a red—unfurled across the floor. Literally the end of the road, each of eighty-five thousand a Simeon the Stylite, all knotted along the shores of the St. Louis River and then Lake Superior. I glided down the hill, one sweeping curve following another. The freeway lights were of federally-mandated wattage, but off to the sides and below, in the neighborhoods—neighborhoods still as traumatized by the freeway as any organ would be upon introduction of the surgeon's blade—the lights were softer, draining into the shadows of the nooks and crannies of ravines, bringing to mind yellow-lit parlors arranged around a large radio through which Roosevelt reported on progress in the Pacific Theater.

Or so I imagined. Could either of my parents possibly be still awake? The road flattened into a straightaway. This was the part of town that occasionally led visiting friends to remark that in some unidentifiable way Duluth frightened them. Smokestacks, railroad trestles, enormous stockpiles of coal, salt, taconite, limestone: towns in the middle of the country weren't supposed to behave this way. The downtown buildings, product of an economic boom no one's grandparents could remember, were dark. I worked my way to an avenue and began a steep climb. My childhood had been spent in a leafy middle class neighborhood not far from the college, but in recent years the prosperity of Boyer, Johnson & Salmi had reassured my father that it would be permissible to build a timber-and-glass lookout on a craggy promontory five hundred feet above the lake. I ascended through lovely pines and birch. The snowbanks were melodramatically high. After navigating the steep driveway and applying the parking brake I armed myself with a canvas bag that could fairly be said to contain most of my worldly possessions. I entered the dark house.

An ember popped from the fireplace on the living room's far wall. The dying fire's audience, my father, slouched in his large armchair, breathing deep the gathering gloom. "Okay," he said, meaning that I had survived the final exam, the fall semester, the drive home, another day of danger, twenty-seven years' worth and counting.

A small tree, decorated but unlit, occupied a dark corner. Besides the orange-rimmed logs in the fireplace, the only light was the winter sky as reflected by snow cover through the enormous lakeview windows. The large room was too dark for me to see the photo of Santorini that did not hang on the wall or the San Miguel de Allende watercolor that had never been purchased. The outlines of a floor-to-ceiling bookcase could be detected, but not *Eugene Onegin*, which was in reality a framed photo of my father on his sailboat at Stockton Island; or *The Education of Henry Adams*, its place taken by a photo of father and boat at McCargoe Cove; or *Henderson the Rain King*—father, boat, Rossport. The jaunty nautical hat that occupied what might otherwise have been Dickens's best years *could* be seen, its small metallic star glistening in reflection of a sudden fizz of last flame. My father's life was not broad, but very deep—after more than thirty-five years of practice, nearly one hundred thousand billable hours deep.

But as I settled in beside him I felt no inclination to judge the life my parents had fashioned. Indeed, I sensed its attraction. The North was romantic in its way: why venture anyplace else? And as for my father's work habits, I hardly seemed in a position to object. We looked down the hill and over the vast blackness of the northern sea. A thousand-foot-long vessel manned by Poles or Chileans who wouldn't make it home for Christmas burned with the brightness of a stadium as observed from an overnight flight.

"It is now permissible," my father said, "to call it a night. Your mother will be very happy tomorrow morning. She hasn't heard much from you since summer."

"There wasn't much time to call."

"I told her that was probably the case."

"I actually enjoyed the workload," I said. This was true. "There was a pride of achievement, soaking in all those cases, getting used to a new way of thinking. I guess you know all about that.

"But it had an unhappy ending." I paused, relieved at committing myself to a disclosure whose delay would have only increased my misery. Very slightly my father shifted his weight. "I didn't finish the exam today."

Why? he didn't ask. A full minute of silence passed.

"I liked law school," I said pointedly. So soon the past tense. "I enjoyed my classmates, no problem with the profs. I got a rush out of how demanding it was, how rigorous." The emotion in my voice took me by surprise. "I got in a study group, a good group. The exam didn't intimidate me. But halfway through I decided not to finish." I tried without success to locate the next sentence. The insufficiency of my explanation appalled me.

"This isn't undergraduate," my father said. "There will be consequences, so don't expect it will be easy to ask for a do-over."

"I'm done with law school, Dad. There's no other way."

"There's something else, of course," he said after a long contemplation. "Some plan you're not telling me, some idea of the next thing, whatever that might be."

"No."

More silence. Finally my father said, in a voice of resignation, "You'll be a parent one day. The strain is tremendous. It's hard enough for a self to get through this life unscathed. Taking on the responsibility for another, your own flesh and blood, is untenable." He sighed, undoubtedly as grateful for the darkness as I. "The worry of parenthood was so great it was crushing me. To survive I needed to stop caring. There was, as you put it, no other way. Concern—I couldn't afford to take that bait."

My bedroom, being a room without a history, was spartan. I undressed and immediately upon lying down realized the extent to which exhaustion had me in its grasp. Of course the beginning of the day, before its actual outcome was imaginable, seemed impossibly distant. But now everything had come to a stop; until I woke, nothing could harm me. My body began to numb with sleep, a wonderful feeling diluted only by that which dilutes the joy of life in general. It wouldn't last.

THE EDGE OF
ALL WE KNOW

My parents' plan, my mother once told me, was for five children in the first ten years of their marriage. So when I was born at the end of a childless decade, no brother or sister to follow, the conditions for a privileged youth, potentially damaging, were established. We were insular, but to my parents' credit I wasn't spoiled, unless being left alone qualified. We were remarkably conservative of habit. My father was not a Babbitt: no Chamber speeches, no appointments to boards and commissions. His practice was admiralty law, an arcane specialty in a profession that prized arcanity. The most dramatic thing that might happen in his world was a late night phone call that two vessels at Sault Ste. Marie had bumped one another. I learned young that two objects in the same place at the same time was a thing to be avoided.

Sundays were representative of our family life. The three of us attended the neighborhood Protestant church, always arriving ten minutes early to secure the same spot (right side, halfway back). Through the fully-attended services we listened attentively; that not a word of any sermon was ever discussed afterwards did not mean, I assumed, that my parents weren't as engrossed with the tales as I was. In my mind Joshua's entry into Canaan was a variation of Lewis and Clark's journey up the Missouri. Daniel's deliverance from the lions was precursor to Captain Smith's reprieve at Jamestown. Without the Abraham of Genesis there could not have been the Abraham who freed the slaves. As I grew older I recognized the advantage these stories had over mere history, their role as vehicles for something more sublime than *events*. Though we weren't by any stretch a demonstrative family, I came to appreciate that whatever was happening Sunday morning had the potential to excite passion. One summer the city library was selling, fifty cents each, books whose time had come and gone. This was a month or two before I left for college. I opened an ancient copy of Tolstoy's *The Kingdom of God is Within You*, yellow paper molting off in my fingers, and I came across the assertion that the coming of Christ rendered the Old Testament irrelevant. And in the margin someone had been invested enough, outraged enough at this impudence, to pencil in *No! Matthew 5:17!* But as I say, this revelation came late, and in fact soon after I left for the University my parents found other things to do with their Sunday mornings.

(There was once a time when I was interested in *why* they found other pursuits more worthy of their time. But there were no other pursuits—the same things they had been doing all week they simply did Sunday morning as well. I puzzled too much about this, eventually concluding that for them abandoning church wasn't so much abandonment, or even simple quitting, as it was rising from the sofa after an evening of television, darkening the screen, and going to bed. For a lot of people bedtime seemed to arrive between the seventies, when I grew up, and the new century.)

After church we would always lunch at a favorite restaurant with a big window framing a portion of the lake. Then we retreated home, each to a solitary preoccupation. In my bedroom I would read for an hour, pick up the guitar for an hour, read for an hour. I was never confident enough to take the guitar from my room. I learned the basic chords and moved on from there. I wasn't unusual–since at least the sixties every school had its legion of budding guitarists, most of them aspiring to someday take the place of an older hero who fronted a band that, pinnacle of achievements, had its own gigs. In our school Jack Babineaux, Jr. was that guitar god. Encouraged by his French-Indian exoticism he had lovingly constructed a persona of long black locks, obscure T-shirts, and jewelry. Though as musically gifted as anyone we had known, Jack had quit choir and orchestra–his identity wouldn't permit the association. He and his bandmates could be found at a certain corner on the school's second floor, and one afternoon, shortly after the final bell, I was emboldened by the sight of Jack deigning to suffer the presence of Shawn Weaver, a quiet, serious boy who also had devoted himself to a guitar. At the time Weaver was a freshman, lingeringly pre-pubescent; I was a year older and Jack was a senior. I slowed to hear Shawn's plodding voice. "I was wondering," he said, "what *S-U-S* means in a guitar chord."

"Do you play?" Jack responded. He was receptive to Weaver, at least superficially, and this caused me to stop. I stood beside Weaver, but a step back.

"A little," Shawn said. I played a little, too; more than a little. I was the real deal, not a novice. This might be an opportunity to win Jack's approval. "I know a lot of the major and minor chords," Weaver continued, "and the sevenths. But I don't get S-U-S. You know, where the music says to play G7, S-U-S, 4."

"That's cool," said Jack. His eyes were fixed on Weaver; both boys were seemingly unaware that I was eavesdropping. "*Suspended*," Jack said. "S-U-S means *suspended*. Right? It's the third of the triad that's being suspended, dangling from half a step up to be a fourth. That's where the *4* comes in."

"Sure," Shawn said with enthusiasm, and in my memory of that moment I realize that even the most egregious cliché was once original: someone had once been inspired to imagine the switching of a light bulb over a boy's head. "*Of course.*"

"Here's the thing," Jack said. "You keep asking me questions like that when they come up. That's what I did with the older guys. You remind me of me."

Which was to my ears so delicious a taunt that I laughed aloud.

"No, really," Jack said, turning to acknowledge me. Now the light bulb was over *my* head. Jack Babineaux wasn't belittling Shawn. *I* was the asshole. This was their conversation, their bond, and who could say I didn't fully deserve the scorn I was about to receive?

But there was no scorn. The same affection Jack was displaying for Weaver he now extended to me. "It's true," he said in a kind voice. "That's how I learned." And then he pulled me into their club: "I mean, musicians need to keep the channels open, right?"

This was the first time anyone had called me a musician. I've long forgotten what became of Jack Babineaux. I have a vague sense that it wasn't a happy story. But hadn't I just glimpsed the model I've been striving my entire life to emulate?

So that was what growing up was like for the only child of Lanny and Priscilla Johnson: a bit of reading, a bit of music, all in blissful solitude, the remainder of the week following the pattern of Sunday afternoons. But that's not right either. I wasn't really an introvert; I had friends. The Norgaard twins, for example. I've already mentioned the afternoons of hockey in their basement. Those were winter afternoons. In fall we drilled footballs at one another and in spring converted the empty lot beside their house to Fenway Park, smacking tennis balls off the green siding of Mr. Sorenson's garage. At least two or three weekends every summer I was asked to join the Norgaards at their cabin on the Canadian border: it was there that I became adept at catching fish and naming constellations. From Bill and Toby I learned what it might be like to have a brother, how family secrets could be leveraged but how, also, siblings were able to bind together against rivals. There were shifting allegiances among the three of us (the twins and I were the same age): sometimes it was Bill and me, sometimes Toby and me, but ultimately they were brothers and I was not. When conflict became too hot we would separate for a few days. I would shift to Amy.

Amy Tiedlow and I had been born the same month, I in Duluth and she in the watershed of the Nakdong River. That we quickly ended up living next to one another (the Norgaards were on the other side, two houses down) is a hard fact for anyone arguing against divine manipulation. Of course I can't remember a first meeting. By kindergarten we had already compiled a history–plastic spoons in the sandbox, trick-or-treating against the sleet, birthday parties. Through elementary years we walked together to and from Chester Park School. Most of the kids thought we were cousins. I've often wondered–what *haven't* I wondered about Amy?–whether we would have become such friends without the proximity. We were comfortable with each other because we knew each other so well; we knew each other so well because we were comfortable with each other. Amy had this recognizable shape, and way of walking, and method of thinking, method of *existing*. She would have agreed to the same about me.

But when did we become attracted to one another? I admit to being unusually dense about this. Two incidents remain in memory. My father installed a basketball hoop for me—or, more accurately, hired two men to install it. I recall a spring evening, one of those evenings, rare for Duluth, when an unexpectedly warm day has settled into the still and pleasant sadness of a somnolent twilight. Amy and I were probably eighth-graders. We challenged each other at PIG, then HORSE, as we had done countless times before. At this particular stage of life Amy, accelerating with her gender, was exactly my height. We were both reasonably good shots. As the light declined we were joined by Dean Tiedlow, five years younger. As sometimes happens, the Tiedlows had needed an adopted child before pregnancy could occur. Amy feigned annoyance at Dean's intrusion, and soon we found ourselves ricocheting the ball off the rim so that it would bound away, Dean in pursuit. He was as reliable as a hunting dog, returning each time out of breath but with our basketball. "You guys," he began to complain, followed by speculation that we weren't even trying to make baskets, might even be trying to miss. Finally Amy banked an errant shot with so much force that Dean announced in an obstinate and aggrieved voice that he was quitting the game. The ball rolled down the street—in Duluth a rolling ball does not soon stop—and Amy ran off for it. "She likes you," Dean told me with a smile of mischief. "She says so herself."

She likes you: an eight-year-old boy had opened the door on a world of misery. The words spoke to a self I didn't know existed. And yet I fell into a denial—a dormancy, you might say. A full two years passed before a November piano recital on a windy, bare-branched, leaf-tumbling, rattling night. I sat with a small audience and watched Amy play a Chopin nocturne, her shoulders turning slowly and methodically, the rhythm of a bird on swelling waters, Amy in her trance oblivious to the river of black hair cascading down a body that curved in unspeakable elegance toward widening hips. I had assessed every other girl in school; never Amy. But what was the use of those girls? Not a one was as beautiful as Amy Tiedlow.

What was a boy to do with such knowledge? Familiarity, which should have been an advantage, was instead the greatest of obstacles. During our high school years it never struck me or my classmates as strange that the boys and girls were in constant agitation with one another. We did not understand–did not even question–why the boys would date girls from the class below, and the spurned girls from our class would respond by dating boys from across town. Nearly half the crowd at our school dances was unknown to me. This was just the way of love, we thought, and maybe we were right. But in retrospect all those years of progressing from grade to grade together had made siblings of us. Familiarity was engendering the turmoil. This realization first dawned, dimly, while we were in college; many midnight sessions were devoted to the distinction between friendship and love, a distinction that could not be reconciled. But what does love mean to a high school boy, anyway? Taking a girl to a movie and yawning with a big enough stretch to engineer a cuddle? Holding her hand at a school assembly as a way of marking a territory? Did being in love mean anything more than putting yourself forward in such a way as would encourage the world to think of you as being in love? During the darkest of times, the end of everything, Amy and I wounded and in tears, we talked about the intoxication that had governed our summer before leaving for college. We had been so young–that was easy to agree on. And what we felt had been more than infatuation or hormones–had been, indeed, love. On that too we found no reason to disagree.

All of that lay in our future. In tenth grade the familiarity that was dooming my classmates' romantic pursuits was doubly dooming me and Amy. I was incapable of imagining what the new universe would be like were I to ask Amy to become a girlfriend. I had no doubt it would be a new universe. How could you profess love and follow it up with HORSE? But in this new universe we would still be neighbors. How could I be a couple with a girl who could, by merely looking out her bedroom window, watch me mow the lawn or argue with my parents?

Lord knows I tried to move us beyond friendship. I planned. At football games I would catch her at halftime–but no, she never seemed to stray from her friends. On the way to school I would run her down and profess my intentions–but no, some new club or project would play havoc with her schedule. She had a life, an annoying fact given that I had none outside devotion to her. Being neighbors meant that occasionally we *did* find ourselves alone together, and the high stakes focused my mind on a complication: I had no tangible intentions capable of being professed. There was simply nothing I could have said that would have made any practical difference. Amy would have appreciated that I was smitten. She might even have told me she had similar inclinations. But then… what? Anyone who has survived adolescence recognizes the conundrum. Schools schedule proms and such to shape the development and control of sexual desire, and in fact it was just that–a prom–that gave me hope. I would ask Amy (we were juniors by now) and the evening would give our relationship meaning. We would be a couple.

Except that Andy Stahl asked Amy first, and she accepted. Of course Stahl asked Amy first: upon learning the news–the moment was crushing–I immediately recognized, too late, that my history with Amy did not make her my possession. It had been fantasy to believe she would hold her life in abeyance until I discovered the means of making us a pair. Andy Stahl was a prize among the girls at our school: wild but not too; respectable but not too; and supremely sure of himself. I could not compete. Yet I couldn't help but see Amy's acceptance as a betrayal. Her acceptance was the first shoe to drop; the next was her happiness, the complete absence of any remorse over what she had done to me. Any hope that Stahl's defects, whatever Amy might decide them to be, would be exposed in the course of a long evening were dashed when, a week after Prom, I happened upon them down at the Canal, walking slowly, hand in hand, appearing from a distance to be teasing each other now and then, speaking occasionally in voices that I imagined to be quiet and knowing, exactly the kind of voices used by lovers.

But neither were Amy and Andy Stahl immune to the destructibility of high school romance. The school year ended and after a month or two each moved on. Another girl took Amy's place and another boy Andy's. Over the next year Amy had a series of boyfriends while I had not a single girlfriend at all. This seemed to be the way of things. Amy's disposition toward me did not change. Occasionally we still spent time doing the things we had done all our lives. During the first snowfall of our senior year we built an enormous fort, Amy cheerfully industrious and my initial pouting eclipsed by the joy of the season change and an afternoon of Amy all to myself. By now our lives were beginning to pick up momentum. All that doodling time of mine–experimenting with my guitar, reading some of this, some of that—was bearing fruit: I thought of myself now as learned, and artistic, and ready to escape Duluth's fog and sameness. Amy had her own future to pursue. A small liberal arts school in Tennessee, of all places, occupied an obscure pigeonhole in distant Tiedlow history and would now be Amy's home for the next four years. She had conquered high school, regularly collecting awards and honors as we raced toward graduation. At noon on our truncated last day of school the senior class was ordered onto the front lawn and a photographer on a ladder took a picture of us; then we dolefully walked away with our freedom. The air was moist, ribbons of silver lacing along the hillside, and nostalgia jumped me. Never again: never again would this group of classmates be together, and right under our noses we had allowed our lives to be stolen from us. All the pointless distractions that had been constructed for us—Homecoming bonfires and hockey jamborees, Valentine's Day concerts and talent shows for good causes—would now entertain a new, younger class. What did it matter that we had scorned such rituals? Now they were gone and the most pedestrian memories were tugging at me. By chance I happened upon Amy walking home one final time and in giddy mourning I communicated all of this to her. "Oh, snap out of it," she teased, which served as an encouragement to persuade her. The afternoon was so enchanting, the approaching evening of commencement ceremony and reception so portentous, that we wandered down into the Congdon Park canyons as a sort of farewell tour. Here we had collected insects for a sixth-grade project, leapt across ice floes during Easter vacations. "A Friday night with no homework!" I threw at her—I was taunting as well—"Never again!"

"Oh," she said dismissively, looking back and smiling broadly. She was in the lead, knifing like a kayak through a sea of wildflowers.

"Setting the alarm early to hear if it had snowed enough for school to be cancelled–gone for good!"

"Listen to yourself!" she cried, eyes widening. "The things about school you're missing are all things about *avoiding* school!" This truth was so amusing that she burst into the utter defenselessness of laughter. She opened her face to me and the reel seemed to be spliced–there was, I mean to say, no passage of time between not kissing and kissing. I had placed us in our new universe: it seemed outrageous, but also preordained, to be tasting and smelling, if only momentarily, the girl who had long ago followed me to see (successfully) the robin's eggs outside Miss Peterman's window. It occurs to me now that that first kiss–it was my first kiss with any girl–was not unlike walking the blue book to the front of the furiously silent lecture hall. The thought became the inevitability.

In memory we were deep into the primeval forest, passionately transformed. And while such kisses followed, in truth the first kiss so startled Amy as to accelerate her laughter. She stared at me in disbelief and gasped for air. Upon recovering herself–I had moved away, for my benefit or hers I wasn't certain–Amy, fearful that her reaction had humiliated me, stepped forward and took my hand. We lived that summer in a fever. Finding love in a flowered ravine became our theme: we took it as a sign, an affirmation that sanctioned frequent escapes into the privacy of the woods. We had as our favorite place a slab of rock perched above a twist in the stream, all pathways of approach obscured by fallen trees. "And to think," I said one cool, damp evening, "everything depended on the chance of me running into you on your way home from school that last day."

"Isn't it odd that *chance* rhymes with *dance*?"

I laughed. "And *romance*."

"Exactly. And because of that, don't you see, through all these generations of songs we keep hearing about chance. It's like *June* and *moon*–the moon's out every month, but June's the only one we hear about because of the rhyme. So people get reinforced with the idea that when you meet and fall in love it's chance."

"You don't think so?" I said eagerly, the wish being the mother, etc.

"Might be something other than chance." The veiled expression of this idea, that our pairing might be cosmically ordained, was so appealing that it seemed to require from me a commensurate response. I told Amy Tiedlow that I loved her. The risk of such a declaration was thrilling. She said nothing. "I'm sorry," I said. "That sounded–wrong."

"That sounded beautiful." She kissed me; I remember the particularities still. "Oh, Tom," she whispered a minute or two later, her voice barely audible. Her eyes saw only me. "You're so sweet."

What did I imagine our future to be? I had no answer. Our lives in Duluth were rapidly coming to an end. I realized that it would be difficult for our love to survive whatever the next four years would separately bring us. And of course we were too young for marriage. Even in my desperation I recognized that. Amy didn't appear to be desperate at all. She was serene. I recall sitting with her in her parents' basement one evening–we were well into August by then; Amy was making a list of things to bring to school–and asking plaintively, "Do you think you'll come home next summer?"

"You think too much about the future."

The balance of power was all wrong. I was acutely aware of this. But being in love required honesty. "You never worry about anything," I complained.

She smiled at me and waited a few moments before responding. "Meaning?"

"Nothing," I said, defeated. "Nothing but an observation."

Shortly thereafter Amy and I broke up. I had actually maneuvered myself into proposing some sort of cooling-off period—I was jumping from a ledge to relieve myself of the awful fear of falling. Amy and I were sitting at my kitchen table now. It was eight o'clock and quickly darkening—summer, our childhood, *us*, all draining away. My parents were off somewhere; we had the house to ourselves.

"Cooling off isn't right," Amy said. "It's not the way we should be thinking of this."

"Well?" I said morosely. I was tongue-tied, miserable, making it easy for her.

"We had our summer," she said, and any failure to grasp her meaning was cured by what came next. "These things don't last indefinitely."

"These things," I repeated, unsure whether to hide the bitterness.

"Do you remember how glum you were when I was dating Andy?"

Never had it occurred to me that this was something she would have noticed. "What does that have to do with anything?" Amy and Andy Stahl: that had been more than a year ago, an earlier epoch in high school measuring.

"There was never any reason for you to be discouraged. I knew it wouldn't last. They just don't." She said this kindly, her face turned to look in at me. The comparison of her

35

mismatch with Stahl and what we had shared that summer was crippling. It was worse than crippling, it was treachery. I was nauseous at how casually she had destroyed me.

This was the context for my entry into college life. I was lonely for home and I was lonely for Amy: how could the two be distinguished? Minneapolis, with its looping freeways and lingering warmth, was utterly unlike Duluth. City life was counterintuitive–the nights were brighter, for example, when it was cloudy. Sirens wailed through those nights. I had a standard liberal arts load, three classes most days but only one on Thursdays. On a brilliant afternoon, trees aflame, I treated myself to a long exploration into the East Bank, imagining all the way across the bridge what Amy was doing that very afternoon, and imagining all the way back what was happening in the lives of younger friends fortunate enough to still be living the life I had lived a year earlier. No objective observer could have expected much from this stab at college. But forty thousand students attended the University and a handful became my friends. Sequestration wasn't an entirely foreign condition–recall those Sunday afternoons at home–and whenever I lost interest in school there was always my guitar or a book that didn't carry the stigma of a professor's reading list. I returned home for Christmas and immediately learned that Amy had brought a boy back from Tennessee. The Tiedlows invited over some neighborhood friends, including the Johnsons, to meet Tobin–how cruelly stupid adults can be–and at the sight of the couple I was freed of the weight that had been riding me since summer's end. Amy and her impressive find were so clearly enamored of one another, so exquisitely matched, that the idea of any sort of future with her was removed from consideration. Astoundingly, this development didn't seem unacceptable at all. And my new life began.

I decided to major in history. The seeds for this could be found way back in fifth grade, when the Norgaards and I hiked to the old crumbling lighthouse at the end of Park Point, all the while looking for fantastic creatures whose bones we would bring back for President Jefferson. But now ideas as well as adventures seemed worthy of study. I read Frederick Jackson Turner; I read *Marbury v. Madison*. Schweitzer's attempt at biography led me to Augustine. I began to revere my professors, who were not my parents, and was so eager for them to be right that I accepted all opinions casually thrown off on the most inconsequential of matters as not merely opinions, or even pronouncements, but white papers.

But. During those college years a maddening double-mindedness first made its appearance. My seminary and law school misadventures can both be traced to this inability to place myself in a coherent story: I could imagine in meticulous detail Magellan's circumnavigation but not my journey into adulthood. On Friday nights I would join a friend or two–sometimes it was a girl–and wander down to Cedar Riverside. This was obviously a life not available to me in Duluth, and on the coldest nights, the black sky an immense vacuum, steam curling from the alleys behind the kitchens, we would stumble home, skyscraper lights at our back and escape as near as the freeways below. Every window was frosted. I would drop into bed, my high Middlebrook Hall window opening to the network of city lights as though in some future age I were descending into a distant planetary colony. The ceiling would spin some, from the liquor of course, but also from what had just been vouchsafed with me, the reggae of Shangoya or the jazz of Rio Nido. (One fortuitous weeknight I wandered into the Coffeehouse Extempore to catch Dylan in the middle of an impromptu set.) And the world was so wide, so inviting. But the next morning I would look down on the gray, the tawdriness, busses blackening the snowbanks, the city a stack of concrete quiet and fearful in the arctic air. Hot water would revive me, and during long showers I would imagine an acceptable life–*acceptable* being the standard to aspire to–as a history professor, maybe a lawyer, possibly even a pastor, in a Midwestern town, maybe even Duluth, grading papers or examining insurance policies or selecting hymns for Thanksgiving Eve services.

I found that I had liked Duluth. I kept quiet about this–my friends would have been incredulous at the idea of four years of college being preparation for nothing more than a return home. But my childhood had been happy. Why couldn't that happiness be re-created? A predictable sequence repeated itself through my undergraduate years. As a semester break approached excitement would rise; and in my first days home I was triumphant, basking like a Medici prince in the familiarity. I might even drive through the college or imagine a storefront law office along First Street. But inevitably the days home would begin to drag. Time in Duluth, certainly for a twenty-year-old, stood still. Soon I would be back in Minneapolis, homesick for a day and then engrossed by the new semester. At night my friends and I talked of tramping through Europe after graduation; in the morning I stood under the shower and envisioned a small town judgeship.

Amy occasionally returned home as well. We saw no more of Tobin, but once or twice she was accompanied by a Philip or Marcus. There was even speculation that she and Marcus were engaged. The Tiedlows hosted a New Year's brunch and ten or twelve of us sat in unfolded chairs arranged as a circle. Polite words were said, and mildly funny words; a few interesting words, even. Stories were swapped as everyone warmed to the situation. My eyes met Amy's from time to time and the truth of a shared life reduced all else in the room to trivialities. No one in the world, certainly not Marcus the Obedient, knew Amy better than I, and surely she was apprehending her clairvoyance regarding me. So she would marry and one day I, too, would marry, and we would live our separate lives, somehow occupying the same consciousness. Marcus was gone by Easter. Amy, home again on break and seeing my car in the driveway, telephoned and shyly asked if I might want to see a movie.

As you might imagine, the development of this story is painful to recall. Amy's persistence had the wonder of an athletic achievement. Not that she began calling weekly or writing letters. But with our shared history and the proximity of our families there always seemed to be holidays and weddings and graduations that found us together, the two people in a room who shared a secret no one else would ever know. I resisted for three perfectly defensible reasons. The first was pride, of course, or maybe something less admirable: *see how it feels to not get what you want.* The second was more nuanced. The Amy I had loved was a high school girl who hadn't yet walked away from my love. I could imagine falling in love a second time with the high school Amy, but that girl no longer existed. And I, of course–the I of that graduation summer–didn't exist, either.

And then there was the third reason. What if she hurt me again?

So I resisted. This occurred over a few *years*, past our college graduations and into the abyss of What Next. Amy responded with preternatural patience. Never a whimper of complaint, never even the hint of annoyance. Certainly I couldn't be so important to her. Yet she never abandoned the quiet insistence that we were bound in a common destiny, which of course we were.

The summer of 1984 found me diploma'd and living in a ramshackle house on Dinkytown's outskirts. My housemates were members of a band we had formed: music would be our future. The walls were hollow, well-trodden runways for mice and, we denied to each other, rats. A nearby rail yard caused the house to shake with the thunderous booms of trains of grain cars being broken apart and reassembled. By early winter we had hung heavy blankets in all of the interior doorways and layered the windows in plastic. The northern wind still blew through. This band–Self Portrait, we called ourselves; we thought it was evidence of wit to tell booking agents we were named after a favorite Post-Impressionist painting–would be one you could dance to, of course, but with the difference that it would be cerebral. We were convinced that Self Portrait was about to break through, to evolve into a different species of music.

I thought hard about this. What did it mean to say the treble clef was "higher" than the bass clef? What had height to do with it? I would sit down at the piano, play a line of C-D-E-F-G, and pronounce to whomever might be listening (John, who was our percussionist, or Scott, who did woodwinds), "Why do people say I just played an *ascending* line? Why can't it just as well be said to be *descending*? Higher/lower is a construct!"

Which would lead us into one of our periodic discussions about planetarium music. Go to any planetarium, watch any documentary about outer space, and the music you heard would be reliably static, quizzical, without rhythm, melody, or, for the most part, harmony or texture. Why was it always the same music, and why *that* music?

"Space is empty," Stoltzman might say. He played a number of brass instruments, usually running them through some sort of electronic scrambling. "So the music is, too." And this of course would lead to a scripted argument over what exactly constituted empty music.

Or I might play a C major chord. "Quick," I would call. "Sound-to-word association."

"Convention," would come the immediate answer. This time the speaker might be Joshua, our electric guitarist. He was also our lead singer, with a style closer to chant than song. "Piano lesson church basementism."

"Okay. And then—" Here I would modulate to an E minor chord.

"Well, that's a horse of a different color. Profundity. Gravity. Wariness, even sorrow."

"Exactly. But all I did was move one tone one half note lower! And it's the difference between *Tom Sawyer* and *Huckleberry Finn*! Why? And why exactly do sounds change moods, anyway?"

In presenting these explorations I'm giving them a belittling treatment, and certainly there was an aspect of the absurd that hung over these exchanges. We recognized that—as often as not we ended up pondering our way to a jam session, "Cherokee" at 312. But these weren't idle questions, not to me. In junior high "Silly Love Songs" had topped the charts most of a summer. Lord knows the song had no cachet with Self Portrait, but McCartney was McCartney, the greatest melodist of the half-century, and here he was beginning a song with thirteen consecutive notes on the same tone. Why should that work? It confounded an idea I'd been kicking around for a year or two: if one collected Western music's most beautiful melodies—"Clair de Lune,"

"Greensleeves," "Danny Boy"–and then studied them, *really* studied them–painstaking, meticulous study–certain commonalities and patterns would make themselves apparent. It might even be possible to divine a formula, not the formula used for teen hits or television jingles, but a scientific equation that would lead to perfectibility. Clearly such a notion was daft. It presumed that something as elemental as music's power to bewitch could be understood.

Minneapolis didn't appreciate us; and what the hell were we doing in Minneapolis anyway? Military juntas were losing their grip in South America and Self Portrait decided it would be daring, yet safe, to move abroad. We arrived in Quito and had exactly two gigs before the high altitude headaches pushed us down the mountain and further south. We found our way to Buenos Aires, a sprawling and residually sinister city that we somehow thought might be ripe for conquest by five musicians from Minnesota. Buenos Aires was exotic enough, of course, what with its crumbling cathedrals and operatic cemeteries. German and Italian couples who looked to be a hundred years old toddled along the streets of Palermo. We had a lot of time on our hands, and finding even fill-in jobs was difficult. One week we ventured north into the pampas to escape the city lights and sleep beneath a dome of southern hemisphere stars. We were like schoolboys, reveling in piles of leaves simply because they had fallen in March.

Our band found a bemused hotelier who allowed us to play in the lobby on Sunday evenings. For all the theorizing, all the over-thinking, our greatest successes seemed to be rooted in simplicity–a guitar-flute duet line, for example, Scott and I navigating the scales in perfect thirds. We were packing up late one Sunday night, the end of four hours of music, when I heard a primordial Piazzolla melody from a radio in the housekeepers' linen closet. I woke the next morning–Monday, traffic, rain–and the Piazzolla was playing in my head. Where had it been through the long night, and what had it been doing? More to the point, why was it Piazzolla that remained, when we had spent the entire evening playing our own music?

I believed that being a Duluth boy in a foreign land was the reason I was having difficulties controlling my subconscious. I was beset by strange and often disturbing dreams. Consciousness didn't give me a rest, either: no previous experience had so demanded that I confront just what it meant to be me, Thomas Johnson, on this planet and in this age. I began to doubt the possibility of ever knowing anything– not how to recognize the essence of a melody, not how to recognize the essence of a life. The essence of *another*. My psyche was the only one I knew. This off-key, unpredictable pattern–or no pattern at all–of elations and despairs: was it shared, in anything close to my particulars, by anyone else? When Stoltzman said that the sound of cold July winds washing through the bare trees made him blue, just how blue did he mean? If I could only have been Devin Stoltzman for a moment, *that* moment. If I could only have been granted a means of comparison. We all struggled for peace of mind, best I could tell. But what did *struggle* mean? And what quantity of peace was peace enough?

Homesickness was an increasingly frequent visitor. The months stacked one on top of another and it seemed to me that spending time in this international capital, beneath the Southern Cross, jacaranda in the gardens and capybaras in the bush, was a silly waste of time. Self Portrait was imaginative and daring, but had trouble finding paying jobs, never mind reorganizing the music world. On paper, our music was revolutionary. The theory was better than the sound; it was better appreciated with the brain than with the ear. In hindsight one incident stands out. A letter arrived one day from Maddy Beckman. Maddy had been in Miss Peterman's class the year Amy saw the eggs and I didn't. We had been friends, the three of us, all the way up. Maddy was everyone's pal—no one disliked Maddy. She had four brothers, two older and two younger, and all five looked pretty much the same: slightly stocky, with heads shaped like large milk cartons. Maddy was unfailingly good-natured. She stayed in town after high school and four years later finished a social work major at the University of Wisconsin-Superior. "I think of you often," Maddy wrote to me. "When I run into kids we know, your name always comes up. Argentina—wow. We should have gone overseas too, that's what everyone says. You're doing it right." And with those words South America was transformed from a dead-end lark to a success. Validation. It didn't matter how lonely I was, how heavily time weighed on my hands. My friends at home knew none of that.

Soon afterwards I dreamt of Maddy. At the time I was sleeping on a floor mattress in a room about the size of the mattress. The doorway (no door) led into a narrow kitchen. In my dream I woke and found my partner beside me on the mattress. She, identity unrevealed, rose and left the room. Left the dream. Maddy was in the kitchen, rinsing vegetables. She asked me in her cheerful way what I had planned for the day, and I suddenly felt compelled to show her kindness, reciprocate her interest in me. I approached Maddy, put my arms around her, and suggested that we retreat to my mattress. In this dream world, then, there was and wasn't morality: cheating on my partner was causing me no anguish, but the cheating was motivated by a desire to please Maddy, in whom I had never had a sexual interest (never mind whether the dream me was actually doing Maddy any good). On the mattress I put my face close to hers and we spoke tenderly, nibbling kisses now and then. But as I got ever closer to Maddy she began a transformation. She was no longer Maddy, but a small, beautiful Asian woman–Amy, of course. With the illogic of dreams (we were face to face) I could see Amy's two small, perfect mounds of buttocks, her beautiful shape and color and perfectly unblemished skin. But not being Maddy, this other no longer cared what I had planned for the day. She no longer had much interest in me at all. Amy remained kind. She wasn't angry with me or annoyed. But she became more and more reluctant to accept the intimacy I was offering. The more beautiful she grew, the more remote she became. And I woke wondering if instead of Recoleta I was on the Peloponnese. Of such dreams are myths born.

I had dreaded the thought of pairing up once again with Amy. Since the end of our high school romance–how ancient that now seemed–it had always been Amy, never me, who had been in pursuit. By the time I returned to Minneapolis all my objections had dropped away. I came up with a thousand reasons to convince myself that it was ludicrous to fear from twenty-four-year-old Amy the abandonment I had suffered at the hands of eighteen-year-old Amy. She was interning at the Minneapolis Institute of Art; I, without the band, wasn't doing much of anything. As I mentioned, in recent years, until I had left for South America, Amy and I had been seeing each other periodically. Now we spent most every evening together. We became lovers, and so the world came into sharp focus. One afternoon we were walking around Lake of the Isles when we overheard a middle-aged woman say to her husband, "Pam and that fellow were walking together, you know."

"They were not," the man replied.

His wife turned to him and said in agitation, "I'm not talking about what they were *not*. I'm talking about what they *were*."

We seemed to become one another, Amy and I. Humans are prone to do this anyway, benefitting the way chameleons benefit. When someone smiles, we smile; when someone is in a foul mood, we are in a foul mood. To do otherwise is an act of defiance. With Amy and me this merging was happening to an astonishing degree.

Amy told me about her little college in Tennessee. For those students who wanted to write there was a school newspaper. Not Amy's interest. For those who were into school spirit there were the football games–again, not for Amy. And for those so inclined there was a youth ministry; as a freshman Amy had attended a couple of services before deciding she did not belong. She devoted much of her time to the art studio, not as an artist but as a student of art. Everyone had her niche.

So Amy was perplexed when I asked her about the existence of a spiritual realm. "Really?" she said. "Why?"

"You thought you knew everything about me, didn't you?"

"What I know is never to be surprised," she said, flattering me. "'Spiritual realm'–is this a new preoccupation?"

"Old as mankind."

"New with *you*, silly."

Was it? "The world makes no sense without it," I said. "That's the conclusion I'm coming to."

"There's your error, don't you see?" I loved Amy's intelligence along with all the other things I loved about her. "Granted, existence is hollow. Pointless. But it doesn't follow that there must be a corresponding existence that is *not* hollow."

"Everything is hollow?" I smiled. I had a little intelligence myself. "Why are you so quick to agree with me about the world making no sense, being pointless? In comparison to what? It can't be pointless unless there is such a thing as a point."

"You'd be fighting all of science. Every day they're learning more and more about God being nothing more than a function of the brain."

"Every day," I repeated dismissively. "Amy, the shortest distance in science is the distance between 'a recent study suggests' and 'we now know.'"

"You don't need religion, Tom." She looked out at the street. We were sitting at the window in a six-table cafe near Lowry Hill. "I mean, have you ever noticed how the people who are religious are those most in need of it? Worriers. Screw-ups. Damaged people, often."

"We're not all damaged?" And besides, I hadn't said anything about religion. But Amy knew me–she always knew me–and in fact less than a year later I was in seminary; in Chicago; in a marriage.

There's a big story there, of course, one I'm not inclined to dwell on. From my distance a recounting makes those years feel haphazard, random, frenetic. One thing and then another. They were that, of course, but at the time a year was a year, long and full, and I was merely following a course that seemed the only option. I never started a new avenue with a thought to where it might lead, or that it would end. Amy and I loved each other—there was never any doubt about that. I worked so hard to convince myself that what I had learned about Amy as we left for college had been bad information.

But I entered seminary for all the wrong reasons. I wasn't thinking about being a pastor. It never crossed my mind to serve anyone, not to mention anyOne. My decision was laughably selfish. I wanted to immerse myself in a search. I was like a boy enlisting in the army to learn whether war might be justifiable.

In our neighborhood, while I was growing up, lived a fervently religious family: the Metzgers. The children were home-schooled. The family eschewed worldly abominations like Halloween and television. The worship services the Metzgers attended—Sunday morning and Sunday and Wednesday evenings—took place in the basement of a large, tired, drafty house on the East Hillside. Perhaps twenty families attended. I know about that house because one Monday afternoon Chuck Metzger invited me to the youth program there that evening. Chuck was in high school; I was three years younger. He was a tubby boy with a disc jockey's set of pipes, brash in the protection God was providing. It was a stormy fall evening—rain swept off the lake in sheets. Ten or fifteen boys of Chuck's age were there. Games, Bible study, treats, and then, in a back stairwell, my conversion. Chuck showed me a small pamphlet with a dove on the cover. He told me about God (I knew about God) and how to ask Jesus to be my savior. Did I want to ask Him to do that? I was embarrassed and resentful and incredulous and obviously could not have said no. Chuck was very self-assured. He characterized the world as being our enemy—it was us Christians against the world, and we were up to the task. He helped me pray. To my astonishment I began to cry. "'Pray' and 'cry'—they're almost the same word," Chuck said. All of this took but five or ten minutes. We rose off the steps to join the others and Chuck said, in summation: "What can harm you if the King of the Universe is on your side?" The idea was an enormous comfort. What, indeed, could harm me? I felt as though I had been immunized against the bullying and mockery that was part and parcel of junior high experience. Even tragedy would be rendered powerless. I was accepted. I loved everyone. The world would not love me back, but this was a source of joy. I wanted to be a rebel for Christ.

At that age I was only beginning to appreciate life's great restlessness. Friday evenings were glorious, the release from school, but by Sunday the feeling was gone. And the horrors of Monday morning eased as the school week progressed. But how could I have suspected that even faith—being touched by the Creator—was impermanent? For it was. I came home that Monday evening eager to tell my parents what I had learned, my enthusiasm thwarted only by embarrassment—nothing like the conversation I felt compelled to introduce had ever occurred in the Johnson household. Days passed and my euphoria began to drain, replaced by life. I never expect to again be as happy as I had been that wet Monday evening. I had received this most profound of insights; I had allowed it to slip away.

Through high school I paid great attention to, and was ultimately betrayed by, the sermons I heard at church. At first I credited my disappointment to inferior pastors, men handed creation's most sublime material and then unable to deliver. In college I would occasionally search out a church (it seems unnecessary to say I went alone) and indeed found impressive pastors, ministers, and priests. But even they disappointed. The sermons, or at least the best of them, would begin wonderfully, provocatively. An argument would be laid out, progress a bit, and then suddenly collapse with a platitude. Logic and reason were called upon to begin the project and then abandoned as it became clear they weren't up to the job. A passage from Scripture was thrown in as the substitute.

This angered me. I genuinely wanted to believe. If only these preachers, who apparently believed, could share with me the reasons for their belief. I wrestled with doubt. By the end of college doubt had won.

After college—it was shortly before the band and I left the country—my mother had a health scare (and nothing more, happily). On the morning of the exploratory surgery I said a silent prayer. So doubt hadn't won after all—doubt, like faith, was proving itself impermanent. But even as I prayed I became aware that the presence or absence of a tumor was not, in those few remaining minutes before she was to be rolled into the operating room, about to change. Any harm to my mother had been put in place long ago. Prayer—God—was powerless. My mom was a living thing in the way a tree was a living thing. The tree would be invaded by disease and die, or wouldn't. Why had it taken me twenty-three years to understand that God has no role in this world?

But on my return from Argentina I began, again, to wonder. What exactly had made me so happy that long-ago Monday evening? Maybe a psychic trick humans are able to perform for themselves. But maybe God.

I summoned logic and reason, just as my discarded preachers had. God must exist, or at least at one time existed. I was, after all, here. There must have been a First Thing. I was willing to give that First Thing the name of God. This of course led, as all such inquiries must, to the problem of random, and ultimately universal, suffering.

Clear evidence–overwhelming evidence–of God's detachment from this world. (What about a next world? I didn't think much about that, though subsequently I have. While once I feared there might not be an afterlife, now the greater fear is that there might be. Who knows what it could be like? And the idea of eternity, any kind of eternity, gives one pause.) I must add that in the course of so much heavy thinking I was well aware that my logic and reason were those of a human, a creature incapable, almost by definition, of such things. Perhaps this is the ultimate knowledge, the real fruit in the garden: we will never know. Of course a seminary is a school, and no school can be premised on never knowing. I studied the creeds, believing hardly a clause. But I respected, even had affection for, the ritual and language and tradition. They were our way–we with our little history, our little tract of earth–of acknowledging something larger. Abandon these things and I would be abandoning the hope of something larger.

All of this was wrapped up in our marriage, of course. Amy hooked a job at the Chicago Institute, explaining Seurat to students. She missed a menstrual period, but only one. The gray of the windswept winter seeped into our apartment, then into us. A thousand things happened, all of them tributaries of one thing. Try as I might, the horrifying truth could not be ignored: there had been a time in our lives for each other, but that time had long passed. An inner sense had warned me but I had ignored the warning. It had been *my* inner sense, no one else's. I had betrayed myself, and the betrayal had cost me my life. I would return to Minneapolis–Lord knows what became of Amy–and suffer for two empty years before picking myself up. On a warm, hopeful, late August morning I entered law school.

Amy left our apartment a few weeks before I moved out of Chicago. Here is the last thing she said to me: "The entire human body is symmetrical, except the heart, which is off-center." For years I used that memory to try and convince myself that in losing Amy I hadn't lost anything. Self-betrayal is itself an intuition.

§

I woke to purple, a light having no source and throwing no shadow. The house was quiet, which told me nothing: my parents moved softly, didn't think to listen to music, and were little given to conversation. It was altogether unremarkable that the first sound I heard was that of a gadget. With profound disinterest a motor, droning methodically, hoisted the garage door outside my bedroom window. I imagined the small chains in motion, and then by association imagined an indefensibly baroque train set I had been given one Christmas, its locomotive, like the head of a snake, slithering along a curve and into a tunnel. Next I heard a car engine, also methodical, spark plugs firing a thousand soft pops in perfect predictability. The car eased from an idle and backed down the steep driveway, the sound of my father on his way to the office eventually evaporating like water on a summer road.

I lay still in indecision; and, after generating a sufficient receptivity to what might await, opened the door and walked to the kitchen. I was wearing a heavy bathrobe that had been hanging on a hook inside the bedroom door: an old hand-me-down from my father, the unintended symbolism so obvious as to afford a kind of protection. My mother, tall and proud of bearing, was at the window, surveying the not-quite black and not-quite white of barren trees, rooftops, and rippled water extending to a horizon layered with clouds resembling folded blankets on a cold guestroom bed. In the style of those years four stools curved around a bar counter. I pulled onto a stool and waited.

"Was the drive home difficult?" There was bravery in her voice–my father had made his report.

"I enjoyed it, actually. It's valorous, if you think of it in a certain way."

She nodded, still gazing out the window. "The drive could have been worse, believe it or not. Our winter came in violently this year." She sighed, despite herself. It would not have been characteristic of my mother to draw attention to her emotions. She was, instead, fortifying herself. "We had that twenty-inch blizzard right after Thanksgiving. The radio said the winds measured sixty-nine miles an hour down at the Canal. It was dangerous. Chunks of ice were falling from the Bridge. We were into the deep freeze after that, ten days in a row before the temperature rose above zero. One morning it was twenty-one below. It was almost that cold this morning. So a long winter is ahead."

"That's what people in the Cities are saying, too."

"It warmed up early last week and that was almost worse. The plows hadn't done a very good job, so banks were spilling into the streets. When you have one-lane streets everything is slow. The cars move very gingerly, you know. I told your father it reminded me of those first walks in the hospital after my surgery. And all the brown road grit–the slop drops down and then plops from the cars. From their haunches, one of those new hires said in the paper. The drain in the garage floor plugged up. Your father was grumbling because he came in with wet shoes and cuffs. And we're always bumping up against cars, so coats and pant legs get chalky. Then how do you find a company that's insured so they can remove the snow from the roof? Some college boys have been around but your father says it's an invitation to a lawsuit."

She turned toward me. We hadn't seen one another since summer, and devoted a few silent moments to examining each other's face for changes.

My father may have decided he could no longer afford to be concerned about my failures, but my mother enjoyed no such luxury. All this winter talk was, it seemed to me, meant to remind herself of the fearsome adversities she was capable of enduring. "We had a Southern California fellow in our section," I said, deliberately bringing law school to the fore. "He was pretty distressed about all the light we were losing through the fall. I told him I couldn't imagine living in a place where that *didn't* happen. All those long, dark winter evenings we're given to stay inside and read. If you're a law student who needs to spends evenings in the library—well, living in Southern California, how do you ever get anything *done?*"

My mother, a perceptive woman, paused. The idea had been to nudge her attention toward law school and then yesterday's debacle, to move her past formalities—talk, literally, of weather—and to what we both knew to be the point of our conversation. So clumsy had been my effort that in a few sentences I had put myself in the position of boasting about ambition and accomplishment. Me, who in twenty-seven years hadn't done a damn thing except the things I had done horrendously.

"Yes," she acknowledged. "But then there are the frozen fingers, and the sore back from shoveling, and the dryness, always reaching for hand lotion and eye drops. Tracking snow that is never white into the house—that's what people who don't live in the North fail to appreciate, that once you have to deal with snow, it's never white. You think your vision is blurring until you realize a fine powder is falling again, like drizzle in Seattle, except at a hard slant."

I laughed in spite of myself. "Does winter really make you so miserable?"

"No," she said.

"I'm curious about what Dad told you, since we hardly spoke at all last night."

"He said—" She looked down, then turned back toward the window. "It's hard, Tom, is all."

"Well, I'm sorry for that."

"Hard, and hard to understand. That's the most difficult part. If your father and I could just *understand*."

"I'll answer any question you put to me, as best I can. I suppose I owe you that."

"Those are your words, not mine," she said churlishly. This change seemed to rouse her from despondency. "We would never say you owe us anything."

"Understood. And the truth, anyway, is that I probably don't have any answers. Not so soon. I'm hoping there will be a little more clarity later."

"Tell me this, though, Tom. What did you mean when you told your father you 'didn't finish.' I'm trying to understand that. I've been trying all night long. If you got stumped, couldn't you have gone on to the next problem and come back? Or just worked your way through it? Surely you could have come up with something. Were you trying to be too perfect?"

The questions were deflating, strongly tempting me toward silence. "It didn't have anything to do with being stumped."

"I'm sure law school is difficult."

The invitation to admit defeat was annoying, inoculated as it was from dismissal by a small truth. Law school had been difficult–this was its attraction, a sort of monastic deprivation–and the exam had been difficult. Had the exam been less difficult, the idea to quit it would not have occurred. But the exam hadn't been *too* difficult. That was the crucial point. It hadn't been difficult enough to require leaving, and yet I had left.

"I don't know," I said.

"You must *know*," she said, giving *know* two syllables. Not exasperation, but a step in that direction. "Did others decide not to finish, too? Maybe the test was just poorly written. Maybe *that* was the problem."

"No." I had no desire to be coy. I wished I had more to say. "I'm not sure what exactly the problem was, but it wasn't that."

"You've hurt us so much," she blurted out, lifting both our spirits. She stepped closer to me and extended her arms. "Doing all this damage to yourself, and your father and I are just helpless."

"It seems like damage now, but will it in a month or two? Damage is relative –"

"Oh, Tom." At a loss, she looked around the room, rubbed her arms. "At some point –"

"Yes?"

"Alright. Perhaps you're correct, what's needed is some distance. I don't want to say something I'd regret." She absent-mindedly found her way to one of the stools, leaving an empty chair between us. "Though I can't honestly think of a single thing I'd regret saying. I'm afraid any regret would come from *not* saying."

"I can take it. Really I can. But maybe there's no point when everything is still so soon."

She gave herself a chance to accept this. "Alright," she said again. "Let's go forward now. Come Monday morning–what then?"

Of course I had thought about that. My father had talked to his partners and obviously there had been no objection to my filling the two-week break as a law clerk at Boyer, Johnson & Salmi. The firm had a newsletter and an announcement and paragraph about me had appeared a few weeks earlier–my mother had enclosed it with a Christmas card she had sent down to Minneapolis. A first-year law student knows nothing, really, but the clerkship was for my benefit, not the firm's. A quick immersion into the world that awaited me elsewhere, most likely, in a bigger firm in a bigger city, but still essentially the same world. Except, of course, that such a world no longer awaited me.

"Unless Dad has other plans, I'll show up as the new hire. Like everyone expects."

"You can make it until January?" she said quietly. "No walking out?"

"I don't think so."

"I'll let you and your father sort out all that. I expect he'll leave you alone at the office. But you'll be here evenings."

"Sure, more or less." Was she hinting I might not be welcome? The thought hadn't occurred.

"The holidays will overwhelm everything, as they always do. And after that? Or is it too soon to talk about that, also?"

"Let's wait and see. I've been awake half an hour. I need a little more time than that for these decisions." I paused but a moment, then cut off any possible reply. "And yes, I probably should have thought of that earlier."

§

I wasn't, though, a child. Through the weekend I worked hard to sort out the implications of what had occurred. Not the practical implications—what would happen, in my mother's pointed question, come the new, empty year—but something more fundamental. How important had Friday been? It had been catastrophic, was my initial assessment. (An uneasy thought appeared: would I have done it if it *hadn't* been catastrophic?) But surely that was a conceit; the one universe in which I was at the center was, after all, my universe. On the other hand, walking away from a three-year commitment after a mere four months was, at a minimum, consequential. The consequences, however—this was important for me to establish—were mine. Again: I wasn't a child. I wasn't some eighteen-year-old who had quit on college after a single semester. Parents would have had legitimate concern, anger, sorrow in such a situation, but that wasn't my situation, or my parents'. Why, really, should they have cared, especially after all the earlier disappointments they had endured? As soon as I satisfied myself with the rightness of this argument, I was blindsided by the obvious fact that objectivity had no place in such an analysis. What was catastrophic to my parents must be, by definition, catastrophic; or, if not catastrophic, at least—crucially—catastrophic to them. This hopeless tautology churned all the way to Monday morning, and so did my mood, irritation following pity following annoyance following compassion, each emotion blending into a general, vaguely defensive, unhappiness.

I built for myself an artificial enthusiasm for the new job. I did this by passing the weekend in enforced isolation, keeping to my bedroom while reading a little and sleeping a lot. I skipped meals, venturing out late to pick from the refrigerator. Whatever the psychic merits of such a strategy, the practical results were highly unsatisfying: come Monday, first light opening the day at quarter past seven, a distinctly unprodigal sun following over the steaming lake by eight o'clock, the thermometer's mercury crouched into a posture of fourteen below, strong winds raking down the hillside—come Monday, the Civic was unresponsive to my endearments and castigations. The block of metal may as well have been a block of stone. My parents owned jumper cables, of course, but these were coiled in the trunk of the Lincoln my father had taken to work an hour earlier. I threw my shoes in a pack, put on boots, and stutter-stepped down three precipitous blocks to a bus stop. The wait was mercifully short. A city bus wrapped in advertisements quickly arrived, its interior warm as an oven—so warm, in fact, that the driver, a long-haired dropout with a thick and well-thumbed Solzhenitsyn on the dash, wore short sleeves. Only half a dozen seats were occupied, elderly in the front, schoolboys in back. With the vast middle to myself I took a window seat and began to appraise the city I hadn't belonged to for almost a decade.

The day would be brilliant—I could see that even now, the sun barely up and long shadows kneading the small yards and alleys. Three inches of snow had fallen Sunday evening, washing the town white and ushering in a new front of subarctic cold. Plows had already been out, and the avenue being navigated had been ground to a hard icy surface. The bus's warmth and motion were calming. The driver's face, as revealed in the large mirror by which he kept the empty seats under watch, was severely vertical—a hatchet face, earlier generations would have said, though to me it most resembled the rigid binding of Black's Law Dictionary. A large woman, made larger by her layers of clothes, leaned forward against her walker. "Did you watch the TV last night?" she shouted piercingly.

"Why," said the driver.

"Did you see about the Eskimos? That show said they have dozens of words for snow."

"And we have just as many," the driver replied with exaggerated forbearance. "All adjectives." Bad weather was of course a staple of conversation in those years, less so now that instant communication has undermined its provincialism. College had displayed for me the alternatives, and during vacations home I had often been struck by the dramatic changes over relatively short distances. Cold, dark Duluth, where taverns celebrated Oktoberfest in September, was always most difficult to tolerate when warm weather was being enjoyed but three hours south in Minneapolis. And even within Duluth the lake and hill played tricks. My father had a story of leaving work at forty-six degrees one June afternoon and arriving home, ten minutes up the hill, to find a temperature of eighty-eight.

A decade away had permitted me to view Duluth with a critical—not to say objective—eye. Part of this was the natural disparagement a self-absorbed young man would feel, or affect to feel, for his hometown. In childhood every rivulet is a river; later, in compensation, rivers are merely drainage. But there was no denying a certain shattered aspect to Duluth, traumatized by the collapse of the steel industry and only now beginning to respond to the national recovery. Development in Duluth, I had heard my father say, was so uncommon that when a new building *was* proposed it was regarded as an eccentricity, a hare-brained scheme. My mother had mentioned to me in recent years the anxiety of living in a backwater (a word neither of my parents would ever have used): when a small law firm closed, or the number of doctors on a clinic's roster fell from seven to three, or a national franchise, popular everywhere else, went dark, the fear was of a slide toward irrelevance. There were lawyers and doctors and drive-throughs and big electronics stores *somewhere*. The world was passing you by. While your life was being conveyed along, days ahead traded for days behind, you were wasting it *here*. This whole line of thought was, of course, in the end nothing more than a cry for validation. *I matter.*

As the nineteenth century regressed into the twentieth, Duluth had blazed on the kerosene of timber and iron ore. That was the era of the big East End houses and the magnates, the top hats and servants. Horace Levine came north from Iowa and established a law office in the Board of Trade Building. Who knows how skilled a lawyer he was, but now, dead fifty years, his reputation was of a man who took cues from his clients, trading off their information. If a deed conveying land near the Clara Pit was needed, because prospects for expansion of the Clara Pit were good, more than likely Horace Levine would by year-end own Clara Pit land as well. He built a great fortune that was lost in the Depression. One hot July night he watched the Marx Brothers perform vaudeville–they were in town to work up bits for *A Day at the Races*–and then, after a few long, soul-searching drinks at the Kitchi Gammi Club, routed his walk home through the rail yard. Whether his death was the result of intent or misstep is not known, local history satisfying itself that there is a point where the two intersect. A poor secretary kept the law office going for a year, typing deeds and dispensing legal advice, until the furniture and books were purchased by Bertrand Boyer. Partners were added over the years, some who stayed and some who did not; if you page through mid-century city directories you will conclude that the legal profession in some ways resembled a high school's dating scene. By 1960 (not long before my appearance) my father had joined the firm. The next few decades saw a couple of small mergers, more hiring, the fortuitous acquisition of a number of clients adept at prospering in lean times.

During my first year of college the Cadotte Building burned to the ground. It had stood on the upper side of Superior Street since 1888–the alley behind it, draped in shadow for ninety-two years, was suddenly bathed in sunlight. The fire occurred one week before Christmas, just like now. Ashes fell through all of downtown, carried by smoky gusts capable of stinging the eyes even two days later. For a week Duluth's entire commercial district, home to banks, brokers, lawyers, and the few remaining retail proprietors, smelled like a hot dog on a stick. The Cadotte Building had been no model–small trees grew out of its walls–but the fire put a scare into Boyer, Johnson & Salmi, which occupied a large suite in a similarly ancient building a mere block away. While the fire marshal and the city inspector argued whether blame should go to poor wiring or arson, my father's firm picked up and left. A venerable warehouse near the Canal was being gentrified, and Ted Salmi negotiated a lease for the top floor. Over the course of a fall weekend the move was made: desks and chairs, typewriters, photocopy machines, books, client files, an old safe, a new facsimile machine. Eighteen lawyers and as many staff. Did anyone comment on the firm's new home being at least as old and vulnerable to fire as the abandoned building? The new offices had large windows looking out over the lake.

This was where the bus deposited me. I was dressed in all three pieces of a suit, my tie the shiny yellow so emblematic of the era five years earlier. Lake Superior was unspeakably beautiful, orange sunlight piercing through billowing geysers of steam. The Aerial Bridge, adorned in ice, loomed overhead massively. The lift was up, lights flashing and bells ringing; beneath, a maroon ore boat nearly a quarter-mile in length, likely one of the last departures of the season, was gliding through the ship canal. I stepped from the bitter cold into the dark atrium, then crossed the floor to a converted freight elevator. An impossibly young woman, blond hair exploding in peacock fashion, entered the car with me. She studied the buttons. "Is six the top, or is seven?"

I wasn't Tom Johnson at this point, of course. I was Lanny Johnson's son, arriving from law school, and consequently my triumphant entry into the legal profession after one paltry semester was filled with dread—I anticipated my welcome to have all the grandeur of the state funeral given the leg of Santa Anna. A general confusion afflicted me: what, exactly, did the firm know about last Friday and its implications? Any information could only have come from my father, who wasn't a talker and, besides, had no incentive to broadcast his only child's latest failure. But quitting school was so enormous an event, so consequential to my reason for being in this place and dressed this way, that I couldn't imagine the news as a secret. The elevator door opened, my fellow traveler drifted tentatively toward a lobby chair, and I fell into the sights of a lively, athletic woman of fifty-five emerging from a corridor. Sandy wore a polyester pantsuit; short black hair topped a pleasant nut brown face. "I'm ready for you," she said.

Sandy had been the office manager my entire life, it seemed. I remembered, and fervently hoped she did not, a firm picnic during which a ten-year-old Tom Johnson ate three or four hot dogs and drank a quart or two of root beer before vomiting onto the top of a picnic table, taking out six plates of food. I had just finished a burlap sack race that Sandy had organized. "We'll put you where you'll keep out of trouble," she now cackled. I liked the sound; laughter was Sandy's default mode. "Under Maggie's eye."

I knew Maggie, too, through mostly from stories delivered by my mother. Maggie was Ted Salmi's secretary, a fan of cigarettes and salacious talk. A belittler of all things male. Maggie had been happiest during the three years of her unhappy marriage; happiness, as is too often the case, would have made her unhappy. She was well into her forties now, a terror to the younger secretaries. Husbandless, childless, her dreams and affections were tethered to her sister's children. But Maggie didn't like them, either, which meant she was basically living for Boyer, Johnson & Salmi, her devotion to the firm reflected by her disdain.

"Maggie's is here, of course," Sandy said, leading me past an empty cubicle. "Don't know where she is this morning. And then here's you." It was the next cubicle, bare but for a yellow legal pad, a dictating machine, and a stack of cassettes each the size of wrapped bubble gum. "Settle yourself in and I'll be back."

The office, I'd already gathered, was swimming in Christmastide. Wreaths covered the walls, and garland was draped along the tops of the cubicle partitions. I'd seen at least one secretary with a ceramic tree on her desk, and wouldn't have been surprised to see that secretary donning an elf's hat. Holiday music was being discreetly piped through the office–Crosby singing "White Christmas," Elvis singing "Blue Christmas," the Mills Brothers chugging along with "Here Comes Santa Claus." But lest irony overwhelm the scene, just as I was wistfully remembering an Andean band in Quito's La Plaza Grande–bombo and ocarina, charango and rainstick, arpeggios cascading as though raindrops were falling on the very strings–the exuberant trumpets of "Sleigh Ride" introduced themselves. "Leroy Anderson," Stoltzman had once said, "is an arranger's arranger." I had spent the better part of a Minneapolis weekend dissecting the piece, attempting to uncover how the packaging of various sounds was capable, in this instance, of invoking nostalgia and whimsy. Those days of dissection were past. Now I just sat and stared ahead, listening.

I felt silly, of course, dressed as I was and sitting purposelessly at an empty desk–purposelessly, it must be understood, in a holistic sense, encompassing both small (I had nothing to do) and large (with no future in the law I had no reason to be here; I was essentially accepting a paycheck to be a burden). Occasionally someone would pass; those who knew me stopped with a greeting. Informed by the newsletter, they asked few questions other than how I liked school, and were satisfied with a noncommittal bob of the head. Most, however, did not know me, not so strange when I remembered that much of the firm's hiring had occurred in the recent decade. Lawyers who could have been my older brothers were working away in their open-doored offices, out of sight yet present in the sounds of their chiming coffee mugs and loud, what-the-hell-Charlie telephone etiquette. "I can't deal with that now, honey," I heard in a boyish voice. "Just call the mechanic." From the next office, older and wiser: "I believe next year will not be what I believe it to be."

I picked up the recorder and examined it, much as a toddler might examine a misplaced blasting cap. The idea was that the memos I would be providing this lawyer or that would be dictated for the benefit of the secretary responsible for typing up whatever insights I might happen upon. My father was a great fan of dictation–many an evening during my high school years I would observe him pacing from the living room to the dining room and back, talking to a lov-ingly-cradled machine. "Chapter 28 of United States Code, section 1333"–I heard that mantra often. Or: "Etcetera, etcetera, etcetera, Pamela, you know the drill." But Pamela was gone now, moved to the Cities like so many others. I flipped in a tape and began a tentative recording. "Test," I said; then, more quietly, "test"; then, most quiet of all, "test." I paused. "One, two, three," I quickly added. The problem was obvious. Talking into a little black cigarette pack–saying the patently uninformed things I would soon be saying–while sitting at a desk exposed to dozens: the idea was inherently preposterous.

And of course it was at this point that Maggie Metaxas appeared. "What's this happy horseshit?" she said, scornfully peering down at a stack of files left on her desk. She wrestled off a heavy coat. The thick wool turtleneck beneath was prac-tical, given the dangerous temperatures, but more casual than seemed to be allowed the rest of the staff. Maggie's face was rough and purplish from the cold. Her black hair shot out

Medusa-like, last-gasp rockets escaping an exploding dark star. She glanced over the short partition to see me in all my foolishness. "You're sure as hell not Kitty Barrister"—Kitty Barrister being, I was soon to learn, Katherine Berster, the law clerk from last summer.

"I never have been."

She watched me without immediately replying. "Lanny Johnson's kid, right?"

"There's a resemblance?"

This made her snort out a laugh. "Where to begin." Into her chair, she began to paw through the files. "I suppose they just left you here to fend for yourself."

"Sandy will be back."

"She's got the twelve-year-old temp to deal with." Maggie extracted a page of notes from the top file. She paused to take it in. "Hell's friggin' bells." She rose from her chair. "Ted!" she called sharply, then departed for his office.

I again picked up the recorder. Would it be possible to speak so softly that Maggie would be unable to hear? To form more than a fragment of a sentence before clicking the machine to a pause? I supposed that Katherine Berster had written her memos out in longhand and then read then into the dictating machine. It wouldn't be beneath me to do the same. And what did I care, anyway, sitting in for a two-week stint and having trouble believing there was anything of value I could contribute to a firm that had actual clients willing to pay large sums of money, conditioned on their legal problems actually being solved?

"Okay," Sandy said in a fast approach, huffing but smiling. "Busy morning!"

"That's good."

"That's good!" she agreed. "You know everyone here, probably more than you want to know."

"No," I objected.

"I'm going to give you the tour anyway. Then come the forms."

So with Sandy as my Virgil we moved from office to office, work station to work station. She took me first to see my father—"It just makes sense, doesn't it?" Sandy said—but he was on a telephone conference, door closed. My father had a corner office, and understanding the inerrancy of workplace assignment—name partners in the corners, followed by offices on the lake wall, then offices on the bay wall, then offices facing the hill, then interior offices; secretaries had no offices, and the mailroom was also the utility room—was like being granted X-ray vision with which to view the skeletal structure of Boyer, Johnson & Salmi. I would quickly learn that if two up-and-coming lawyers gave me separate assignments, priority had best be given the lawyer whose window view was better (though something in me—contrarian? failed seminarian?—consistently defaulted toward the diminished view). On we moved, from a real estate lawyer to a divorce lawyer, a bankruptcy lawyer to an estate planner. I said hello to Bertrand Boyer, whom I had known all my life, though not at seventy-nine; he had a couch in his office for napping, and death seemed to have migrated from threat to a promise he intended to enforce. I said hello to Ted Salmi, blunter and more headstrong and hard-charging than I had remembered, a warrior out of a Kalevalan pine swamp. Ethnic features, I observed, become more pronounced with age. (This was even more true of Mr. Abelman, squinting at ledgers in the accounting office and, having made the regrettable trade of hair for eyeglasses, now resembling nothing as much as a Yiddish tailor examining the seams.) I met all the staff. I met Kay Knapp, whose son was apparently on his way to the National Hockey League, in ten years; it was important to Kay that her son do well, I would learn, but more important that the other boys do poorly. I met Toni Torelli, who had actually been in my high school graduating class; we both charitably denied remembering one another. I met (and quickly forgot the name of) the plumed temp with whom I had shared the elevator. I met Nicole Haraldson, who, like Toni, seemed to be about my age. On her desk were photos of three splendid children.

"This is where you'll probably be spending most of your time," Sandy said as she directed me into the library. "That's what Katherine did."

"I'm sure." I began to examine the volumes that lined the walls.

"Curiosity," Sandy laughed. "Not a wonder that you chose law. Your destiny, most likely. Come to my office when you're ready. I'll be prepping the paperwork."

The library was modest, a conference room with a large table surrounded by eight chairs and shelves on three walls. The room had the smell of old bindings. The Minnesota reporters took up an entire wall, every opinion issued by the state's Supreme Court since the Union had been joined. There was tradition in such accumulation. In making this observation I wasn't thinking of the law firm, though an eighty-four-year history represented something of value. My thoughts were of the state's heritage, which of course had been built on law from the emancipated colonies, itself a product of English law. Blackstone. The four Inns of Court. Here, truly, was something of value. A hearing instead of a dual. In the Middle Ages, Professor Priley had taught us, land had been conveyed by the symbolic delivery of a clump of sod from grantor to grantee. The nagging issues of proof, authentication, and memory, the very joinder of independent wills, were addressed one by one in the development of deeds and boundary descriptions and recording statutes. Refinements were introduced. This all accompanied–enabled, one might say–the rise of empire, the fitful nurture of democracy and individual rights, the flowering of art, the creation of Western power and civilization. The law was, in short, worthy of preservation. It was ennobling. It was, like the priesthood, a calling.

I slid a volume from the shelf and opened its yellowed and flaking pages to, randomly, *Thomas v. Barton*, decided in 1921. The case had originated in one of the western counties: Thomas and Barton had been neighboring farmers. To open more land for production Barton had drained a slough and planted potatoes in the old lake bed. Thomas, who had depended on the vanished pond's ducks, and who in any event believed much of the bed to be his, brought suit. The Supreme Court cited similar cases, some of them even then a century or more old. The court considered the respective needs of Thomas and Barton, suggesting with deft subtlety family histories and traditions, visions and aspirations. Perhaps–I was extrapolating now–Thomas had inherited his farm, and had memories of father and son running a trapline through the lowlands. Perhaps Barton had a daughter he had promised to send to the teachers' college, assuming just a bit more income could be squeezed from the land. What sort of result might best serve not only these neighbors, but also society?–the court considered that facet as well. The justices did not know Thomas or Barton, presumably. And yet as I turned the pages the care bestowed on these two men, their preferences and livelihoods, their rights and dignity, quieted me with a profound sadness. After reading the eleven-page opinion–the ruling didn't matter–I turned to the front of the volume for the names of the seven justices, a couple of surnames being vaguely familiar. It goes without saying that all seven, as well as Thomas and Barton, were by 1989 long dead. I felt an admiration and a debt, and of course I felt these things bitterly.

§

Whenever gravity pulled particularly hard, as now, my uncon-scious defense was imagined retreat into the woods. Our family seldom left Duluth. (My father sailed, true, but for him sailing was psychic hygiene; an invitation to join him would have been about as likely as an invitation to sit beside him in the dentist's chair.) The Norgaards, however, spent numerous and glorious summer days up the shore and among the Canadian lakes. I was often their invited guest. One memory in particular has stayed with me through the years, the setting being the chill of a northern July morning, tents perched beneath lordly white pines, and a small stream gurgling from the corner of a placid border lake. The noisy fuss of a jay had roused me, and while the twins and their parents slept I set off to navigate the boul-ders crowding along the water. I was probably thirteen. From a height of five or six feet I lay on my belly, the hard slab of basalt already warming in the early sun, and watched for fish. I saw none, but what I noticed was the peculiar way the stream was really two streams, a surface current but also a deeper current; neither, I could see from the floating pine needles and water bugs and bubbles, was moving at the speed of the other.

In nature the discovery was sublime; as applied to life, *my* life, ridiculous. And so it was that while what I knew to be a turning point was playing itself out—and twenty-five years have proven me correct in my assessment—the current of the mundane, the quotidian, pulled me at day's end to the shopping mall over the hill, among the cliffs and swamps. Part suburbia, part Indian reservation—but of course on a well-lit bus at half past five, mere days from the year's longest night, the mall and everything else in the physical world could only be imagined, the bus's long windows being black as mirrors in a cave. If I were expected to return to Boyer, Johnson & Salmi for eight more days, more shirts than I had had the foresight to bring to Duluth would be needed. There were other odds and ends as well—a day among people who were actually able to manage life suggested that I might be entering a stage where practical considerations should be given a hearing.

Having never actually worked in my life, not in the way that was expected of a contributing citizen, I was unprepared for the exhaustion justly rewarded me for nine hours of toil and tedium. The day had been a patchwork: greetings and introductions; instructions and make-work assignments; embarrassing inquiries (bothering Sandy for staples); and stretches where there was little to do, stretches where I (and everyone) wished I were elsewhere, and pretended that to be true, eyes averted and words left unexchanged. "You'll be back," Maggie said as five o'clock neared, despite all evidence to the contrary. "For forty years. It's what people here do." The bus, stopping and starting with herky-jerky repetition, was not conducive to a revival. We paused at each intersection all the way up Central Entrance, picking up passengers in groups of one. Waiting to be deposited into the cheer of

72

late fiscal fourth quarter commerce, we sat in silence, staring ahead blankly the way passengers must in wintertime Minsk. There being no reason to decamp at the pawn shop or tattoo parlor, the bus filled like a balloon attached to a helium tank at a school carnival. I gave my seat up to a woman apparently on her way to return a microwave; she smiled at me over the box. It felt good to stand.

The cold between bus and mall entrance was invigorating. But once inside, the garishness was immediately upon me, bad music and roaming bands of teens and a general, dispiriting commotion. Our Duluth mall was no match for the colossi I had grown to know in the Twin Cities, unfortunately: I longed for the anonymity unlikely to be afforded me in my hometown. Head lowered, I threaded through groups moving in the slowest of gears—meander, hesitation, standstill—to find the anchor department store most likely to have the least expensive, minimally presentable clothing. A question for a clerk, an emptying of the wallet, and in short order I was on my way with three shirts, one white and the other two white. The bus driver on the climb up the hill—no Russophile now, but an anchor-on-the-forearm, 249-league-average, no-nonsense union rep sort of fellow—had given clear instructions that the return bus would be leaving from the other side of the premises, ostensibly to regulate crowding but more likely due to some arrangement with mall management to increase exposure to all manner of record, dress, poster, videotape, toy, and candy shops. Years had passed since I was last in this shopping mall. I remembered, as though re-watching a childhood television show, the woman behind the counter at the low cal food shop—still there, incredibly, older and tubbier. I duly noted the new (to me) craft and trinket shops shouting for attention, each make-shift and nomadic, offering little aesthetic pleasure, daily gross receipts undoubtedly measured in fives and tens. Much of the holiday music I had endured during daylight hours was omnipresent in the food court, cheerless familiarities meant as comeback vehicles for graying pop stars: the music of any generation will inevitably sound to that generation's children like novelty tunes. Yet just as there appeared to be a full and absolute merger of reality and caricature, I turned into a small atrium, a blessedly colorless DMZ between Santaland and escape, and what to my eyes did appear but two dozen high school students in Victorian costume. Chairs had been set out and roughly one hundred parents and other wearies were finishing a round of applause. I took a seat as an ensemble began a challenging and lovely Burt carol. Alfred Burt was doubly loved by me—for his music, of course, intricate and yet virtuous in the simplicity of its conception, but also for the back-story. Burt had been in all respects an anomaly, a minister's son raised in Michigan's Upper Peninsula, a jazz musician who composed a carol each year and mailed the sheet music out as his Christmas card. Had cancer not taken him at an exceptionally young age, Self Portrait certainly would have hunted Burt up. I listened to "Sleep, Baby Mine," and in those four minutes began to lose myself in the song's restlessness, beauty, and promise. At the same time I was aware of how ominous, even depressive, was the re-creation of Burt's ghostly winter wind—a fit for dark and solemn winter, perhaps, but a sound that would never be tolerated any other time of year; unimaginable in summer, for example. The voices soon gave way to a brass choir. My skepticism was calmed by a restrained "God Rest Ye Merry Gentlemen." Some busyness then ensued—sheet music, mutes, glances toward a reassuring teacher. "The Holly and the Ivy" followed, world-weary but bravely hopeful.

The bus was up to the task of ferrying us back toward town, not up to doing so comfortably. It was an accordion bus, two long sections pivoting crazily as we roared into the night, a wall of pungent diesel exhaust graying our wake. I stood near the rear door, one elbow jabbing the kidney of a big college boy and the other tapping the nose of a forlorn grandmother. The ride had the contingency of a log rolling contest. Stops were sudden, and because the bus's mission was tied to the mall, few people climbed on or off. Most of us would not be released until downtown, transferring then to the relative comfort of smaller neighborhood busses. At each stoplight—there were many—stood a three- and four-shop strip mall. From the bus's interior they could only be seen in outline, but when the doors flung open I beheld a taco shop, or a liquor store, or cleaners. Then, at the next intersection, an automotive shop, a bakery, thirty-one flavors of ice cream. A young woman stepped through the rear door, directly in front of me. She wore a ski jacket with a dirty lift ticket dangling from the zipper. A knit cap topped dark hair—Minnesota dark, I should say—that grazed the shoulders. She had an athletic look, tall and limber; the way she bounced up into the bus caused me to picture her in gym shorts, the two horizontal creases behind each knee. She was holding before her, and her eyes were fixed on, a cone of peppermint ice cream, jewels of Christmas red and green sparkling among the pink.

"What would your mother say?" I asked.

"What?" she answered, eyes wide in disbelief. "What?"

I am reporting this from a distance. I was, incredibly, a mere three years short of thirty. I had been *married*. But twenty-seven now seems to me impossibly young. From either perspective, then or now, it is good to be occasionally reminded that adults can act like adolescents—or, rather, that adulthood is not so much a separate category as a variation on adolescence's themes.

"Eating something so fantastic," I said. "And right at dinnertime. What would your mother say?"

She examined the ice cream, then me. "Do I know you?"

"And it's a good thing you don't." I appreciated the sensibleness of her caution.

At this point she slowly, charmingly, took a healthy lick of ice cream. "Good idea," I said. In her wake a Siberian pocket of air had entered the bus. "You wouldn't want it to melt."

"My mother wouldn't care in the least, even if she knew, which she doesn't."

We were silent. For that matter the entire bus was silent but for mumbled conversation here and there, a testament to the numbing aspect of mass transportation, or the mall, or the weather, or possibly Christmas.

"Did you go to the U?" she asked, turning her attention from ice cream to this odd provocateur. "I feel like you must have."

"As a matter of fact, yes."

"Which campus?"

"Minneapolis."

"Maybe I saw you on intercampus or something."

"No, I'm pretty sure we've never met."

"We wouldn't be talking if we'd never met, would we?"

"Why not?"

For the first time she looked into my face directly. She held the gaze long enough for me to appreciate the sable of her eyes. Her face was not round, but more of the shoebox variety, flawless skin swaddling an exquisitely expressive mouth. Her teeth were as perfect as a dentist's daughter's. Despite the dark eyes and hair (the possible result of some unspeakable atrocity committed during a warring expedition centuries ago in the old country), I guessed her to be of standard-issue Scandinavian stock; her skin tone was the same as that of virtually everyone on the bus and at the mall. The danger of inbreeding crossed my mind—as a fancy, of course, not as any type of concern. But that such a thought could arise during those first minutes of conversation was not nothing.

"I guess I need to know if you meant what you said. There's nothing wrong with ice cream, you know. There's worse."

"Salad's better."

"I get the feeling that if I'd walked on with a salad you would have had something to say about that."

"I hope I would have."

She gave this some thought, then seemed to lose herself again in ice cream. The bus began its steep rumble down Mesaba Avenue.

"Let's have a salad together," I said. "A whole meal. We can talk."

She smiled and looked toward the window, its opaqueness giving way to downtown's cluster of lights. "What would we talk about?"

I shrugged. "Why you're eating ice cream in sub-zero temperatures?"

She laughed helplessly, disarmingly. My intentions could not have been more transparent. They were clear to the grandmother at my knee, who for the past mile had been carefully watching. They were clear to a handful of others in the vicinity, all staring resolutely at the floor. Was this girl trying to make me believe she had never been the object of such (admittedly clumsy) attention?

"You're making fun of me."

"No," I protested. I told her my name.

"Are you serious, then?"

"About the ice cream? Or about grabbing something to eat?"

"Yes."

"Yes."

We were on Superior Street now, slowing for disembarkation. Those fortunate enough to have claimed seats rose, crowding the bus intolerably. Pressed close to me, Ice Cream Girl turned her head away. The doors sprung open and we flooded out as though water from a punctured jug. "Right here tomorrow," I said, anxious that she would disappear into the crowd–anxious that I would be reduced to *chasing* her. "Six o'clock."

"No"–hope dashed; and then restored: "not tomorrow."

"Then Wednesday."

She turned with a look of exasperation. I had saddled her with something she had not, but twenty minutes earlier, given a thought to expecting. She pursed her lips and waggled the top of her head back and forth, considering. Maybe; maybe. Then she turned and was briskly gone. I waited for my transfer and rode up the hill on the life force Alfred Burt had gifted me.

§

To this thin reed did I cling for my new life. A willing suspension of disbelief was required–I knew that. But I also knew hope could burn through me without exhaustion for another forty-eight hours.

Again: all is memory and speculation. Currents move in their separate planes, independent of one another. The grandmother on the bus knew nothing of me—not my family, my childhood, my misadventures and grievous mistakes, my *history*. In the same way I was comprehensively ignorant of a girl careful to disclose nothing but an apparent sentimentality (peppermint at Christmas) and independence (ice cream at five below). Even in my spells of gravest doubt I had no problem imagining a set of eyes on high, watching me board that bus and a girl order her cone, pleased by the intersection that awaited us. There was no reason to think God could ever grow bored: the girl ordering ice cream had as much a history as I, a family and childhood and triumphs and missteps. There was so much danger and promise in what the two of us did not know.

By Tuesday I was no longer Boyer, Johnson & Salmi's novelty. Without comment three lawyers—the secretaries of three lawyers—delivered memos requesting that I delve into one thing or another. What should be done when a corporation, charged with providing its shareholders notice of a critical meeting, had no addresses for the bulk of those shareholders? What was the consequence of a chain of deeds being recorded out of order? Was a will invalid because the notary's commission had lapsed a month before signing? I set up shop in the library and began my research. This was not unlike law school; this was something I could do. The day advanced satisfactorily. At noon I sat in the lunchroom with the secretaries. Here I again slipped back toward novelty. The women found me cute and somewhat ridiculous, and for an hour were able to forget the possibility of my status with the firm changing dramatically over the next few years—they might, in other words, resent me someday, but could toy with me now. I ate a sandwich and apple brought from home. The questions I received were more difficult than those I had spent the morning researching. Was I happy to be home for a couple of weeks? Would I be back clerking over the summer? I used false modesty as my cover, deftly refusing to provide anything like the good faith answers common decency required. My status with the firm would never change—would never rise, anyway—but there was no need to go public.

Through the day the outside temperature rose. The weekend's Plutoesque cold was not in fact sustainable. My car returned to join the living; using wrench and pliers cold enough to remove gloved skin, I had wrest the battery from beneath and given it pride of place inside my parents' entryway all night long. As I drove back on Tuesday evening my thoughts were of a pair of skis I had spied in the garage's rafters. I inspected them on my way into the house; a plan was developing. Once inside I was greeted by the plastic-on-plastic clap of a spent conversation. "That was your father," I heard. "He's leaving the office early. We'll hold supper for him."

The three of us had experienced virtually no communication since my first hours home. This was awkward and ultimately pointless: avoidance couldn't last long, certainly not with Christmas fast approaching. Guilt nagged at me as well. I was living in their home, eating their food, working the job I wouldn't have had but for them. I probably couldn't give my parents what they wanted—an explanation and a plan— but I might possibly be able to make them understand that my failure to provide answers wasn't malicious. So as we sat down ninety minutes later—something had delayed my father in leaving the office—I opened the conversation. "I've been genuinely welcomed downtown," I said. "It's felt good to be at the office."

"Good!" my father said.

"You know many of these people, Tom, isn't that right?"

"Not as many as you might think. And I'm learning you don't really know someone without working with them eight or nine hours a day."

My father gave a grudging laugh—a sneer, actually, but I was determined to hear it as a laugh—of recognition. "Oh yeah."

"Who are you working with," my mother asked, "and what sorts of things are they having you do?"

"Well," I began, and proceeded to thread my way delicately. My father and Ted Salmi pretty much ran the firm, Bertrand Boyer having passed into semi-retirement. A bad word from me, a carelessly disclosed confidence, could have consequences for the lawyers who desired to one day be in the position my father now held. Earlier that morning a late arrival by one of the young corporate lawyers had delayed the answer to one of my questions. That couldn't be mentioned: in my father's cosmology late arrival signaled a character defect. Nor could I relate overheard remarks passed between two of the young female lawyers to the effect that the firm lacked a certain appreciation for the demands put on working mothers. Also off-limits was the lunchroom, rarely visited by the lawyers and therefore prized by the secretaries as a refuge. It wasn't that I had heard criticisms of any sort—not of my father, or any of the other lawyers, or the firm. Not even of their jobs. But in two lunch hours I had become privy to: grocery prices, radio station comparisons, an exchange of Christmas cookie recipes, a biting review of an elementary school choir concert, a middle school boy's idea of a racy joke ("Why don't witches have babies?" "Because their husbands have Halloweenies."), and a near-constant flow of commentary about husbands, almost all of it disguised in exasperation so thin that the affection easily shone through. In short, all these women had lives fully independent of Boyer, Johnson & Salmi. I wasn't sure my father would have received such information favorably.

"Whatever happened to that clerk from last summer?" my mother asked.

My father's attention was on his plate, a winter mix of heavy meat and dark vegetables. "Don't know who you mean."

"Sure you do. Bill Berster's daughter."

"Katherine," I said. "Katherine Berster. Kitty Barrister, in Maggie-speak."

"Maggie," my mother said, blending reprimand and appreciation with a detectable envy.

"Maggie is a force of nature," my father said.

"There are lots of Maggie stories, Tom."

"At some point," my father said, not uncharitably, "it would have done everyone good, not the least Maggie, to have had a talk about boundaries."

"I think she understands boundaries pretty well," I said. "Enjoys leaping over."

"No dispute there. But in any event, if there ever were a time when such a lesson could have been learned, it's past."

"Long past," my mother agreed. "Do you have a problem with her, Tom?"

"Maggie? I hardly know her. I just know what I've observed. I've never met Katherine, but I have some sympathy for her."

"She was with us three months. Maggie's been with Ted for years."

"Might not have been the best idea to put Katherine next to her," I offered. Like so many opinions, this was one I didn't know I had until it was uttered. Though the thought seemed so uncontroversial that I hardly considered it an opinion at all.

"That would have been Sandy's call. Take it up with her."

"Obviously I–"

"Shop talk," my mother objected, sensing what was developing.

"Or wait for more than two days of observation."

"I'm not taking anything up with Sandy. I never said I would. It really doesn't concern me."

"When a firm's been around for generations there are some things that get done right, some that don't. But for every mistake there's a course correction. Someone comes in for a few days, he might not have the judgment to understand that there's a reason for the things he disapproves of. There's a history."

"I don't disapprove." My best self wanted to say this rationally, sympathetically. Without conscious decision I said it defensively.

"Your father's very protective of the firm."

"I can understand that. He's devoted a lot to it." And then I added–the decision, again, was made so quickly as to seem unconscious; and who makes such decisions, anyway?–I added, "He's sacrificed a lot."

One sort of man might have engaged me on this point; there was, clearly, a conversation eager to break out of the egg. Another might have recognized the danger in such engagement, especially after recent events, and drawn back with a demurral, or maybe self-deprecation, or simply by changing the subject. Oh, there were all sorts of ways my father might have responded. I'm not for one moment trying to minimize my own responsibility; this new unhappiness that had descended on our family was, after all, of my making. And it must be said that possibly, *possibly*, neither my father nor I could be charged with what was ensuing; or, rather, that we were at this point powerless to avoid the damage. We were riding a wave of inevitability, suffering at the end of a chain whose first links were events that could no longer be recalled: for three transgressions, and for four. One sort of father might have recognized this. What my father actually did was draw into himself. He said not another word, instead eating quickly and then retreating to the bedroom to pack for what my mother told me would be a three-day business trip to Cleveland. He was booked on the next morning's 5:15 flight.

The ski trails that wound through the hills above the Lester River were mostly empty. With the sound of a blade slicing paper I moved from shadow to light to shadow. At the top of a long incline I paused to take in the canyon below, a frozen waterfall descending from a birch forest. The air was biting but tolerable. A south wind sighed through the branches, pine boughs bobbing slowly. On the drive home I followed Glenwood Street up Oatmeal Hill: more birch, more balsam gyrating in the breeze. The Thanksgiving weekend blizzard had arrived wet, and snow still adhered to the northeast sides of tree trunks. The windows of eighty-year-old two-stories offered a warm and buttery yellow, broken now and then by the frenetic cavalcade of television screens. The captives hypnotized by those screens would have been unable to apprehend the surrounding beauty. Venus was bright and the moon a tear in the night's fabric. A narrow train of white clouds crossed the sliced moon and extended into the dark solstice blue.

§

There was no reason to expect this unnamed girl would appear. Indeed, one of the revolving moods afflicting me throughout the day was a regret that I had ever struck up our silly conversation in the first place. It had been done on a whim, obviously, the way a hundred things each day are done on a whim. You decide to ball up a page of notebook paper and launch it toward the basket across the room. You decide to wear the red tie, not the yellow. Choose the oatmeal cookie over molasses. I had chosen banter over silence. Did it make any sense that such a trivial decision live on into the next day, and the next? My actions puzzled me, largely because I could no longer imagine just what it was I was pursuing. I couldn't remember what Ice Cream Girl looked like. A description stayed with me–hair to her shoulders, dark eyes, a thin figure and somewhat tall stature–but those were only words. The whole thing was spur-of-the-moment flirting, nothing more or less.

This mood of regret was simply a mutation of impatience. Was this really what I wanted to be doing, throwing myself into a new... undertaking, let us say... only days after my final exam stunt? There was merit to the idea of putting one catastrophe to bed before initiating another. And this went to the heart of the matter: Ice Cream Girl, for whatever untraceable reason (this bears emphasis: just what *was* it I had in so short a period of time found attractive, found worthy of exempting from my default mode, rejection?), had struck me on Monday evening, in those few seconds of her sudden appearance, as necessary to putting my past behind me. My recent past, certainly, but the middle and distant past as well–the whole misbegotten package. This admission brought me to something like bemusement. I was betting quite a lot on quite a little. If she were my rescue line–or, more precisely, if a *relationship* with that girl were my rescue line–then the odds of survival seemed on the longish side. So another mood surfaced, one of contrived indifference. This was all a fancy, I told myself; of course I didn't believe it involved anything more than harmless fun. I liked this view. It kept my hopes down and preserved my self-esteem, such as it were. But there was no denying the pose was a pose. Manufactured. How else could I explain why I devoted my lunch hour to walking the half-mile downtown and scouting out possible dinner locations (slim pickings, I must say)? Or why the minutes moved at the speed of three minutes, one o'clock creeping to two, resting some, then slowly plodding to three?

Six o'clock was beyond the end of a Duluth workday; most of the downtown offices were by then emptied, their occupants home making supper. The crowd near the bus shelters in front of the Holiday Inn had largely dissipated. I casually wandered from indoors to out, then back, hoping to see her first, but mostly hoping to see her at all. I continued to steel myself for disappointment–at her failure to appear, of course, but also at a different, less alluring, appearance. My reaction to her on Monday night had had as much to do with me as with her–much more with me, probably, riding high on art and recklessness's promise of escape. I was entirely capable of deceiving myself. At any moment hung the possibility of encountering a woman of deflating ordinariness.

"Hello," she said in a stagey voice. The greeting came from over my shoulder—she had been searching too, obviously, had spied me and approached. (Did I conform to *her* memory?) I turned and found her standing close. She was (nearly) identical to the girl on the bus: same ski jacket and knit cap; same eyes. Same small, exquisite mouth. Her hair still swept the top of her shoulders like over-long curtains bunching on a living room floor. There was no ice cream, unsurprisingly, but the only other difference was a pair of fairly exotic rings dangling from her ear lobes. Improbably she extended a hand, which I took. We were standing close enough for my elbow to dig into my ribs.

"I'm Linda," she said, giving our hands a controlled snap of formality.

"I'm still Tom."

She nodded, greeting proceeding apace. "Do you have a car?"

"Well, yes, a few blocks' walk."

"Alright."

"You want to drive somewhere?"

"I've made us salads. I couldn't very well bring them along."

It was undoubtedly a blend of chauvinism and protective instinct that caused me to hesitate. An invitation cast toward a stranger on a bus was one thing. It was my thing. Now I was on the receiving end. "Drive where?"

"To the salads."

"But where, you see, are the salads?"

"In the refrigerator. They'll keep."

We began walking. Her legs were thin, taut; even weighed by mushers' boots they had a bounce. "Did you play sports?" I asked.

She laughed. "No one has ever asked me that before."

"You move well, if you don't mind me saying."

"In school you had to take gym. I was terrible. I didn't like it at all. I ski, though. Sheryl and I ice skate when we can."

"Where did you go to school?"

"Here in town. They're mostly all closed now."

"You're a native?"

"Sure. Not too much longer, I hope." She laughed at herself. "Well, I guess I'll always be a native, no matter where I end up."

"Where do you want to end up?"

"Somewhere else."

"What is your full name, Linda?"

"Brekke," she said, snapping the syllables like peanut brittle. "Do you know Dr. Brekke? Dr. Ed?"

"I've never had an appointment with a Dr. Brekke."

"That doesn't surprise me. Daddy's a gynecologist."

"Never heard of him. Sorry about that."

"You're not from town, then?"

"No, I am. But not recently."

She thought about this and presumably realized it had the potential of opening up a long story best left for later. We were then mostly silent until we reached my car. "Do you work in this building?" she said, staring up at the rows of windows embedded in dark brick.

"Ever since Monday."

"At the law firm?"

"Boyer, Johnson & Salmi."

"And you're a Johnson." The name I'd given her two nights ago had, then, stuck.

"Do you know Johnson?"

"If you're entitled to say you don't know my father, shouldn't I be able to say I don't know yours?"

"More than fair." This was the thing about Duluth: you could encounter a complete stranger on a bus and she would know your father's law firm. The oddity wasn't that she knew *Johnson*, but that I didn't know *Brekke*.

She told me to drive across the Bridge. On the other side of the Canal lay a miles-long sandbar, one street riding the spine, houses on each side and water beyond the houses. Those houses were a patchwork, laboring class interspersed with eccentricities. They were tightly packed, though now and then lots opened to reveal the bay marina and shipyard to the west, the dunes and fall-off-the-world's-edge lake to the east.

"I don't think I've ever known anyone who actually lived on the Point."

"When we moved to town Daddy insisted on it. He can be very forceful. People say not everyone is tough enough for Duluth, but Daddy says that's wrong. Not everyone is tough enough for Park Point."

"It's his source of pride, then."

"Yes, you could say."

"Does your mother feel the same way?"

"Living out here still scares her a little bit, even after all these years."

"Being bridged?"–being, in other words, at the mercy of a lift bridge that frequently severed access to the mainland.

"The winters, mainly. If the wind is wrong it can be claustrophobic." This was well-known: every few years the newspaper was able to run a photo of snowdrifts climbing to second-floor windows. "But little things, too. Do you know about the sand spiders? We can't really have basements because of the water table. There are crawl spaces instead. Every spring when the ground thaws these little spiders rise up. They're everywhere."

Then we were silent for a minute. "So this is your parents' house we are driving to." The idea made Linda seem less incautious, which I supposed to be a good thing, but it also made her disappointingly young.

"Yes. I moved back after college last year."

"Until you leave for anyplace else."

"Yes."

After a few miles, the neighborhood thinning while the houses bulked up, Linda leaned over and extended a pointing arm across my lap. "There," she said, craning her neck; and looming to my left was a trophy of a house crowning a modest slope of sand. I pulled into a stunted driveway and followed Linda through the front door. The house was a cousin to the one my father had built. Whereas the Johnson house was low, as though ducking beneath a gale that might blow it from its mountaintop, Dr. Brekke's monument longed, like the spiders the good doctor's daughter had described, to rise from the sand. The ceilings vaulted high and formed a series of interlocking triangles that opened the house toward the lake. Silhouettes of Linda's parents were slouched in deep chairs anchoring a darkened sunken living room. A television crackled in the corner; in the same way that my parents would sometimes watch hospital shows, the Brekkes were watching a courtroom drama. "Is that you, Linda?" her mother called perfunctorily. We peeked in from the entryway. I was grateful they kept their eyes on the screen.

Linda led me into the kitchen, which flowed into a dining room. Here was the point of such a house: windows reached breathtakingly toward the ceiling. The scene they revealed was blackness spotted with the bright reflection of track lighting. There was a pleasing Four Elements feel to the room, the glass shielding a stone floor and an imposing table of unembellished wood. A fireplace, like a missing front tooth, centered the brick wall dividing the kitchen from the living room; were it not for a vigorous fire it would have been possible to look from one room into the other. We could vaguely hear sound from the television, and of the house's four occupants I alone did not know how much talk from the kitchen might seep into the parents' lair.

After an initial busyness—Linda pulling out plates, silverware, glasses, food; me awkwardly making things worse, all the while discreetly admiring the flare of her hips—we settled in at right angles, which seemed to me in my newly-adopted caution, my *chasteness*, odd. inappropriate. I was pretty much flummoxed by this turn of events. No reasonable guess could have moved me, in the space of less than an hour, from a downtown bus stop, pining for a glimpse, to the heart of a stranger's household. Sitting at the family table. There had been a disquieting innocence about this lark of hers—something theatrical, almost. But not theatrical, too. Unassuming. She had youth going for (against) her—a year out of college would have put her at about twenty-three. I was bothered by the relative formality of my dress: although I had tossed jacket and tie into the backseat of my car and pulled on a chilled sweater, I was still wearing business armor to her comfortable turtleneck and jeans. "Not bad," I said, a cud of lettuce in my mouth. And so we settled toward conversation, letting life play itself out in some sort of congenial pre-sex world.

"You went, then, to the University," I said. I had an incentive to lead the interrogation, offense being the best defense. "What did you study?"

"Jewelry."

Which struck me as odd, obviously. Having no response I laughed.

Linda kept her smile, but added to it a look of concern.

"As in your earrings?"

"Sure."

"You made those?"

"Sure."

"As a hobby? Surely there's no such thing as jewelry. Not as a—major."

"What did you major in?"

"History."

"And there's such a thing as that." Her smile broadened. "I mean, it's… everywhere." She lifted her hands, palms up, and gazed into the track lights in bedazzled wonder.

"Fair enough. Okay, jewelry." I paused. "Really?" Part of my incomprehension derived from Linda's straightforward appearance—attractive, yes, but straightforward. Not a hint of devotion to fashion or glamour.

"That's the way it works, you know. Daddy came from nothing and worked himself all the way up. He was the first Brekke to go to college. In his world a doctor was the greatest thing he could be, and no one thought he could be that. It was inconceivable. But he did it so we could do something else."

"Like jewelry?" Of course her insight had occurred to me once or twice—riding the wooden subway in Buenos Aires, for example, guitar slung over a shoulder. But I appreciated the insight nonetheless. "'We,' you said. And you mentioned a Shari? There are other Brekkes?"

"There are three daughters. I'm the youngest." Without further questions she began to introduce her sisters; this was clearly a subject of intense interest. "Karen's the oldest. She's thirty just last summer. Can you imagine that? Karen, thirty?"

"It happens. Is she in town, too?"

"No, no. She's always hated winter. She knew in high school she wasn't long for Minnesota. She's in northern California."

"What does she do?"

"She's an artist, like me. She paints. She's a potter."

"You're an artist?" My experience with Self Portrait, now relegated to the dustbin of history, had somewhat soured me on the idea of artists. Amy had valued art.

"I've always been an artist."

"Your jewelry?"

"That's what I do, and it's really important to me–it's everything, really–but it doesn't have anything to do with me being an artist. Not really. You're an artist or you're not, the same way, oh I don't know, a volcano's a volcano whether it's erupting or not."

I smiled, which seemed more politically astute than rolling my eyes.

"If I stopped making my jewelry tomorrow, which would be devastating, or stopped drawing, or painting, or ceramics, any of it, I'd still be an artist. My *identity* wouldn't change."

"You'd just be dormant, like Vesuvius. A dormant jeweler."

"It's a calling. It's not an occupation."

"Once again: fair enough. Is Karen married?"

"Not anymore," she said, lowering her voice. For the first time all evening a frown appeared on Linda's face. It made her look older, a preview of Linda at her sister's age. It also made her look uncomfortable, as though unhappiness were incompatible with the idea of an artist, her idea of an artist. "It's an issue with Mom and Daddy, as you might imagine."

I nodded, allowing a few moments of silence to serve as my condolence. "And there's another sister."

"Sheryl."

"Is she an artist, too?"

"No; Sheryl, no." Linda giggled and shook her head with delight, unable to shrug away a silly smile. "What should I say about Sheryl?"

"How much older is Sheryl?"

"Two years. She's the middle child, in all senses. Our parents are very pleased with her."

"She's followed the straight and narrow."

"Not really. She's –" Linda angled her head as though peeking under a bed–"kind of boring." A laugh popped out. "We love her for it. Daddy *really* loves her for it."

"Parents like boring children. There's no doubt about that."

"For Christmas this year she's asked for new tires for her car."

"What did you ask for?"

"Oh, something I saw in Minneapolis."

"Not tires."

"And she has a very practical degree and a career. She's a nurse."

"Which would make a doctor father happy."

"Daddy doesn't really have much to say about nurses, I don't think. But he likes that she's here and has a job at the hospital and can probably keep it for forty years if she'd like."

"That's the boring part, then. Keeping a job forty years. Being a nurse doesn't sound particularly boring."

"She got her very own loan and bought a house up on Observation Hill." Linda's eyes widened. "Sheryl has a mortgage."

"Does anyone live with her? Is she married?"

"Just her."

"Could you move in?" I swept my hand in a semicircle, taking in fireplace, vaulted ceiling, and window. "Not that there isn't a reason to stay right where you are."

"I'd never fit. Sheryl's home"—another giggle—"is about as big as a box."

"Well," I said. We had finished our humble meal, Linda's salad and water. "I want to hear what it was you saw in Minneapolis."

"Do you really?"

"Of course."

Again the enthusiasm welled up. "I was in one of those shops along Lake Street and I came across this color wheel. You know what a color wheel is, don't you?"

"Like a paint chart?"

She gave me a scolding look. "This one was hundreds of years old. It was a print, I should say, of a color wheel developed long ago. What made it unique was that personality traits were paired up with the colors. There were dozens of colors—a hundred, maybe—and each one had a character trait."

"It sounds like something you'd see in a booth at a county fair." This was a harsh assessment, given how important the print apparently was. It was her Christmas wish, after all. "So

Sheryl wants tires and you want a wheel. Not so different, Linda." Adding her name was a conscious decision. It softened the criticism. It was meant to have an effect. And it did, though the effect was on me. It was the first time I had spoken her name since our greeting, and saying it gathered my blood.

"You wouldn't be saying any of this if you'd seen it."

"Who did you ask to buy it for you?"

"I mentioned it to Mom. It's kind of hopeless, though. I don't see her driving down to Minneapolis, and even if she did it would be hard to describe what shop I found the color wheel in. And hard to imagine her going in, anyway."

Of course I immediately thought of fetching her that print. "Is there some basis," I asked, "for connecting colors and personalities? Red is war, I guess."

"Tom," she said–another stirring in the loins–"it is so much deeper than that. I could never make jewelry without knowing who I was making it for. Not to match with skin color or eyes, or hair, but to match with, or contrast with, the inner spirit. Beauty isn't really the object, not in so many words. *Truth* is."

"Are beauty and truth different things?"

"Mostly they're not. But think of two roads running side by side, what do you call –"

"Parallel."

"–parallel, and for miles and miles, until one ends. Just stops. But the other continues. Beauty is the road that stops. Truth continues."

The warring instincts: to laugh at the thought, but love her who expressed it. Must the instincts be incompatible?

"Where were you coming from on the bus the other night?" I said. "Home from work? Do you work near the mall?" I thought of the trinket shops and imagined Linda behind a glass counter, selling earrings on consignment, asking a hapless boy to describe his girl's inner spirit.

"I took a few days off from work to run errands," she said. "Appointments, Christmas shopping. I'd been out looking for gifts for my sisters. You?"

"Me? Running errands also. Outfitting myself for work."

"Which you started just this week." She waited for me to finish the story, a difficult task with so many stories to tell.

"Well," I said, "to begin at the beginning, it never occurred to me to major in jewelry. Maybe it should have."

"You're trying to say we're very different."

"Opposite sides of the color wheel. Then again, I too went to the University. So we should start there. I was probably getting out at the time you were coming in. And then five years later I went back, now to the law school."

"What did you do those five years?"

"A bunch of things that led to law school."

"If lawyering is in your family, that makes those five years interesting. Like you were giving yourself every opportunity to not go to law school. Am I right?"

"I moved to South America."

She leaned back and laughed a deep, husky laugh. "Oh, I like this."

"But I never thought of myself as avoiding law school. Just getting other things out of the way."

"As simple as that?"

"Nothing's as simple as that." I had been treading carefully, weighing what to release and what to hold fast. Now I felt secure in making a disclosure. "Like so much else, I was of two minds about law. On even-numbered days—make that even-numbered hours—I imagined myself as sort of a late twentieth-century Abe Lincoln, traveling around to far-flung hamlets, trying cases before juries of local farmers and teachers in their old nineteenth-century courtrooms. And the rest of the time I saw myself in international finance, New York one week, London the next, Tokyo the third. All sorts of numbers, all sorts of money. It would have been a denial, really, a life where work crowded out everything else."

"You're an odd person," Linda said, displaying a tentative smile.

"There's a thrill in being named, I guess. The oddness I admit. It comes from this double-mindedness. Part of me would like to paddle into the Canadian wilderness as far as I can, putting as much distance between me and the world as possible."

"I don't see that in you."

"And part of me wants to pick up and move to New York. It's not that I don't know myself. It's that I know myself too well. I wish I didn't." All of this was accurate enough, if a bit puffed up in self-importance.

"Knowing yourself is a means, not an end."

The line felt practiced, but much the improvement over talk of ice cream and salads. "It's a tricky business," I said, "knowing yourself. You pull at the thread and pretty soon you've lost the sweater."

Now her smile broadened. "You say funny things."

"You're just laughing at the metaphor. People do that by instinct."

This seemed to interest her. She leaned forward, supporting the side of her face with long fingers, a favorable pose. "Why do they do that?"

"They go to the truth, metaphors. When the Linda Brekke highway goes from two lanes to one, the lane that goes on, Truth, might as well be called Metaphor."

"You mean, like, nothing can be known without reference to something else?" She said this less out of curiosity, more as though she were laying a trap. Of course I considered, briefly, the matching of personalities and colors, a metaphor if there ever were one. But that would be conceding too much.

"Yes, that's what I mean." I paused. "Think about what you just asked, the words you chose. 'Nothing can be known without, like, referring to something else.'"

She gave me a quizzical look. Now her fingers were working over her earring, caressing, stroking.

"*Like.*"

"Oh, that. That's just a sloppy tic. I admit it. Daddy calls me on it all the time. I'm not alone—everyone does it. It annoys him. He says he hears it all day long from his patients. 'I think, like, the baby's coming early.' He hears it from the nurses, too. 'There are, like, a hundred patients who want appointments today.' It's an occupational hazard, he says, of spending your days around young women. Daddy's a chauvinist. He says everyone knows what it's *like*, but no one knows what it *is*." Linda awarded her father's cleverness with a proud smile.

"And I say there's no difference: what it's like *is* what it is."

This sounded too much like an aphorism. Saying it embarrassed me, strangely. Linda brought her hands to the table as if to signify that this part of the evening was over. "Good," I said, nodding down at the artist's hands. "I was beginning to feel like Dorothy." Because there had to be more to the evening. Linda couldn't walk away from so obscure a reference.

"Dorothy Gale of Kansas!"

"Yes!" I cried happily. "That's what made the witch so menacing, wasn't it? She always had her hands to her face."

"It wasn't that her face was green?"

"As soon as you opened your mouth I knew that's where you'd be going."

"People hold themselves all the time," Linda laughed.

"That's true. That's very true. People putting their hand on their hip."

"Or holding their wrist."

"Women are constantly touching their faces. And skimming their palms over their rumps."

"That's practical," Linda objected. "That's for dresses. But the general point is true."

"Is it vanity, do you think? Drawing attention?"

"I think it's more like reassurance. I mean, it can't be vanity. Think of the way people put their hands up to their faces when they see something bad, like a fall. Or hear bad news. It's like they're holding themselves together. Like there's a core to people that must be protected. A gravity. So they don't spill apart."

"Yes," I said, holding her eyes as long as she would allow. "Yes."

Linda was the one who suggested we see the beach; wanting to agree, I nevertheless protested that I had insufficient clothing. But Linda hunted up extra socks and an old pair of her father's boots which, despite the mortifying and laughable symbolism, I stepped into. "Don't think of me as your father," I said, accepting her invitation to recklessness. And then, thinking of my own father's old bathrobe, hanging on my bedroom door: "I'm always wearing the clothes of the previous generation." Linda had no opportunity to respond, as I tripped over the doorsill the moment the words were uttered. She, leading by a few yards, looked back and burst into laughter, crying out (yes she did): "Billowing bale of bovine fodder!"

We descended through a series of dunes, distancing ourselves from the large, lighted house as though space-walking away from the mother ship. Linda had a flashlight; her swinging arm created a frenzied sand comet that raced toward me and then far ahead. Despite the recent moderation the night was intensely cold. We dropped down from our grassy trail, arriving on a beach barren and hardened by sub-zero temperatures. Wind had cleared the snow. Linda stopped as we neared the gaping blackness ahead. We heard the gentle lapping of water. But there was ice, too: we knew this from a hushed grinding and gnawing, as though a mouse were hard at work inside a wall. At times the interaction of ice and water created a canticle sound. I looked down the beach to see the city at a distance, streetlights climbing the hill. Above these white lights were the silently-winking reds from the antenna farm towers. The winking was soft, a pulse. We were being watched; protected.

"Basically–" Linda began.

"Uh oh."

"Uh oh why?"

"'Basically.' It's like 'essentially.' Shorthand for 'what I'm about to say really isn't true.' Warnings of an imminent lie."

Linda said nothing. Had we known one another better she would have reproached me, but then again her silence *was* a reproach. I had subjected her to an evening of cross-examination, a habit I had recently learned and hoped to unlearn. And now my tomfoolery had profaned a sacredness I had acknowledged myself by using a lowered voice. The vast lake, dark and cold, stretched before us, sliding.

"When I'm out here," Linda finally said, also in a quiet voice, "I see each star as its own world, having its own troubles and its own joys, and looking at us with the same wonder as we have for them."

I was willing to tolerate deviation; one must, in any pairing. But the patent ridiculousness gave me pause. It was deflating. "Any life hoping to live on a star would certainly have its own troubles," I said.

"And its own joys," Linda insisted.

We were now walking side by side–walking slowly and not hunched or chattering, despite the exposure.

"You believe in astrology," I ventured. "Naturally."

"It's not so much a matter of believing in it as living it."

But of course. "What sort of classes does one take to satisfy the requirements of a major in jewelry?"

"Some are pretty technical. Some aren't much more than business classes–markets and economics of gems and stones, and so forth. The truth is that I was somewhat the odd duck in my program."

"Why would that be?"

"Jewelry is just a manifestation. Do you know what I mean?"

"Of being an artist?"

"It has to do with color, it has to do with magnetism and poles. It has to do with cosmic elements, really–where do you think minerals come from? It's all related, and what it's related to is a common denominator."

It's not any of those things, is what I was thinking. A sloppy mishmash. Then again, what's the saying? It's your own best thinking that got you here?

"I couldn't let the evening end without telling you a truth," I said. "Not a Truth, big T, but a small truth. A non-beautiful truth. I was a law student until I quit. Gave it up without any reason I can identify. I don't know if that's important to you or not, but I couldn't not tell you."

She said nothing; most likely she was still thinking of jewelry's place in the universe, and my news struck her as hopelessly commonplace, as anti-jewelry. I reminded myself that we had met but two nights earlier. A mere five days had passed since I walked out of that lecture hall, that life, but of course to Linda it was a prior life. She was not equipped to understand how recent and consequential my abandonment of law school was, in the same way that children, even grown children, can never appreciate the weight of events occurring in their parents' lives even short months before their own birth.

"So our lives are in the same place, wouldn't you say?"

"I don't know," I answered.

"You're done with law school. I'm done with things, too, Tom. You're being prepared for the next thing. Maybe you don't know what it is."

"That's right. I *don't* know."

"But that doesn't matter. The universe knows."

"Those stars. What is *your* next thing?"

She laughed. "Work a bit, get some money, buy a car."

"No more bus rides."

All the while Linda had been exploring with her flashlight–groping, as it were, for Truth. We were walking among driftwood, some mere sticks, other pieces as large as log cabin

PAUL KILGORE

timbers. All had been stripped bare by the water, the endless kneading and probing. We came to a stretch of shoreline already ridging with ice, the beginnings of the prodigious canyons over which the college kids would be swarming near Easter week. The water continued to lap, puddling us in quiet. A train could be heard in the far distance, beyond the long point and across the Canal and far up the hill.

"Do you see that?" Linda asked brightly. She pointed an arm into the sky. Distantly overhead I saw the flashing red of an airplane. Linda directed the flashlight to her wrist watch. "Right on time, every Wednesday and Saturday night. Where do you think it's going?"

North, is where it was going. There was nothing to the north, not for a plane that high and at that hour. "I can't imagine."

"Reykjavik. It leaves Minneapolis at eight-thirty and flies right over the tip of the lake on its way out. They'll be in Iceland before you and I are waking tomorrow morning."

"And we're watching it from the beach."

"Yes." She turned off the flashlight as if that subtraction might change anything. "The edge of all we know," she said, "is as close as that."

§

Edward Brekke. Ed. Gynecologist. These were the first words I wrote. There was no intent to describe or comment—straight facts were all I was after.

Nothing was written about Linda's mother. Linda had given me, that first evening, nothing to work with besides a trepidation over living on the Point.

104

I've kept, all these years, boxes of my life against the back wall of the storeroom behind the office. A squirrel gets in now and then without doing irreparable damage. There's a small window that looks away from Dead Wolf, facing instead a cluster of jack pines that are on my list to thin. The boxes themselves came from the law firm; a *Boyer, Johnson & Salmi* logo can still be seen. There are legal documents—copies of closing papers, tax returns, things I needed to keep seven years and kept twenty. There are papers from the probating of my parents' estate. There are items of sentimental value, too: photographs, of course, as well as cards and letters that were and are important to me. Years pass without a thought of the contents, and then I might add or retrieve something (my most recent addition: a children's picture book). Not long ago I pulled out a remarkably well-preserved sheet of lined paper. It was from a narrow-ruled notebook I had used in Priley's contracts class. I had, all those years ago, thought the sheet significant enough to save.

Karen. Oldest. Northern California. Thirty. Painter/ potter, etc. Divorced.

I had wanted to remember what Linda had told me that evening at her house. My notes, hastily written out after I had returned home, had not been intended for twenty-five years later. The page was meant to be a reference sheet, something I had hoped would not be needed (and in fact was not needed) after the elapse of a week or two. I wrote on that sheet what I knew that night, which is not the same as what I knew a day earlier or later. December 20, 1989. I wrote what Linda had told me because her family could not be an afterthought. I wanted her, and them, as *my* family. It amazes me now how quickly I made up my mind, how reckless my intentions look from this distance. But I wanted to belong, wanted Linda Brekke's future to be mine.

Sheryl (Cheryl?). Ed's favorite (?). Ice skating. Tiny house on Observation Hill. Nurse. Linda + 2 yrs. Straight and narrow.

§

And then in all respects the world I woke to Thursday morning was a new world. During the night Lake Superior had generated an enormous northeast wind; I was roused at three-fifteen by the rattling of my window. On my way to work I drove down the hill through fine grains of snow so dense that the effect was one of fog, whole sheets of atmosphere jerking crazily with the gale's whims. The streets were blown clean and polished down to their ice. Pulling into the lot in Canal Park my Civic lost grip and grazed the support of an advertising sign that was itself being torqued by the storm.

Against reason I trudged across Lake Avenue and approached Superior before giving myself over to the workday. By evening the entire corner of the lake would be jammed tight with blown ice, but now water was rolling in as tumbling gray cylinders, hundreds of yards long, smashing into the shore boulders and throwing pebbles and ice pellets toward me. The lake sound was low-pitched, cavernous—it was the sound of ships breaking apart, doomed for the bottom. The wind sound, though as loud and frightening, was different: it rose and fell like a fire, tearing at the eardrums.

My face, having been opened to the nor'easter's fury, naturally reminded Maggie of diaper rash. A person cannot be faulted for her observations, I suppose, or even her imagination. No more than three days had been needed to teach me that it was odd to see Maggie so frenzied at such an early hour. She stood over a scattering of paper and cassette tapes on her desk; the fixture muffin and coffee mug were nowhere to be seen. "What's going on, Maggie?" I asked. Without a word she stormed off to the coffee room, saving both of us her reply.

Maggie wasn't the only person charging about. Beth Hokanson, whose habit was to stop at all eleven work stations between the coffee machine and her desk, walked briskly by without so much as a mention of whatever malady might be afflicting her that week. Toni Torelli, too, passed without a word, her expression vacant as she worked out the implications of some new problem, much like Lazarus coming to grips with being sentenced to a second death. The some new problem, I soon learned, was exactly the type of problem law firms depend on to meet payroll. One of Ted Salmi's biggest clients, a railroad, had in October signed a purchase agreement to buy the assets of a smaller but troublesome competitor. Even in my short tenure I had heard war stories of the negotiations—late nights running into early mornings, revisions of revisions, posturing that had led a rival team of lawyers to depart for the airport before returning to the conference room. The agreement had contemplated a first-quarter closing, but now, the week before Christmas, a gnawing discomfort over the implications of some obscure accounting issues had caused the two railroad presidents to demand that the transaction be wrapped up by year-end. Ted had been telephoned at nine o'clock the night before, about the time Linda and I were on the beach, gazing at stars. Junior lawyers and key staff had then been given the message (there was no reason for a green law clerk to know anything about any of this, of course) and by seven Thursday morning the firm was humming with midday urgency. Sandy Bartholomew, a sort of field commander, had been the one to fill me in.

"This is what we do," she said, leaning over the top of the partition above my desk. "But you know all about that." She had a broad smile; crisis, to her credit, put Sandy in her element. "People will be working Saturday and Sunday, too. It doesn't matter that Sunday is Christmas Eve. It won't surprise me to see people here on Christmas Day, at least in the afternoon."

And what might those people be doing if not at the family table, or passing the Stille Nacht flame, or watching their children unwrap presents beneath the tree? "You'll be part of the due diligence team," Sandy said. "Mark and his group"–Mark being Mark Soleski, Ted Salmi's protégé, young and energetic and exceedingly hail-fellow-well-met–"will give you the assignment, but I can tell you now that there are a lot of legal descriptions to proof."

Sandy laughed with delight as she departed, a peak of happiness bell-curved flat by Maggie's reappearance. Maggie held a stack of thin manila folders as though she were carrying wood for the fire. She allowed them to cascade down, like a spread deck of cards, onto my desk. "From Ted to me," she said darkly; then, with a glimmer of light, "and from me to the law clerk." Each folder–there had to be two hundred–contained two instruments, one historical and the other newly-created to effect a piece-by-piece transfer. "Find yourself a damp young secretary, give her one set, keep the other, and make sure everything fits together."

I began to look over the documents–deeds, easements, assignments, amendments, a treasure trove of fastidiousness. Truth be told, I was energized by the task; by the whole atmosphere of purpose, really. I was part of a team. We had something of worth to do, something that someone (holders of railroad stock) valued. I was, basically, essential.

The storm outside paid little attention to human construction: window panes were shuddering and the sea gale seemed to be coursing through the building's ventilation system. A law clerk would have no access to windows, of course, being embedded deep in the interior. But from the doorway opening into Mark Soleski's office I was able to gaze over his desk, over Mark himself (he was hunched over, running numbers), and out across the bay and up the river valley. The view was severely limited by the snowfall, light but horizontal and moving with great abandon. Mark looked up. He had a large, jowly, gas tank sort of head; apnea was his destiny. His smile was broad and genuine. "Law school is theory," he said, "and I never liked that. I wanted to be doing something that actually mattered. Well, this matters!"

"Everyone in the office seems to have a hand in this closing."

"It's a big one. The type that comes around maybe once a year, if that. There are so many issues. We can talk about those later, but right now there's no time."

"No."

"You're here to help, I'm hoping."

"Sandy mentioned you were coordinating things. And Maggie dumped a whole slough of documents on my desk."

"Good," he said, rising from his chair. I had no idea how skilled a lawyer Mark Soleski might be–no reason to think he was anything other than highly competent, which seemed as great an accolade as one might hope for—but his good cheer portended a long and prosperous civic life. Had law school worked out for me (had *I* worked out, is the better way of putting it), there was no telling where I would have landed. Abe Lincoln or Wall Street or anywhere in-between. Until this week I had never considered Duluth a possibility (though aware that my parents, to varying degrees, thought seriously about just such an eventuality). But standing in the thick of the joyous battle I could easily imagine myself as *Mark's* protégé, moving someday into the slot he would be vacating to fill Salmi's slot. None of this could happen, of course, not anymore. I had shut the door on an entire life, not that anyone at the firm knew anything about that. My life, it occurred to me—the thought came while eyeing a gilded baseball bat anchored to Mark's wall; how could he not have been a superior athlete at school?—my life, as I say, was really not one life but a whole series of lives, none lived beyond the first inning.

"Good," Mark repeated, snapping me out of silly, daydreaming self-pity. "Signing off on the conveyance documents is critical, needless to say. Put your head down and plow through them. Take a five-minute break every half-hour to maintain your concentration."

"My sanity," I suggested, a sort of intentionally lame attempt at wit. Mark was pulling me in.

"Attaboy!" he crowed. Mark slapped my shoulder as he hustled off to check in on another member of the team. I watched him step quickly down the hall, broad shoulders and hips, faultless clothes. He had been blessed with an imaginable future.

To work. I spent a few minutes taking in just what lay before me. I had once heard that while preparing for that first landing the Apollo astronauts had had no idea whether the lunar surface was rock or unforgivably soft sand. Folder A contained a cloudy copy of some sort of township land permit, booked and paged and dated long before television or another world war. Tucked behind was the work of B, S & J: an assignment of permit rights. How difficult would it be to confirm that the assignment's information, mere numbers and dates, matched those of the permit? No damp secretary required. I disposed of Folder A in less than a minute. Next came a set—Folders B-1 through B-8, each containing variations of an option agreement and the freshly-minted December 31 assignments that a young lawyer or two under Mark's tutelage had produced overnight. This review took a bit more concentration, but a pattern seemed to be emerging. On to Folders C, D, and E-1 through E-5. I was in a hermetic container by now, oblivious to the white noise of the storm and the industriousness at the desks aligned down the hallway. I opened Folder F, took in a co-location agreement similar to a half-dozen I had already seen, then turned to the relevant paragraphs in the accompanying transfer agreement. An error was waiting for me like a snake beneath a pile of laundry, and when it appeared, and the shock of its appearance passed, my impulse was to doubt the error; or, rather, to locate the error with me, not the document. But soon I regained my balance. The error validated me: by spotting it I had contributed. Then just as quickly a second error appeared—a series of errors, in fact, forming a pattern that made me question my review of the earlier sheaf of folders. I reached for the dictating machine to begin a record of what I was finding. A dozen small cassettes were scattered in the desk's top drawer. I fished one out and dropped it into the machine.

"Memo to Mark Soleski," purred a feminine voice. By quickly-acquired habit I had played the tape's opening moments to be sure I wouldn't be talking over something deserving of preservation. This was definitely deserving. "Re: analysis of tax implications of royalty agreement amendment." The voice was quiet, a pillow talk whisper made all the more seductive by its tentativeness. "August twenty, nineteen eighty-nine." I held the machine to my ear. Of course there was but one explanation. The voice was Katherine Berster's, spoken softly to protect Katherine from ridicule. Maggie's ridicule, obviously. "I have reviewed the relevant provisions of the Tax Code regarding income coming in. Those provisions include –" and what followed was a series of section numbers spoken directly from Katherine's lips to my ear, expressed as sounds that might as well have been the sound of my name.

"Oh, she was fine, as far as I could tell. Really quiet." This was a new voice, that of litigation secretary Kay Knapp, rising in Doppler pitch with her breezy approach down the hallway. "Her hair was quite a sight. Reminded me of a hydrogen bomb." Preoccupied with Katherine, I didn't see Kay or the intended recipient of her observation. They passed by me and as they did I heard that intended recipient laugh.

How many voices does one hear in twenty-seven years? How many *categories* of voices? Some, like my mother's, I had heard from the very beginning, and still heard today. Others, like my grandparents', I still heard, but only in memory. Some voices were added along the way–those of the Norgaards, or my friends from college, or Self Portrait. Some I had heard intensely for a defined period, Amy's being the obvious example. And some I had gone almost my entire life without knowing, only to have them fill a thin line of recent bandwidth. Marian Blake and Charlie Boyle from law school, occupying four months of a life. Clay's baby-faced wife Tess, whom I had spoken with for possibly ten minutes over maybe three conversations spanning four out of a few hundred months. Ten minutes out of a million–millions?–of minutes in a lifetime, my lifetime. The laugh I heard wasn't Tess's, but it was a laugh I knew, a voice that claimed a mere thread of space, but claimed it indelibly, on the bandwidth. I couldn't place the voice, other than to know it was not a B, J & S voice. Everything I am describing I processed, if *processed* can be used to describe a semi-conscious comprehension, in possibly one or two or three seconds.

And there was more than a laugh. "Appearance conforms to myth, actually. It's complicated." Before I grasped the words' meaning, to the extent they had meaning, I identified the type of person–the type, not the person–who had spoken. Engaging. Thoughtful. Loopy. Alluring. Kind. Careless–free of care, I mean; free of worry. Unpredictable but tolerably so. Incapable of harm. Joyful. Did the women glance in at me as they passed? No matter. I stood quickly and looked over the partition to see the receding figures of Kay and Linda.

The mind that couldn't persevere through seminary, couldn't persevere through a single semester of law school, would not be permitted to fail me now. I scanned over everything Linda Brekke had in two meetings said. Should any of it have been understood as communicating that she was employed by Boyer, Johnson & Salmi? That she knew anything of me? There had been some ambiguous talk while we walked to my car the previous evening. *If you're entitled to say you don't know my father, shouldn't I be able to say I don't know yours?* My father's firm had no use for jewelry majors or color wheel aficionados, but if there were a practical side to Linda–a set of clerical skills that could generate enough income to buy a car, for instance–it seemed possible, then likely, then inevitable, that Dr. Brekke's daughter had been hired as a legal secretary. Which meant she would have seen the newsletter announcing my pending arrival. At what point after her hop onto that bus had she become aware that the Tom Johnson in pursuit and the son of Lanny Johnson, the boy coming back home from the university to work in daddy's firm, were one and the same?

At *some* point. And yet she had said nothing. Possibly none of it had mattered to her, her job being nothing more than a paycheck, the prestige of a lawyer no prestige at all. Of course this must be how she felt; nothing in her make-up suggested the slightest interest in someone fitting my description. And yet she *was* interested, or seemed to be; or was not, at any rate, not interested. She likely thrilled to my disclosure about quitting school–that would be consistent with what I had learned of Linda in a few hours of conversation–but that had not come until later, down on the beach. Like a returning horsefly her decision to say nothing tormented me. From one view it could have made me happy, but this was not the view I chose. Couldn't her incuriosity be seen as manipulative? She knew more than I knew she knew, and she knew she knew more. I had set aside the dictating machine and the silly cassettes, turning back to the folders distractedly. Not for any portion of the next hour was I unaware that Linda sat at the end of the hallway, occupying the same corner station that had for the past three days been occupied by her temp.

Should I approach her? Now? Would it be better to wait until the end of the day? What would be, in the word even one semester of legal education had taught me to appreciate, appropriate? What would approaching Linda mean? I couldn't imagine what I would say or what she would say in return. And so, in the same way that I would drown myself in a hot Middlebrook Hall Saturday morning shower, comforted by the thought of reviewing insurance policies, I turned to the folders with a vengeance. At 11:17– upon jerking to attention that was the time of day I saw on my desk's digital clock–Linda's cry rolled down the hallway, flooding as indiscriminately as water.

I took it at first as a cry of merriment, having not yet been bestowed with the revelation that human expressions of joy and lamentation may be nearly identical. I pushed my chair back and stood, staring down over the desks all the way to the corner. And then I stepped into the hallway and moved closer. Linda held a telephone receiver to her ear almost as an afterthought. "Oh, no!" she cried, shaking her head and staring at something that did not exist. "Oh, *no!*" she shrieked again, more emphatically, words that were sounds, not words, the cry of a wounded animal whose entire world has dropped away, yielding to the trap. Tears appeared with a startling suddenness and tumbled rapidly down her cheeks. Her anguish carried throughout the office. Linda was naked, shorn of all pretension and vanity. A half dozen people hovered near but not too near: Toni Torelli stood beside her own desk, a hand over her mouth; Kay, seated, stared hard at a document in what I took to be a well-intentioned if ineffectual attempt to provide Linda some privacy; and Nicole Haraldson, who had been carrying a file down the hall, stopped dead in her tracks as her face violently reddened. One of the young lawyers peeked from his doorway helplessly. The person who happened to be nearest Linda was Maggie Metaxas, and she without hesitation leaned in, her spread fingers vigorously rubbing the sweater on Linda's back. Maggie spoke loudly, appalled at the effrontery of what was being visited on Linda. "Dear" is the word I heard, proclaimed as exhortation. I heard it three times.

The others then approached, hands to Linda, an immediate dropping away of all manner of code and barrier that had been governing the work life of every woman in the office. And not only women: Mark Soleski, drawn by the commotion, gently laid his hand on the arm of Nicole, who was now sobbing with fear and sympathy. The thing that had been an imperative—a *railroad purchase*—existed no longer. I mean to report this as truthfully as I am able, so there is no use denying that I felt, besides a monstrous helplessness and self-loathing at my instinctive passivity, a strange thrill—overwhelmed quickly by grief for Linda, but a thrill nonetheless—at the freedom granted all of us to live apart, to have found a core of life that exposed the tawdriness of everything we had constructed from that one empyreal gift entrusted to us. The web of unspoken rules— how to look, how to speak, how to regard one another, how to regard one's self; what was a proper subject for discussion and what was not; what was expected, and the absolute necessity of complying with those expectations—all of this had in a few moments been ripped apart. Linda may have been less tethered to these things than the rest of us, but what part of her was I seeing now? Linda with her talk of jewelry, her grainy laugh, her two roads; Linda with her peppermint ice cream—all of these seemed puny beside her enormous capacity, dormant until this moment, to be wounded. We were all by our actions now confessing to that same capacity.

But Linda was not being merely wounded. She was being destroyed. Before our eyes a part of her—a part located in her heart, in her soul—was being killed.

She slumped forward, her eyes vacant. The world that was beginning for Linda was not one capable of being seen, not here. But she would see it soon enough, and never be able to not see it again.

ANYTHING
BUT THIS

Sheryl Brekke, I was to learn, had been a quiet girl, not to say shy. Being five years behind her sister, she naturally took to mothering Linda. For a few years their parents treated the younger girls as twins; a number of photographs had Sheryl and Linda in matching outfits, or sitting on the same pony, or buffing their way through a shared Saturday evening bath. As they grew each of the three sisters found her place. It was Karen who came home at one-thirty the night of the Homecoming game and vomited a belly of beer onto Ed Brekke's Persian rug. It was also Karen who snuck out one evening and had the misfortune of backing her mother's car into her father's, a two-for-one calamity that got her grounded (for all the good it did) an entire month. At the other end was Linda, the youngest, predictably independent and happy to isolate herself from the family's Karen-inspired (or, more accurately, parent-inspired; Karen was born Karen, after all) unrest. Ed Brekke may have expected high achievement of Karen—he *did* have such expectations, paying dearly to send her to a private college from whence she was soon tossed—but by the time Linda came of age she was free to do things like go to the University of Minnesota and major in jewelry. Between these poles was Sheryl, who got B's in high school and then B's in college and was perfectly happy to get B's in all aspects of the remainder of her life.

Sheryl liked animals. She had a hutch behind the house and fed her rabbits with eyedroppers. She had a puppy. She memorized most every page of *Misty of Chincoteague*. Sheryl's animals had unimaginative names: Flopsy, Mopsy, Snowball; Buddy; Salt and Pepper. When Buddy ran away, Sheryl, who was eleven at the time, made six big cardboard signs that she fastened to poles up and down the Point. The signs described the beagle, gave the date he had gone missing, and then added, below the family's telephone number, "We love him so MUCH!" A neighbor spotted Buddy out near the small airfield two days later and he was returned. That night he slept fifteen hours at the foot of Sheryl's bed, growling through dreams.

Sheryl liked to bake. Cookies were her specialty; when she was in junior high school her mother put Sheryl in charge of family desserts. There were the inevitable mistakes: missing salt, flour or sugar doubled or halved. Once she and Linda fell into a dispute over a recipe's use of "heaping teaspoon," Linda's position being that salt did nothing but sit until someone moved it from canister to bowl—it was not capable of "heaping" any more than it was capable of performing any other act. "Heap!" Linda chided her sister, the word more ridiculous with each repetition. "I've never seen salt heap!"

"It's not the *salt* that heaps, it's the teaspoon!" Sheryl indignantly replied. "One heaping *teaspoon!*"

"Spoons don't heap, either!" This continued until both were so angered by the absurdity that they turned to whether there might be such a thing as a heaping teaspoon of water, Linda—of course—seeing this as a different matter and arguing that water could indeed, in certain situations, heap.

This story was related by Linda in the B, J & S lunchroom to a rapt audience, laughter, as it so often did, metamorphosing into tears, and then back again. Over weeks

I saw that the dichotomy wasn't between laughter and tears, but rather between both, on the one hand, and their absence. Linda was no longer living in the absence.

Sheryl liked home activities: cutting paper, shaking rugs, knitting, folding towels while they were warm, connecting the garden hose and sprinkler, filling the bird feeder, copying recipes, popping popcorn, playing the piano, reading girl detective stories while lying with outstretched legs on the couch. She was tactile, as were all the Brekkes. She also had a sense of proprietorship, concerned with bringing in the mail and keeping tabs on the outside light.

Ed Brekke taught all three girls to ski, for the same reason he would never have taught them to bowl or play pool, but Sheryl's favorite sport was ice skating. The rink was eight or nine blocks away; on winter weeknights Sheryl and Linda would leave immediately after supper, tied laces over their shoulders, one skate hanging in front and one in back. There were actually two rinks, one with boards and nets for hockey and one that simply rounded off into snowbanks. Between the two was a warming house, the smell of timber, a heavy door on a whining spring, and the clunkiness of skate blades on plywood. On lucky nights hockey moms might be present to sell candy and hot chocolate in small crumbling cups best held from the top by fingertips. Outside a radio station's offerings might be amplified for the skaters, releasing to the night sky the tail end of rock soon to be sold as Classic, this being around 1980. It is strange to think that while all this was occurring I was likely in my first year in Minneapolis, my life filled to the exclusion of all the world—to the exclusion, certainly, of two giggling sisters on a Park Point rink—with its own preoccupations. Sheryl and Linda would play tag or mimic figure skating maneuvers. Occasionally they would join schoolmates in pom-pom-pull-away. They did this night after night, never aware of the significance, never aware they were riding a countdown.

Though a homebody, Sheryl Brekke, like her sisters, had an independence about her. (Being a homebody was part of that independence.) She, again like her sisters, suffered no concern over what others thought of her. Sheryl avoided most of the high school rituals, staying home from basketball games and dances to watch black-and-white movies on television. She drew the interest of a boy during her senior year, but no one in the family knew what type of relationship it was; mostly he came over to do homework, and then after a couple of months he stopped coming over. ("Did *you* have boyfriends?" I asked Linda when she was telling me this; she let the question go as though unheard.)

Nursing was a perfect fit, the family thought: practical, not given to silliness, and, when looked at in a certain way, similar to caring for a household. Sheryl stayed in town to get her degree and was immediately hired by one of the hospitals for night shifts on a post-surgical floor. She purchased a small house in a dying Italian neighborhood of steep streets and ledge rock; from one of her windows she could glimpse the harbor. Once she invited her parents and Linda for dinner, but the four of them, together with the table, chairs, and food, did not fit. Thereafter family meals took place on the Point; Sheryl usually came on Tuesday evenings, before work. Another boy might have entered the picture–while stopping to deliver something on a Saturday afternoon Linda noticed on the refrigerator the schedule for a men's curling league.

Sheryl had been well-prepared for Christmas. Her tree fit snugly in a corner of the front room, boughs intruding over the arm of her couch. Presents for five (another hint of a boy) had been bought and wrapped, though not tagged. The book on telescopes was clearly intended for Dr. Ed; the embroidered pillow, Sheryl's mother; the scarf, Karen. A small stationery box held two tickets to see the college's winter production of *To Kill A Mockingbird*. An almost identical box held a hand-written ticket for "one homemade French dinner for two." One of the gifts was meant for Linda—but which? And who was to receive the other? "Mystery Number One," Linda would eventually call this. All the gifts had been placed beneath the Christmas tree.

Piecing things together, Linda was able to learn that Sheryl had been reading *Mockingbird*; the bookmark had been on pages 207 and 208. She had, that Thursday morning, made herself some oatmeal and toast; the bowl, filled with water, was in the sink, and there were crumbs and a butter knife on a small plate left on the kitchen counter. She had changed out of her uniform, which was back hanging in the closet. The bed was made, so she likely hadn't napped. The morning paper was on the top of the kitchen table, opened to a half-finished crossword puzzle—Sheryl had known the prez after G. W. but not the pen name of Mary Ann Evers. And then—Mystery Number Two—she had left the house. She would have known, coming home from her shift, how treacherous the streets were becoming. She would have heard the plows—large as tanks and loud as an emergency, lights flashing, sparks jumping from the blade, rotating discs spraying road salt like gunfire—as they raced up and down Mesaba Avenue. Where had she been going? Why had it been more important to go then, at midmorning, than to sleep and wait until the storm eased? Her little Chevy had fish-tailed down the hill—the loops of her tire tracks swung from side to side, the police had needlessly pointed out to Dr. Brekke—and slid sideways through the light and into Mesaba.

Linda did not return to work until January. I was continuing on as a clerk; I was taking a well-deserved pause in my legal education, the newsletter reported. On Linda's first morning back the staff, one by one, stopped at her desk. Each stayed perhaps two or three minutes; my desk was too far away, of course, to hear what was said. The three female attorneys (there were four at the firm, but one was in court that day) also stopped, staying not quite as long. Of the remaining attorneys maybe half stopped for visits that didn't seem to exceed twenty or thirty seconds. I don't mean to cast blame; I am willing to charitably assume a universal fellow feeling. I merely note that decency is a learned skill as well. Myself, I hung back until late morning, when I passed Linda's desk and told her I was sorry. She thanked me. No more than twenty words were exchanged. At morning's end we were among a dozen others in the lunchroom, but our eyes did not meet. Linda was kept busy receiving truly kind words delivered with an amazing effortlessness. Linda's sorrow seemed not to be hers alone, but shared. The compassion Linda was afforded by the firm's secretaries–who had known her little more than half a year–shamed and inspired me. I resolved to speak privately and deeply with Linda before day's end. But after lunch Linda left for home.

The week wore on. It was easy for me to imagine what Linda must have been thinking of me, when she thought of me at all: the guy on the bus, the *glib* guy on the bus, the guy having nothing better to do than strike up taunting conversations with strangers who interested him. The world I occupied was not one she occupied, not anymore. She had no desire to go back to that world–wanted with all her being for Sheryl to still be alive, obviously, but not to go back to a world of banter and caprice. As if going back were even possible. The world Linda had left behind was no world at all. It was a fiction, make-believe. It was a distraction, an avoidance of the actual, as well it might have been, the actual being little better than a horror show. But truth couldn't be called untrue simply by being a horror show. This is all a caricature of what Linda thought, but it was close enough, especially since I imagined it without any of her assistance. So in a way I was myself passing into the actual, imagination being a twin of creation.

§

It was with surprise and gratitude that I received Linda's invitation. This happened shortly after noon on the Friday of her first week back. She leaned over my desk–I was busy on some post-closing clean-up; the railroad purchase had been completed by year-end, as it obviously could not not have–and asked in an I'll-understand-if-you-say-no voice if I wouldn't have dinner with her that evening. This tentativeness also took me by surprise. Apparently Linda saw invitation as a move, if only slight, from safety. Why should that be–or, more to the point, why did she feel the need?

We sat in a booth of a small, largely empty Chinese restaurant on Superior Street. Winter was still reigning supremely. Our booth butted up against an iced window; the temperature of the air pressing against my back (aided by a north wind unimpressed by the streetfront pane of glass) was ten or twenty degrees lower than that of the air hovering between us. Linda looked tired, of course. She had looked tired all week; it had been her defining characteristic. I had been torn between wanting to observe Linda and wishing to avoid her—the two of us being in the same office seemed on the whole a disadvantage. Drawing on adolescent experience I occasionally went out of my way to pass her desk, then changed plans to avoid encountering her at the copy machines or in the mailroom. After a day of this I told myself to grow up, i.e., stop caring. I kept to the library as long as I could justify. January, and thereafter, yawned ahead.

On one level there were, surely, many things for us to discuss. I hadn't spoken with Linda, not really, since before I knew her to be a secretary with my father's firm. Her salad, our brave moonwalk onto the beach and even braver presentations to one another—all of that seemed impossibly ancient now, events from a world that no longer had places for us. A new year can do that anyway: the white vacuum of January swallows up the close, bejeweled anticipation of Christmas, the old life's purpose and assumptions distant as those of a grandparent's childhood. But the chasm over which we were regarding one another had nothing to do with any of that. In Linda's mind wouldn't I be irredeemably tethered to her sister's death? Whatever designs I had had on Linda necessarily evaporated with her mother's telephone call. And weren't those designs (again: whatever they might have been; I had been acting on impulse, no thought given to what lay beyond the headlights) the only basis for my interest in her? What were we to one another now?

She began with small talk. This continued for perhaps fifteen minutes—what Kay had said about her son's latest hockey game, Sandy's impending Florida vacation. The minutiae of office life had a therapeutic effect, raising Linda from exhaustion to a sort of happy bemusement. "I heard the best Maggie story," she concluded. "For another time. I don't feel like telling it now." She paused, looking off toward a crazed but silent television mounted high in a dark corner. "The hard thing to figure out about grief," she said, "is whether it is strong or weak."

"Very strong, I should think."

"Very strong." Linda looked down at the plate of food that had just been delivered, noodles and steamed vegetables. She was gathering herself, I could see; this dinner would not be a half-hearted affair. "The first thing it does is show you the truth, which is such a miserable thing. There's nothing beautiful about truth. We talked about this, didn't we?" She was looking at me searchingly now and her inquiry was genuine—the December evening whose every turn of conversation I had practically committed to memory had obviously been of less significance to her. "About truth and beauty— that's right, we did."

"Two roads," I reminded her.

"Well, I was wrong about all that. Truth has nothing to do with beauty. Truth is emptiness. Everything else is beauty, maybe, but it's all add-ons. When I leave home now the only thing I see is emptiness, and God it's a terrible, bleak thing. It's all loneliness. Family doesn't help. *This*"—here she flapped her hand back and forth between us, like the tail of a fish moving against the current—"doesn't help, because we don't come and go together. Everyone is born and dies on their own days—you know? We're on our own. No one can help us. I get on the bus and overhear people talking and laughing. I think"—now she gave a little gasp of emotion—"how can they be so *happy*? What world are they in? Because it's not my world. And yet we're only sitting ten feet from one another!

"And then I look out the window at the trees that I used to think were beautiful, even in winter, *especially* in winter, and the birds that were beautiful, and the lake—none of it is beautiful. All of it is remote and meaningless. The trees are just sticks. The lake is just water that's here because"–bitterness had crept into her voice–"it came from uphill and there's no downhill for it to drain to. Meaningless. And none of it gives a damn about Sheryl or me or our parents. This is so hard on Mom. And Daddy, well–" Linda's speech had been accelerating, and she paused now to reassert some control. "I mean, the world is filled with things–trees and buildings and animals, everything–having nothing to do with people living and dying and suffering."

"Nothing," I began before having the good sense to stop. Nothing, I had intended to say, had changed, not the trees or birds or people on the bus, meaning that life, not now found in such things, could *never* have been there. Life resides someplace else. But of course that was just me toying with an idea, life between the ears, while Linda was (the phrase came to me easily) facing down death. Which was a cliché, but even worse, a misapprehending cliché. Linda wasn't facing down anything. The last thing on her mind was "death"; she didn't give a damn about "death" or any other idea encapsulated in language. This was about her sister.

"But here's where grief is weak," Linda continued. "There are times when I feel like nothing ever happened. I don't mean forgetting that Sheryl is gone. That happens, too. When it does it's a terrible thing. You know, those few seconds in the morning, after waking, when I'm back pre-accident, half-awake, half-asleep. And then it comes upon me that she's gone. It's like getting the news fresh all over again. Or during the day, getting lazy and falling into the old way of thinking–'after work maybe I'll see if Sheryl's busy.'"

"That doesn't show grief being weak," I offered. "It's not an example of weakness. It shows grief being diabolical."

"It shows grief being diabolical," Linda said, leaning into the edge of the table. "Absolutely. But there are times when I'm fully aware that Sheryl is dead, and everything that that means, but I'm not mourning. I'm not even sad. It's worse than that, actually. I feel *joyous*." She stared hard, daring me with her apostasy.

"I haven't seen you joyous at work."

"Oh, yes, there's a –" She hesitated but a moment. "Jesus, Tom, I've got to say it to someone. There's a *freedom*. I mean, nothing in life can ever hurt me again. I'm cut loose. After a tragedy everything's excused. And there's a *clarity*. I know things you don't, Tom."

This I *had* noticed. I would not have called it joy, or freedom, or clarity–I had no name for it, truth be told–but there had been no mistaking a separation between Linda and the rest of us. I had seen Linda naked; that was as good a way to express it as any. The word seemed apt, sex being at its core a surrender of self, the whole idea of protected identity compromised. The conceit of withholding. Kay and Toni and Nicole and Soleski and Maggie and I and everyone at the office now knew Linda better than we knew any of the others, and better than Linda would ever know us. There was an imbalance, the strange thing being that Linda's exposure, her destruction, had played to her benefit. Being sacrificed had given her power– given her life, in a way–rather than stripped it from her. *After a tragedy everything's excused*: what else could this mean? Sitting across the wooden bench I was taken with the idea of Linda's emancipation being a shared emancipation. It was perverse, but was I not being granted the very intimacy I had been pursuing by more conventional means? The thought was in some ways repugnant–I recognized that. I saw the corruption of desiring to share with Linda whatever realm she had entered through her suffering. She had been seared; I hadn't. There had been a trauma in watching Linda receive news of her sister's death, but any grief I felt, or was feeling now, was wholly vicarious. I had never met Sheryl; had not, indeed, heard her name or known of her existence before the evening preceding her death. Lord strike me down for claiming too much.

I appreciated the ease with which Linda spoke, the way she felt free to hold an idea while turning back to her meal, or pause to gather her thoughts before proceeding, the way friends do. "But there are things I don't know, really basic things. The *most* basic things." She giggled a small, girlish laugh, here and gone, before looking at me with a deep sadness. "I don't know whether Sheryl's dead."

"Disbelief."

"I mean, I never thought she could die. I'm not naïve. I *would* have thought it could happen, if I'd thought of it. If I'd thought to think. But I never thought of it at all."

"People can't live keeping death before them," I said. "It would be paralyzing." This was half-true: paralyzing, sure, but people *did* live in expectation of catastrophe–*I* did, for example. To one cursed with a highly-developed imagination, yesterday's misplaced letter leads to the unpaid premium, the uninsured fire, the recriminations and divorce; and then how is time with the children to be divided at Christmas? It's not as far-fetched as it sounds. My life had demonstrated the creativity of misfortune.

"And now that it has happened–like I say, half the time I just can't believe Sheryl is really dead." Once again, the intensity: Linda leaned forward, her glass earrings, sea green in color, swaying with the momentum. "Tom, I so need to see her body," she whispered with urgency.

"Is that possible?" I said delicately.

"It could never be possible. Sheryl no longer exists. Her *body*"–another involuntary gasp–"no longer exists. I could look day and night and not find it. It's not anywhere in the universe anymore. How can that happen?" Her eyes were suddenly glistening. "I expect her to call me. I have this incredible urge to go to the hospital in the middle of the night and find her on her shift, sitting at the nurses' station updating a chart. I almost believe that if I just look in the right place, at the right time, I would find her. One night this week I took Mom's car and drove up to Sheryl's house. Not because I'd forgotten she was dead. Because I didn't *believe* she was dead."

This was all making a tremendous impression on me, needless to say, the words expressing such thoughts being spoken by someone so obviously alive, so fundamentally *existing*. Linda's face was directly before me in all its three-dimensional physicality, the little movements of her throat muscles, the flitter of eyelids, her entire being a subtle vitality of breath and pulse. A minute eyelash–*Linda's* eyelash, and therefore *Linda*–had broken away and was adhering almost imperceptibly to the waxen skin rising to the bridge of her nose. If a high-speed camera had taken a hundred frames of Linda over these few seconds, each would have shown a different expression on her face, reflecting a whole series of micro-gradated emotions, barely observable but, crucially, observable–comprehensible–received by me with eyes trained through epochs to understand her, to share life with her. And we were supposed to believe that such a thing as a human could simply evaporate out of existence?

Linda eased back, a conflicted look on her face. "Do you know what I did that night of her accident? I left the light on in my bedroom all night long. I turned the radio on, too."

I shrugged, not understanding, needing her to continue.

"You tell me. Fear? I was afraid, sure. It sounds so childish, but part of me was afraid that in the darkness I'd see Sheryl."

"See her in a nightmare?"

"You tell me."

Linda slid up against the back wall of the booth. She sat erect and looked across the empty room. Over the course of the evening two or three customers had come in to pick up white paper bags of dinner. The voices in the kitchen were distant; occasionally I would hear the laugh of our high school waitress. Neither Linda nor I had made much progress with our meals.

"Life can change so fast," Linda said absent-mindedly. "Don't make plans. Don't wait."

"Sheryl was loved," I said, fighting the helplessness. "I hear that in everything you're saying, Linda. She knew she was loved, too."

"Yes. I'm so thankful. I feel that a lot these days, gratitude." The words didn't sound strange to me at all. I recalled someone once observing (at seminary, most likely) that it's when the worst suffering is visited on people that they are most grateful. Not for the suffering, of course, though possibly for the opportunity to suffer, for the intuition, mainly, that in suffering they are nevertheless being cared for. The observation struck me as true when I heard it and it did the same now. Yet I felt compelled to ask whether any urge toward cosmic blame existed.

"Blame?" Linda shook her head once, dismissing the idea. "There's no space for that. What I feel is pretty much the opposite." She slowed her speech, picking the words carefully. "Life just goes on and you never realize–I never realized–that every day, through all the mundane, you're building a life, piece by piece. It takes a tragedy to see that. So I grow up and leave for St. Paul, and make my choices, and come back. Happen into a job at Boyer, which would never have occurred if I hadn't aced typing back in high school, a lifetime ago, and if I didn't need a car now. It's all so improbable, every advance a surprise. But at the time every little choice is the best choice, the only choice. Inevitable, like the seasons changing. But not to be predicted."

"Life."

"And here I am. You think you're building your life, but someone else is building it for you."

"I don't follow." Though I thought I did.

"You never met Sheryl, right? I mean, you couldn't have." Throughout our dinner the thought never left me that Linda was in turmoil; collected now, but three weeks into a long turmoil. Yet I was struck again by the different perspectives from which we viewed each other. Bluntly: I thought of Linda quite a lot, not to say obsessively; but when we weren't conversing she apparently gave no thought to me at all. There was no way to assess any blame for this, obviously, or even disappointment. Not now. But it meant something. "She was…" A smile flickered. "Oh, Sheryl.

"She had little things about her. She was sensible, but not always. She was afraid of comets."

I surprised myself by laughing. Linda took the laugh properly, as encouragement.

"She never said why. But I was talking about comets once and she wanted to change the subject. She said they made her nervous.

"And once when we were in school I made a fruit salad with apple slices and bananas. It was just fine, but Sheryl said I spoiled it by putting the bananas in first and then mixing in the apples, rather than the other way around." Linda giggled but with eyes that were distant. "I admit that sounds more like *me*." Linda used a long finger to dab away a tear. "One more thing," she said, opening her purse for a tissue, "is that she had one gray hair." She now gave a congested, teary laugh. "One. It was a silvery strand, very luminous in the right, or wrong, lighting. Mom told her to color it or pull it, but she wouldn't. Mom said a girl in her twenties shouldn't have gray hair, even just one. Especially just one, since it called attention to itself."

I nodded, helpless as she began to cry, tears coming fast.

"The point," Linda said, "is that that was Sheryl." Linda pressed on, refusing to pause for the tears. "There was never anyone else in the world with those combinations, all the little parts put together in just that way. You'll never know her, Tom, because all of it's gone, the million things that were only her. All gone." This was too much. Linda wept openly, propping her elbows on the table and pressing her palms into her forehead. I reached across and ran my hand up and down her forearm. A minute or two passed before Linda gave herself a gentle reprimand, sniffing deeply and then taking a big breath. "Okay." She pulled more tissues from her purse and began to gather her coat. "There's another point, too. I would bring up comets, or ask what would she be doing about her hair, just to see what she would say. And anything I would do in school, or jewelry I would make, the real fun was telling her about it. Actually the real fun, the *most* fun, was *thinking* of telling her. *Anticipating* it." She stood up and reached into her pockets for gloves; I took her lead. "So that's the other point." Linda looked at me directly and plaintively. "I didn't realize until Sheryl died that everything I was doing I was doing for her."

We walked to my car carefully, arm in arm as a stay against misfortune. I drove her home. We were quiet the entire ride, waiting patiently for the car to warm. Her silence was broken once by a hiccup. When I thought she might have fallen asleep we arrived at her parents' house. Linda gave a wan smile and shyly turned her head. Without a word she let herself out, pushing on to where I could not follow.

§

We began, then, to see one another regularly. Part of this involved interacting as little as possible at work, where a conversation of any substance could easily swamp our employment obligations. Secretaries are more perceptive than lawyers, women more perceptive than men, and consequently it wasn't possible to keep from at least part of the office the existence of a relationship. What sort of a relationship was a different question: Linda and I did not ourselves know the answer to that. My father would not have been likely to detect anything but for the fact that he was married to my mother, who didn't expect me for dinner the Mondays, Wednesdays, and Fridays when Linda and I would make our way to Peking, the austerely-named small and empty restaurant hidden beneath the winds ghosting down Superior Street. But this gives too formal a description to what was actually a makeshift arrangement, for at least once a week Linda would stop by my desk late in the afternoon, usually with a tired, vacant look on her face, and tell me she simply wanted to take the bus home and spend the evening alone.

The dinners we did share were unpredictable, Linda being in the spike-and-flatline stage of mourning. She could be quiet and sad, or caffeinated and silly, or thoughtful, or simply uninterested. None of these moods were false. Never did I see the precise pre-loss Linda; I didn't expect I ever would. Had I arrived home from law school one week later the pre-loss Linda would have been a Linda I would never have known.

We didn't always talk about Sheryl, of course, though much of our conversation would not have occurred had her death not happened. We made small talk, sharing bits of information we had picked up at work, odd things that had appeared in the paper. I chided her for holding back, that first evening at her home, the fact that she, too, worked at B, J & S; she responded, in Linda-like fashion, that it had been too soon for her to decipher the mystery of such a coincidence. Occasionally solemnity would weigh us down—one Friday evening we were at our booth a full four hours. Once we had nothing to say to one another—hardly seemed to know the person we were with—and parted after barely thirty minutes.

The logistics of our time together were spectacularly unimaginative. We would ride in my Civic a few blocks to the restaurant, then, at the close of our evening, cross the Bridge so I could deposit her home. Here a certain formality did enter in: as I pulled into her driveway Linda would become unusually proper, thanking me curtly for the ride and occupying herself with securing mittens and hat. A few times she invited me in, invariably to show me this or that pebble of jewelry she was working on. On these occasions the living room was quiet, Linda's parents and their televised sedative nowhere to be found. Linda provided bits of information regarding the Brekke family workings, but she also had a protective instinct likely impressed upon all the girls during their upbringing. Dr. Brekke had taken charge initially, interacting often with the police and city maintenance, going so far as to visit the plow operator, at home while on a merciful leave of absence, to hear his version of the awful event. But after a couple of weeks the permanency of his daughter's death seemed to clothe him in listlessness. Linda expected her father would now throw himself into his work; instead he lost interest. The most confounding aspect of Dr. Ed's transformation was his new-found indecisiveness. To her father, Linda said, indecisiveness was with rare exception unpardonable. Indecision could lose lives at work; at home it was a mark of moral sloth. But now there was a tentativeness about Linda's father, manifested most obviously in his confusion over how to handle Sheryl's funeral. Like Linda, Ed Brekke had needed to see the body; but there was no recognizable body to see. Linda's father seemed to suffer the same absence of finality of which Linda often spoke, the same disbelief. The extreme winter served as a pretext for doing nothing immediate. Linda had overheard her parents speak of a memorial service in the spring, when Karen could come back out, but the tone in which they spoke was so distraught that Linda deemed it best to not ask questions. So the subject of closure was left floating, unresolved.

The "when Karen can come back out" justification seemed particularly weak. Linda's sister apparently had little holding her down in California. The cost of an airline ticket would not have troubled the Brekkes. Karen had flown to Minnesota the day of Sheryl's accident, arriving late in Minneapolis and flying to Duluth the next morning. After a week she left with promises to return often. There was always drama when Karen and her parents were placed in proximity, but of course all of that sank into insignificance now: everyone, Linda told me, left everyone alone. Karen and Linda had taken it upon themselves, the day before Karen's departure, to begin putting Sheryl's affairs in order–cleaning out the refrigerator, tidying the house, identifying bills that needed attention. Linda could foresee that most of this would fall to her, her parents being largely paralyzed by the remainders Sheryl had left behind: her clothes, her college books, the kitchenware she had begun to accumulate.

Sheryl's death had been big news in town. The death was pathetically tragic in its own right (not the least because it had occurred a mere four days before Christmas), and Dr. Ed's relative celebrity intensified the coverage. My father didn't hear the news until he returned from his Cleveland business trip. My mother learned of the accident the day it happened, seeing the story on the six o'clock news and then hearing from me the B, J & S connection when I returned home from work. The three of us fell into a civil existence. My father didn't ask how long I intended to stay at the firm and I didn't ask how long the firm could justify keeping me. My mother, aware that I was spending time with Linda, refrained from any but the most general of comments. She did not suggest that I bring Linda to the house for dinner.

"Get ready for this," Linda said to me one evening soon after we'd arrived at our booth. She was sitting in a pose of casual happiness, back to the wall, one leg stretched across the length of her bench and the other cocked, knee to the sky. With her fingers she was provocatively twirling the dark hair above one ear. "I've been meaning to tell you; it's too good to let go. I got the story from Beth." And she proceeded to recount an episode from Maggie Metaxas's tumultuous marriage to a man, Linda took pains to establish, enamored with physical attributes he felt obliged to share with women who weren't Maggie. The story put Maggie and Charlie–Charlie was his name, Beth had said–in a bar, Charlie spending the evening ladling a lot of interest on one woman in particular, and then another woman in particular, Maggie growing more and more angry, culminating in Maggie bursting into the men's room when Charlie, who had bid up the bar tab all evening, was standing at the urinal, which provoked Maggie, in bitter inspiration, to belt out, in a voice loud enough to be heard out on First Street, "He's Got the Whole World in his Hands."

"Even funnier," Linda said as she worked to control the laughter generated by her own telling, "was Beth's comment. She said in a very sober voice that Maggie knew all the song words from when she was a little girl in religious training. And then Beth said"–another mirthful eruption–"'You never know.'"

This story, barely entering the realm of the risqué for two twenty-somethings by now quite familiar with one another, was Linda's first acknowledgement of the existence of carnality in the world. We had touched one another now and then, but only in a decent sympathy appropriate to the Brekke family's new reality–*decent*; *appropriate*; as though the subject of our discussions, and the attendant emotions, were not creating a tremendous tide of empathy rushing hard toward physical intimacy. I held her arm. I brushed a tear from her cheek. She took hold of me on icy sidewalks. That Friday evening I convinced myself of signals portending a change. It was a pleasant, promising evening. Sheryl's name did not come up and I could see in Linda's eyes a corresponding gratitude. But when I arrived at her parents' home she bounded away with a chirpy goodnight and the broad wave of a sibling.

Sheryl's accident had occurred on my sixth day home. Back then, my mind still in Minneapolis, everything was next-next-next, like a canoe zipping down a cascading river, cause and effect, one thing leading to another. But now a long unknown stretched ahead, little explosions of consequence separated by nothingness.

§

Linda's grief, as she noted early on, was persistent. It relished surprise. It was willing to give ground for the impact of reappearance.

"Remember when you said that grief is diabolical?" Linda asked one evening. "Didn't you say that? One of the things it does is force me to tell about Sheryl's death over and over again."

"Who would make you do that?" This was often my role in such conversations: Linda would introduce a thought and with short observations or questions, often rhetorical, I would smooth the way for full expression. It bothered me a little (though I tried to resist the selfish impulse) to know that without my markers Linda's tendency was to let her mind drift and follow it away from me. It was the pondering that was critical, in other words, not the presence of someone to receive it.

"I've heard from so many people these last few weeks. High school friends of Sheryl's, mostly, or college friends, late getting the news. It's jarring to them because it's new—to them it's as though her accident happened that very day. They're in shock. And I have to give the same story, beginning to end, time after time. Some of them want a lot of details."

"Irritating. Worse than that, I suppose."

"They're in shock," she said again. "I've been thinking about this a lot, how people move at their own speeds. We're alone, Tom, we really are. I mean, we're on the same planet and we live by the same day and night, which tries to make us all one big human family, sleeping at the same time and being awake at the same time"—this was Linda-talk; I was becoming skilled at detecting its approach—"but we're all of us operating at our own speed. That Thursday of the accident Sheryl's friends were happy as could be, looking forward to Christmas, I'm sure, lost in a thousand little details, and I was…" Her voice trailed off; her eyes put her far, far away. Just when I believed she had lost her train of thought she turned back to me. "Sheryl was already gone. Sheila Norton was one of her best friends. Sheila never knew until I called her that night—how *could* she have known? And there's another friend from nursing school, Patti Rislov, who lives in Iowa now, she called my folks around New Year's because she'd been trying to get ahold of Sheryl to hear about her Christmas. She finally ended up calling Mom. Patti had no clue about what had happened. It just makes you re-live it all over again."

Linda was true to her word: she had given this much thought. "There are some friends, old classmates and others, who may never find out."

She then returned to disbelief, a prevailing theme. "Mom lost an uncle she was really close to. This was years ago. He dropped dead at a young age. The other night she told us that one of the things she learned was that grief doesn't come immediately after the death, but later, after the truth has sunk in." Linda took a big breath. "Think about that."

"Is she right?"

"I don't know when that later is. It's so hard for me to believe that Sheryl is dead. The last time I saw her she was alive. Now she's just *gone*. But does that have to mean she's dead? I half expect Karen to call some night and say that Sheryl showed up at her door. What I truly feel—strongly, Tom—is that Sheryl's someplace, if I only knew where to look. I mean, I've thought of everywhere."

Another evening Linda made a point of extolling the furious pace of that day's work, frequent revisions to a thirty-five-page brief and a looming five o'clock mail pick-up. "I wish all the days were like today. The slow days are the worst."

"Too much time to think," I offered.

"Life goes on. It has to. But"—she rummaged for the right word, her head nodding as though in counting—"it's *infuriating* that we have to move on, that we just *accept* death. Such a huge loss, such a devastating loss, and we do *nothing*."

"Because there's nothing to do," I suggested. In these conversations there was no shame in lingering on the obvious; as a lubricant it was sometimes demanded.

"Of course I know that." The *of course* wasn't wholly unnecessary; Linda, grounded though I'd seen her, could at times display a constitutional aversion to levelheadedness. Artists have means at their disposal to teach death a lesson or two: that was the sort of thing I was always prepared to hear her say. "But it's just pathetic that we're so helpless. The only thing we can do is live like we did before, as though nothing happened." Linda wasn't clear on her next step, but it was evident even then that she had no intention of living like she did before.

Fear was another topic. The telephone, Linda said, was a menace–having taken her mother's call at work, every ring triggered for Linda the threat of another horror. There was her father to be concerned for. There was her mother–she, too, might die in any number of ways. And Karen. This was just the start. Far-flung family, friends old and new–all were poised to harm Linda. "Even you," she conceded near the end of a particularly tender evening. "Sometimes I think about why we're friends–why I should want a new friend, is what I mean. One more person to lose sleep over." She laughed. But the words had been important enough to speak.

"I was up at Sheryl's house last night," Linda once said. "She keeps this basket on the kitchen table with papers in it. Karen and I pulled out the bills but last night I spent some time going through the rest."

"Anything of interest?" Smoothing the way.

"As a matter of fact, yes. She had received three estimates for work."

"What sort of work?"

"Practical Sheryl. She wanted a new roof. And I did notice some water damage in a corner of her bedroom. She also asked for a quote on painting the trim, which is peeling. All three specified gray paint, so that must have come from her." Linda began to smile.

"Daring. It must be especially galling to a jewelry major." And in fact the necklace swinging from Linda's neck that evening had been uncommonly exotic, Ontario amethyst anchoring a rainbow of looping fabric.

"On one of the estimates there was a note that said, 'Yes, we can install a weather vane.'" Linda broadened her smile.

"So artistry in fact runs through all the daughters. You and Karen don't have the market cornered."

"Imagine a weather vane. I'll bet she wanted a rooster. But I'll never know." With this last thought Linda's smile disappeared as though she had overheard an insult.

"You could honor her wish."

"Maybe." The idea seemed to have no traction. I was greeted with the distant look that had by then become familiar, Linda following a road that led her away. "I'll never know," she murmured. And then the words that had become a refrain: "Life can change so fast."

§

Mostly I listened. What Linda had to say didn't always involve Sheryl. Life, she would remind me, goes on. She talked about: the way Kay Knapp's obsession with her son's hockey career really wasn't healthy; how tireless a worker Sandy was; the inefficiency of the heating system at work, temperatures sometimes varying by six or seven degrees from office to office; whether I thought the elevator foolproof; why Duluth didn't have a decent movie theater; the still-elusive color wheel; the difficulty of finding even passable produce in winter; whether I seriously thought there was nothing to astrology; was a used car worth the risk?

Mostly I listened. But occasionally I would take the initiative. "Does Sheryl's death make you more or less frightened of your own death?" I asked. We had spent so much time together by then; such a question was permitted.

"Oh, less," Linda answered quickly. "Less, absolutely. I'm more frightened of *others* dying. That's true. But myself? No fear, anymore."

"Because Sheryl went first?"

"Something like that."

"If she can do it, you can do it?"

"It's like if a comet hit the Earth…"

"As Sheryl apparently feared."

"… and destroyed everything, not just the dinosaurs, but everything."

"The dinosaurs are already gone, Linda."

"And all the people died."

"Universal death."

"That wouldn't be so bad, would it? If no one was left behind, there'd be nothing we'd be missing by dying."

"That's true. Very odd, but undeniably true. We would rather be killed by a comet than cancer. It's the lack of inclusiveness that's objectionable."

"One thing Mom and I have talked about is the nightmares we've been having since the accident."

"Do you have them often?"

"No, there have been just a few nights. Two or three times I've dreamt about Sheryl as if she was still alive. Each time we talk about the accident, about her being dead."

"Who is talking about Sheryl being dead? *She* is? Sheryl?"

"Yes, Sheryl. But the oddest thing–you reminded me of it by mentioning cancer–is that last week I had a nightmare that didn't involve Sheryl at all. Not consciously, anyway. But isn't a dream *all* subconscious? Anyway, the nightmare was that I had been diagnosed with terminal cancer. It was so real–I never realized how powerful an imagination I must have. It was so hopeless. Honestly, it was more hopeless than reality, than Sheryl being killed."

"There's no past or future in a dream," I said. "It's purely and inescapably *present*. The present is terrifying, if that's the only thing. Nothing to apply hope to—no place for hope."

"That's interesting," Linda said thoughtfully. "I mean, the present is all we have."

"As so many pop songs have reminded us."

"And yet that idea—of having only the present, no past or future—is intolerable."

"There it is."

"But I don't think that's it, Tom. All day long I kept returning to that cancer nightmare. I imagined getting a real cancer diagnosis, also hopeless, every detail exactly the same as in my dream. I'm convinced the real diagnosis would not be as terrifying as the dream diagnosis. And your past/future thing is interesting, but I don't think it's right. There's no God in a dream. That's the difference."

"Is there a God once we wake?"

"We must think so."

"We crave meaning. There's no way humans could *not* have invented God. Our first and best invention."

"Because God gives our lives meaning?"

"There's nothing more meaningless than death being capital F Final."

"But wouldn't living forever be just as meaningless? If we went on endlessly—where is the meaning in that?"

I was impressed. "The essence of being human," I suggested, "is not that we die. It's that we're unable to detect meaning."

"Unable to *detect* it? Tell me this, Tom. Tell it to me. Is there a meaning to detect?"

I shrugged. I couldn't keep a smile from my face, I was so enjoying this.

"You went to seminary."

"I left seminary."

"So you've thought a lot about these things. All for naught?" She wasn't about to let me off the hook.

I paused, considering how to reply. "Linda," I finally said, "in the worst of times I've turned to Taoism. It helped, and the natural course of events helped, sandpapering down the despair, and eventually I no longer had a need for Tao. But the furies returned, and I went for Buddhism. That helped also, until I no longer needed Buddha. But life back-filled in, the way it just keeps coming, and there was Jesus. Until I no longer needed Jesus." I looked at Linda unblinkingly. "No, I'm not a person deserving of respect."

Later that night she said: "The reason I'm not afraid of dying is that, when you get down to it, I don't want anything to do with a world that could take my sister."

§

During the last week of that long January Linda asked if I wouldn't like to meet Karen. The question came suddenly, as she was on her way out of the door at workday's end. I was holed up in the firm's library, trying to determine whether an abandoned mine pit filled with water was subject to state regulations governing lakes.

"How would I do that?"

Linda stood in the library's doorway dressed in her ski jacket, midnight blue knit mittens and hat in hand. "She's coming back on Friday for a week. Mom's picking her up at the airport."

"I'm free Friday night." I said this with a smile; both of us surely understood, tacitly, that we had nothing going besides each other. Linda mentioned few friends, practically none in town. And I was nine years removed from high school. Every friend from when I last lived in Duluth was by now long gone.

"You can meet her at Sheryl's house on Saturday. We'll all be up there. I'm going to be moving in." She said this casually, as though having given no thought to how I might react to the news. But why should she? In fact the disclosure troubled me, vaguely at first but then with more force. I was excited for the change, our status quo being most likely unsustainable. But the unexpectedness of the announcement seemed an indication of how inconsequential a place I apparently occupied in Linda's world.

"What is the thought behind that?" I said. "Moving into Sheryl's house." Had I, before that moment, understood how dependent my future was on Linda's? It was like slipping on ice, wondering how badly you've been hurt in those few seconds of immunity before the red tong of pain. I'd been excluded from her decision to move; Linda, who had told me everything, hadn't told me *that*. Reasonably or not, I was aggrieved. There was something else: a fear, never felt before, that Linda, having just been asked to give a reason for moving, would not answer well. She was perfectly capable of telling me her decision had been prompted by the stars. It was dismaying to grasp how important it was to me that she not say that.

"It just makes sense," she said; a pleasant surprise, as I hadn't expected this would be her measuring stick. Of course I was aware, of course I was annoyed, that I was fending off this ambush with conservatism, wishing away what made Linda Linda. "The house is sitting empty. And living at home was fine for awhile –"

"But only awhile," I said, eagerly completing her thought. "I'd be happy to help you move."

"There won't be much of that. Sheryl had furniture. I don't have many things, which is good because the house doesn't have room anyway. But we'll be emptying some things and doing a little rearranging. We'll keep busy. It's a better way to meet everyone."

And with a laughably abrupt shift of outlook that was the clearest indication yet that I *sought* to tie my fate to Linda's— that I had feelings for her—I understood from Linda's words that my place in her world was actually one of prominence. For I hadn't actually met her family—hadn't met Karen, of course, but also hadn't even made introductions with the girls' parents. The prospect, I was embarrassed to admit, was slightly foreboding. I'm not devaluing Linda by saying that Dr. and Mrs. Brekke would have been within rights to wonder why I was interested. There was the age difference, for one thing—four years being not so great a difference, but nevertheless a difference. The gap in years was a coded way of thinking about a gap in experience, which was itself code for the albatross of my having been married and divorced. Seeing myself as stained, how could I have faulted the Brekkes for reaching the same conclusion? Linda knew about Amy, the disclosure having been made at possibly our second or third evening of refuge at Peking. Linda had been—I *believed* her to have been—thrillingly indifferent. (Of course that sword had two edges.) I doubted her parents would have learned of Amy from Linda, but Duluth could be a small town, its professional class even smaller. And certain parents can crave information about the misfortunes of their peers.

By that Saturday the January thaw—understood to be a false promise, of course—had arrived with vigor. The streets and avenues cross-stitching the humps of the great ridge that extended from the river valley, to and beyond the Canadian border, were black with the skim of water. The sky was blue, but to arrive at that blue the eye was required to climb through wisps of condensation rising from the snowbeds. Sheryl's house, tiny and square and often remodeled by amateurs—there was no telling when it had been built, but its present appearance seemed to fit a returning-G.I. zeitgeist—was accessed by a steep climb of wooden stairs, perhaps thirty steps, with railings on both sides. I parked on the street, there being no driveway, and looked up the unpainted and improvised stairway. Mounds of glistening snow, the result of ten weeks of shoveling (most recently by Sheryl's father), pressed in against the railings. The late-morning air was pleasant on the skin. Without bothering over a hat or gloves, my heavy winter coat left unzipped, I climbed to the top.

The steps led to a small deck fronting the house. Boxes crowded the deck—whether on their way in or out was difficult to tell without snooping. I picked my way through to the door. Each of the house's visible sides had a single window, a small rectangular pane of glass looking toward downtown and, around the corner and facing (if not providing a clear view of) the harbor, a somewhat larger rectangle. The decision not to subdivide the windows, or provide shutters or any other type of ornamentation, gave the entire house a shop-project look, a class of seventeen-year-olds' first experience with shingles and caulking and PVC pipe.

I opened the aluminum door, then the brick red wooden door, and let myself in. A narrow entryway led to a cramped kitchen. Boxes covered the table. Sheryl's white-bleached cabinets were open and largely empty. The Con-Tact paper—cows, silos, and sunflowers on a robin-egg-blue background—curled here and there at the edges.

"Hello," I called.

"Oh, hello," Linda volleyed back from a room down the hallway. This was followed by another voice, female but quieter and not directed at me: the continuation of a discussion my entry had slowed.

I unlaced and stepped out of my boots, then ventured carefully down the narrow hallway leading from the kitchen. A door on the left opened into the living room—couch, floor lamp, small television, small desk with metal chair. The Christmas tree had been removed but needles and nubby bits of branches littered the rust-colored bas-relief carpet. I looked to the hall's end and into a bathroom painted a thick sea-green. The outlines of large tropical fish lazed their way across the shower curtain. The door on the right, past some hallway closets, led to the house's sole bedroom. Linda and her mother were fitting the mattress of a squat double bed. Linda's father was gazing out the window into the uphill slope of a neighbor's backyard.

The aura of quarrelsomeness was strong. For a moment I considered backing out of the doorway, stockinged feet concealing my withdrawal. There were pine needles to be picked off the living room floor. A freezer to be defrosted. But Linda's mother caught a glance of me. Without a word she turned back to her daughter. "Have it your way, but I say it's a mistake."

Linda gave an exaggerated sigh, notable because I had never before heard her—not at work, and certainly not with me—accept the mantle of regression. And for what had she stooped? Linda and her mother were squabbling over the arrangement of some trinkets in a drawer. "Don't argue with a jewelry major"—that would possibly have been an acceptable throwaway to ratchet down the tension, but of course Linda's parents and I were new to one another; and, more to the point, everything needed to be seen through the prism of this house being so recently Sheryl's. I didn't have the courage to speak. And what place did I have, anyway, in the history of a mother and her daughter? The thought running through my head was this: There is no better indication of the world's brokenness than the instability of family exchange. No matter how hard one might try to be the perfect child, it's a doomed effort: an inadvertent offense is waiting; or, to avoid committing the slight, the child will accede to the earlier architecture, the teenage pushback against instruction.

Linda straightened up and turned, looking at me with wonder. Bite the apple and this is what you see. She was not the girl on the bus, at the desk, in the diner booth. Being placed with her parents diminished Linda. "Well," she said. "Thomas Johnson"—*Thomas*: a first, and fascinatingly chosen—"and Edward and Joanne Brekke. Meet one another."

"Hello, Tom," Mrs. Brekke said, but her face was still in her daughter's drawer. Dr. Brekke murmured but kept his attention on the snowbank. Linda resumed unpacking, stuffing an open drawer with sweaters until it looked like a deviled egg.

"What can I help with?"

"Oh," Linda said, drawing out the word. "Did you see the boxes outside? Some can be brought in and the rest can go down to the car."

"But which is which?"

Linda paused, evidently to get her bearings. There must have been something disorienting in forcing these two self-sufficient, willful constructions of her life together; bananas and apples, as it were. Wordlessly she squeezed past me and into the hallway. I followed.

"I should have called you," she said, speaking at full voice but looking ahead. "Karen didn't come and obviously it's a big deal."

"I was going to ask."

Entering the kitchen, Linda turned toward me and softened. "She didn't call until Mom was waiting at the airport. It was bad all the way around. Dad had to drive out and tell her. By the time he got there the plane had already arrived."

"No Karen."

"No."

"What happened?"

Linda looked around the room moodily. Outside the window, plucked strings of water were falling from the roof-line gutter to the deck. The sun shone brightly through the thinning moisture. "Karen said she didn't feel up to coming back."

"Oh."

Linda read disapproval in my voice, a willingness to choose sides. "It's a very difficult time. Mom and Daddy and I have each other, but Karen's out in California by herself."

"What did your dad say to her?"

"Say to Karen? He reacted the way he reacts to everything now—silence. Mom did the same, but for her it's a different silence."

"Pissed."

"Yeah."

"She probably thinks Karen could have decided sooner."

"Karen *could* have decided sooner. We all could be doing things better, now."

There was ambiguity in this; there was forewarning. Linda fished into a front pocket of her jeans and pulled out a ring with three keys. "Mom's car–well, mine now–is the green one up the street. The Mazda. There's some bags in the trunk, if you'd like to bring them up. And those boxes to the left of the door"–she leaned forward to peek out the window, breasts against the pane, her straight hair bobbing as she lowered her gaze–"can take the place of the bags."

The busyness of this assignment was appreciated. My first trip back up the stairs brought me to a crowded deck–Linda and her parents were sorting and moving boxes, learning themselves about the advantages of distraction. On my second trip up I turned to see Linda's father, arms full, three-quarters of the way down the stairs. I took a step back, immediately provoking his objection. "No, no," he said, quickly and athletically retreating to the top. I followed him up–face to face we stood, Dr. Brekke in a retreat that he had commanded. When I reached the deck, allowed Linda's father to pass, and then entered the house, I found the kitchen empty. Linda and her mother were back in the bedroom, and it's entirely possible the conversation was about me. Joanne Brekke stepped into the hallway and from twenty feet gave me a good hard look. "We didn't make introductions properly," she said. "We've been too preoccupied to do things properly."

I held my ground, arms full of bags being my excuse. "I'm so sorry about Sheryl."

"Thank you," she said, a rote answer she then repeated with unexpected gentleness. Joanne Brekke was a handsome woman of medium height, her curly brown hair cut short.

Today she was dressed for work, but even in a frayed sweatshirt there was an elegance about her that arose from self-possession. A pride. I guessed all this from the way she carried herself even in the cramped, uninspiring corridor, dignified while struggling to manage the shock of being a mother of two.

Linda called her mother back into the bedroom for an opinion. Without Karen there was no reason for my presence, but even if she had arrived it would have been difficult to say what place I had among this family, on this of all days. Idly I began to look over Christmas cards and photos Sheryl had taped to the rounded door of the refrigerator. Even casual observation filled me with sadness: so many connections, so many stories. A photo of a wedding-day bride and groom. A Sheryl-aged woman, her arms wrapped around a gorgeous German shepherd. An open-mouthed baby in an infant's swing. A young couple in Adirondack chairs, shorts and T-shirts, beer bottles in hand. Smiles. A sheet of green paper staked with a magnet unfolded its panels of holiday doggerel:

So that was my life
In 1989,
More than you wanted to hear.
Your love's been received,
And you've received mine,
God BLESS you in the New Year!

Comets. A silvery strand of hair. I walked out into the glorious midday. The sky was cloudless from lake to hill, one horizon to the other. From the deck's back corner I saw that the southerly wind was already beginning to open ice from the shore; patches of water, colored with the loveliest blue, sparkled in the sunlight. Our ears were opened as they hadn't been in months—from far down the hill I heard the slam of a car door, the bark of a dog. All of this was a loosening of the grip, a freedom to feel sadder yet. The world as it existed on Sheryl's last morning had only seemed permanent. The storm and ice had only been passing. They could have been avoided, waited out. This thought led me to the pointless reproach of synchronicity: Sheryl could have left home thirty seconds earlier or later. So many lives would not have been ravaged.

Ed Brekke stood on the deck, patiently waiting on wife and daughter. He was leaning up against the railing, black ribbons of street below, beyond them downtown's modest buildings. Dr. Ed was a tall and trim man, sturdy, hard-muscled. He wore boots that rose halfway to his knees, a telling conceit: Ed Brekke was just the man to face the day, ride the high plains. His head was shaved clean.

"I'm sorry," I said.

"Yes."

"It's really unbelievable." This was not a response likely to impress, though delivered with the deep sadness I was feeling.

"Did you know Sheryl well?"

"I never had the opportunity."

He began to move, straightening and turning to take stock of me. "You're right, Tom. Unbelievable is precisely what it is." His voice was deep, thick as butter. "But I'm learning that life is the process by which the unimaginable becomes imaginable."

The day soon dissolved, a run to the hardware store to buy light bulbs followed by a run to the grocery store to fill the refrigerator. Without fanfare, practically without notice, each of us went separate ways. But upon Joanne's invitation I arrived at the spacious Park Point house near nightfall and the four of us, seated among the stone, glass, and high beams, laughed our way through grilled fish steaks and wine. There were many Sheryl stories to hear: the Brekkes had without discussion decided that, at least for this one evening, Karen's absence would be graciously excused, memories of Sheryl would be a source of love rather than anguish, and acceptance would be chosen as the path toward reconciling themselves with the reckless veer the course of their lives had taken.

Then, slowly, to the living room. Ed provided more drinks, Linda fussed with this and then that. Eventually we four settled into a lengthy and mercifully tedious television drama, Dr. Ed in his big chair, Linda and her mother together on the couch, and me uncomfortably conspicuous in a straight-backed chair far from any other piece of furniture, a crippled vessel floating out to sea. Meant to suggest a latter-day film noir, the story was incompetently plotted and paced, contrived surprises popping up whenever it was time to pitch a sale. Most every scene took place in an alley or vacant warehouse or among waterfront fog, meaning that the screen and the Brekke living room were dark until the repeated ambush of bright lights and warlike volume signaling another ad for cars or liquor or pills. At one point the brightness revealed that Linda and her mother had moved together, each resting an arm or hand on the other. Drama or commercial, dark or bright, quiet or blaring–it made no difference: no discussion animated the Brekke living room. Cheering or mocking the show would have been the easiest form of conversation, possibly even a catharsis, an opportunity for the family to share something other than loss. But all was quiet, the insulting infantilism of television accepted without complaint. Finally, after a tiresomely predictable twist of fate ended the evening in a confusion masquerading as mystery, Joanne rose and switched on a floor lamp, putting on display Ed Brekke, sagging deep in his chair, words lost on him; and Joanne Brekke, drained from the pummel of one day into another, but grateful that *this* day had come to a close; and, finally, Linda. She remained on the couch, gray-faced, eyes wide and blind. Unaware that she was being watched, unaware even that the penetrating grief was capable of being observed, much less lightened.

Linda walked me slowly to the door. She quietly thanked me and I quietly rebuffed. Life seemed about to turn: the next morning Linda would move a few remaining items with her to Sheryl's house, which would then be *her* house. A new way to accommodate Sheryl's death would need to be found. Winter, the day's southerly wind had promised, would not last forever.

I kissed her–quite an amazing thing, occurring as it did a full six weeks after our acquaintance. I kissed her softly and held the kiss, the palm of my hand lightly and bravely settling on her cheek. We enjoyed the fruits of familiarity, of trust, our kiss being a comfortable extension of so many previous evenings shared. Comfortable, but charged. When we finished Linda smiled up at me. We exchanged no words. Linda didn't linger at the door: when I reached my car I turned back to see a dark entryway.

§

Predisposed to see patterns, or perhaps manufacture them, I naturally ruminated whether this assortment of developments–Linda's move, our kiss, even the tease of a planet rotating us away from the solstice–suggested that a future was being shaped. In turn this line of thought made me wary, the truest statement a person can make being *I don't understand a damn thing about anything.* The Brekkes on Saturday may have been the most devastated people I had ever seen. And yet on Monday morning I heard Linda and Toni's laughter erupt from down the hall. They were laughing about nothing, it turned out; even grief can be vulnerable to lethargies.

The Mazda was one of those developments seemingly engineered by fate–a tool, in other words, of malevolence. Succinctly stated: Linda worked at my father's firm for the purpose of acquiring a car; now she had a car. This nagging insecurity was another confirmation of something I had once called falling in love, a phrase–indeed, a concept–I had sworn off post-Amy. Both Linda and I were in ridiculously tenuous stages of our lives, Linda driving her mother's car, living in her sister's house, and working a job to which she felt no allegiance; and me living with my parents and collecting a paycheck I had no business collecting. Neither of us had an idea as to where the future would take us, or where we wanted it to take us. I had crossed music and seminary and law school off my list. Nothing in life is permanent–I knew that. In theory I could revisit past choices. I had no interest whatsoever in revisiting those choices. Well, music–being music–still tugged, but experience had taught me not to expect it to pay bills. The college radio station devoted an evening to Dylan and the student at the microphone mentioned between cuts that the following year Dylan would turn fifty. The student was incredulous; I was, too. That night I dreamed I saw Dylan back down in Minneapolis on a West Bank stage. "Now that I'm fifty," he announced to his audience, "I see no reason to ever play a minor chord again." Then he broke into "Tangled Up In Blue," his guitar falling silent where the minor chords should have been.

At work I was becoming a quite efficient researcher. Sometimes assignments would pile up, but more often I found myself underworked, providing by midweek the memo that wasn't needed before Friday. Everyone became more familiar with me, of course—I assumed, and certainly hoped, that they saw me no longer as just Lanny Johnson's son. Lawyers would occasionally stop at my desk to do little more than converse: had I been out skiing lately (yes, more often than not), or did I have plans to get my music into one of the local bars (emphatically no)? I also seemed to have earned the trust of the staff. To them I was pretty much a mascot. One benefit of my observed but ambiguous kinship with Linda was that no one asked me about companionship outside of work; and, an even greater benefit, no one attempted to introduce me to their neighbor's interesting and well-thought-of daughter.

Mark Soleski asked if I might be up to an out-of-office assignment, something closer to tangibly profiting a client. Something a lawyer might actually do. Lawyering was not in my future, but that was no reason not to immediately accept Mark's invitation. He wanted me to inspect one of the port grain elevators that dotted the harbor line. Mark's client was an international conglomerate that owned the elevator; somewhere in Chicago or London or Johannesburg was a boardroom with a mounted map and a pin locating Duluth. The grain elevator was horribly overtaxed by the local assessor, Mark said; that was the client's position and so that was ours as well. "But I can't very well appear before the tribunal without someone from the firm having actually examined the property," Mark told me. "Find out how the place works and then give me your report. It'll do wonders for my credibility. And the client will appreciate being charged seventy-five dollars an hour rather than one hundred and forty."

"Is that what you're billing me at? Seventy-five?" My salary was twelve dollars an hour.

"It's not a secret. It's called leverage." He said this with a broad smile.

I smiled back. Mark Soleski was eminently likeable. "You'll get a full report," I said, as though I were off on a combat mission.

Which wasn't so far from the mark. The first thing to say about a one-hundred-fifty-foot-high, eight-million-bushel grain elevator is that it can fairly be considered the world's largest bird-feeder. Pigeons circled like monkeys above the witch's castle. I entered the small office beneath the towering cylinder and introduced myself to a supervisor. He looked me over doubtfully. Above his desk, which was cluttered with tickets and receipts, invoices of all manner, was a 1983 calendar distributed for some mysterious reason by a timber salesman. A smirking and shirtless blond held forth a chainsaw. The supervisor walked me next door to the office of a subordinate named Jay—a Packers calendar, here, this time for 1990—and the start of my tour. Jay dared me into an industrial elevator and we ratcheted higher and higher, the shadowy expanse of the silo unfurling itself for us as we rose. At the top an unfenced catwalk extended to an ancillary storage unit; Jay resisted the temptation to suggest we cross it. We gazed out a window for a magnificent view of the terminal and the bay, beyond that Park Point and the Aerial Bridge, and beyond that the expanse of the great iced sea. An epiphany of a sort came upon me: perhaps the reason Superior held us in its spell was the flatness of it, the fact of a plane, a geometric figure one does not otherwise find in nature. There was no time for pondering: in no-nonsense fashion Jay led me back to the elevator for our descent to the floor. *Beneath* the floor, actually, and into a large overflow cellar knee-deep in grain. Jay grinned and nodded toward a large lever switch on the wall. "If I pull that, all power will be cut off from the silo."

"Absolute darkness," I acknowledged. "I can take it."

"And then I will count to ten before switching the lights back on. And when I do you'll wonder what happened to the grain on the floor."

"Why will I wonder that?"

"Because every square foot of it will be covered by the backs of rats."

We talked some about that, and about the pigeons, firmly establishing an animal kingdom theme. It seemed to excite Jay that this held my interest; he had one thing to sell, and I was buying. We walked outside and he showed me the railroad spur that carried in the grain. Carried it in sloppily–piles of grain lined the tracks like sawdust on the floor of a carpenter's shop. "The deer in those woods," Jay said, pointing to a small grove of popple, "are the best-fed in the state."

"And the biggest?"

"It's not even close."

"Are you ever tempted to bring in your rifle?"

"I keep it in my office. I scope them all the time."

"Ever take a shot?"

Jay kept quiet, weighing my trustworthiness before deciding in the negative. "We're in city limits," he said circumspectly.

We walked out onto the pier. "This is our quiet time, obviously. But once the locks reopen, it's pretty crazy." He explained the transfer of grain between silo and vessel, his eyes and coy smile pleading with me to ask the obvious question. When I obliged he seemed to swell with pride. "Oh yeah. If you saw the size of those carp, feeding all summer and fall on grain, you'd never wade into the water again."

My report to Mark Soleski contained none of these details, his focus being on valuation rather than titillation. He was impressed enough to spread the word that Lanny's boy was good for more than reading dusty reporters and pontificating into a little black box. Ted Salmi, of all people, asked me to accompany him to court. "You might as well see something worthwhile," he said in his rapid-fire happy staccato. Ted wanted to condemn a twenty-five-foot-wide strip of land through the back of a scrap metal yard to make way for a power line. The lawyer opposed to this, a thin, shabbily-dressed man I had once heard my father speak of dismissingly, was seated at counsel's table when I followed Ted into the courtroom. Beneath his jacket Ted was wearing a sunburst yellow sweater vest. "How the hell are you, Wally?" he bellowed. Wally didn't look well. His hands and feet were twitching, then his head. He sighed deeply two or three times until, unable to suppress his misery any longer, he said to no one in particular, "Those damn Vikings." The newspaper that morning had reported that the football team had fired its coach.

"Wally, this is –" Ted began, but his show-and-tell was cut short by the thump of a door being opened, followed by the entry from behind the bench of Judge Larson and a severe-looking court reporter. We all rose to attention.

"That's fine," the judge said stiffly. "Please be seated." He organized before him the motion papers that had been filed, summarizing for the lawyers the matter they had placed on his docket, each of the judge's assertions preceded by a tentative "if I'm understanding this." Then Wallace Bergquist began, explaining how Peter Rollina was a local boy, had always thought of Duluth as his home, had graduated from Denfeld High School, playing hockey and baseball and lettering in both, had married a neighborhood girl, begun work at his father's filling station, been a go-getter–always a go-getter–and Rollina Salvage had been a good neighbor, Peter paid taxes like everyone else, and understands that he's just the boy David here, the power company is the Goliath, and if one taxpayer wants to take the property of another, even if it pays for it–that's irrelevant, and not to be considered by the court–that's a grave matter, not anything the Founders ever envisioned happening, not in a situation like this, which is why the law imposes strict requirements, such as a petition must be filed, containing very specific and narrow allegations, and the court should review closely the petition filed by Mr. Salmi, and three affidavits must be filed in accordance with unforgiving deadlines, and the documents must be served on Rollina Salvage, and there too strict deadlines apply, and Mr. Salmi will need to prove to this court's satisfaction that his client has complied with these deadlines.

"Has there been compliance?" Judge Larson said. "Are you alleging there hasn't?"

"The court will need to look at that closely," Bergquist said, and so then and there his motion was lost. But Bergquist continued on, and then Ted responded, keeping his remarks brief.

"Thank you, gentlemen," the judge said. "I'll take the matter under advisement. You'll receive an order within thirty days." Wally Bergquist, still distraught over the loss of a coach, and probably the fate of Rollina Salvage as well, packed up and exited quickly. The judge lingered at the bench, captive to the paper that surrounded him.

"Your Honor," Ted said, "I didn't get a chance to introduce Mr. Johnson. He's a law clerk with us this winter and a damn fine one. University of Minnesota Law School. The memorandum of law we filed, every word is his."

The judge brightened. "Welcome, Mr. Johnson. You're at a top notch firm."

"Thank you, Judge."

"Does Mr. Salmi's practice appeal to you?" The judge gave a discreet smile to Ted, *Mr. Salmi* being protocol; the two had known each other since drinking days during law school. "Power companies and railroads, that sort of thing?"

"I wouldn't want to rule anything out."

"No, I'm sure. At your stage the only thing you're focused on is finishing school and passing the bar."

"Yes, sir."

"Ted, why don't you prepare an order and send it my way. I'll look it over."

"Thank you, Judge."

"I mean, it's just a little strip at the back, isn't it?"

"That's what it is."

"Well, send me an order."

"Not bad," Ted said as he charged back to the office. I was at his heels, struggling to keep up. "Lying to the face of a district court judge."

I thought about what Wally Bergquist had said in court, and then tried to recall what had come from Ted, and finally it dawned on me that I was the one Ted was referring to. I was the liar. Ted Salmi's sensitivity to what I considered conversational lubrication, even if occurring in a court of law, put things in a different light. I must have looked shocked; glancing back, Ted smiled with satisfaction. "Just keep that in mind." He said nothing more while I panted and he beamed through the duration of our Light-Brigade-like charge back to the office. I had nothing to fear from Ted Salmi. (I had nothing to lose, for one thing.) But I found myself replaying my short conversation with Judge Larson: what precisely did he say, how precisely did I respond, what did I mean by what I had said, and—the eternal question, the constant—why hadn't I done things differently?

"Here's a question for you," Shelley Radulovich said upon my arrival. We were the only two in the lunch-room, Ted's hearing having occupied me into early afternoon. Shelley, skirted and cross-legged, was spooning out a carton of sweetened yogurt. On the table before her rested a banana on a napkin. "You're pretty good friends with Linda, aren't you?"

"Yes."

"I mean, I've heard that."

"We're friends."

"I like her a lot. She can be really funny. Do you know what she told me last week?" Shelley paused to scrape out the bottom of the carton, working her spoon with the tenacity of a prisoner about to break through. During my initial weeks at the firm Shelley had struck me as shy by disposition. She frequently sat alone at lunch, listening and smiling but seldom wading into the swamp of dropped G's. But that had changed. I had learned from Linda that a few weeks back Shelley had survived a rite of passage, mailing out a letter from Bertrand Boyer thanking Duluth's first female commissioner of neighborhoods for a lifetime of pubic service. There followed a closed door, some shouting and tears, and an afternoon of sick leave, all of it, once surmounted, resulting in a more confident and chatty Shelley.

"I'm always eager to hear something funny," I said.

"Linda's got interesting ideas, sometimes. She's really into art. She said that in college she studied gems or something."

"It was jewelry."

"Jewelry. She's especially into colors, which seems sort of weird."

I knew what Shelley meant. One might expect a jewelry major to be intensely interested in hair dyes and nail paints and make-up. Linda had time for none of that. "I don't think she's interested in color as a decoration," I said. "Color just for the sake of color."

"No. No, not at all. She said colors and personalities go together, they match."

"I've heard her say that."

"We were talking about how one thing you learn when you're new to a law firm is that there's no such thing as a 'lawyer.' There's a business lawyer, and one for wills, and one for divorces, and litigators—it's a hodgepodge."

Hodgepodge I liked. "A lot of different personalities," I agreed. I was thinking of stocky Frederick Fallingstad, toting up tax returns as though actually wearing green eyeshades. And Brenda Kieffer, a trial attorney, throwing a cold pot of coffee against the wall.

"That's what Linda said! Her idea was that if the personalities aren't all the same, their offices shouldn't be either. Everyone should have a different color scheme. Paint, furniture, everything." Shelley paused, looking thoughtfully into her empty yogurt carton. "I don't know if she meant the colors should match the personalities, or whether they should somehow influence them. Change them, you know." Shelley paused again, likely waiting for a reply. A few more moments passed, and then she looked up at the clock and stood decisively, gathering from the table the remains of her lunch. "It's interesting, though. Funny."

§

Linda happened to be out of the office that day. Earlier in the week she had made casual mention of some sort of morning appointment. My expectation had been that she would return for the afternoon. But she did not return.

The following morning I was out of the office, my duties as law clerk continuing to expand. This time I was up at city hall, reviewing building permits and zoning maps. I should say now that I didn't really understand all of what I was doing–not what I should be looking for at the grain elevator, or listening for in the courtroom, or even how assertive I needed to be in trying to get my hands on property records. My legal education had been limited to one semester and half an exam. (Though I admit to a benefit from having a lawyer as a parent–something about observing how a task is approached, and when it's time for that task to be done.) But I was beginning to sense the contours of the world in which a lawyer, or even an adult, operated–the difference, you might say, between expected and unexpected, or acceptable and unacceptable. I could see the universe's edge. I felt a sense of accomplishment when the young woman behind the counter nodded at my request and marched back toward a large set of metal cabinets. "Come on," she said with mock impatience.

I looked at her as closely as I dared. "You wouldn't happen to be Lisa Szczury," I ventured.

"Good, Tom," she answered. Lisa and I had graduated together nine years earlier. But that Lisa—as opposed to *this* Lisa, who was as unremarkably presentable as could be, a Level II-B civil servant ordered up from Central Casting—had been recklessly wild, devoted to dope, nursing vodka in a root beer can in the school cafeteria, sporting tremendously long frizzed locks, biker clothing, and always a sneer. Truth be told, I wasn't sure she had graduated with us, our paths having been diverted by senior high scheduling, one off to Problems of World Political Systems and the other to Social Studies I: Law Enforcement in Our Community. But here she was, showing me the zoning maps.

"How long have you worked at the city?"

"Since school."

"It's a good gig?"

The question seemed to strike her as inauthentic; as too much trying. "You can't beat government benefits."

"Don't you want to ask what I'm doing up here?" I teased.

"Oh, Lord," she murmured. And for a reason I couldn't fully comprehend her presence made me happy in a way I hadn't been for a long while. It had something to do with being transported back to school days, certainly. Back to safety. Back, primarily, to a time *before*. I opened a cabinet and, while scanning the bindings of a row of volumes, couldn't keep a grin off my face. And with a grasp so acute as to credit Him who made me, I knew, just from the feel of my face, what that grin looked like to Lisa, and how she would react—how she *was* reacting. She was, I knew, smiling as she turned away and left me to my foolishness; and I knew, without seeing, what her smile looked like, the playfulness of indifference.

It was noon by the time I returned to the law firm. I dropped my pack on my desk and went straight for the lunchroom. I had given Linda little thought through the morning, but the stubborn fact remained that she had never returned from yesterday's morning appointment—an undefined appointment that was now suggesting to me something consequential, possibly something worse than consequential. The lunchroom was full, but Linda wasn't among the crowd.

"There's a chair back here," Nicole Haraldson called. She had seen me scan the room.

"In a moment," I said, giving her a wave and then backing out of the doorway. The halls were noon-hour quiet: no typewriter chatter, no opening and closing of cabinets. I walked to the end, to the corner where Linda had her desk. She was staring at a contract marked intricately with arrows.

"Working through lunch," I said in relief.

She said nothing. She didn't lift her eyes.

"You've been keeping yourself scarce since Tuesday."

Still no response. Her mouth was closed tightly and her head was bobbing almost, but not quite, imperceptibly. Well I could imagine the accelerated heartbeat.

"Say, Linda."

She then did look up at me, seemingly distracted by the interruption.

"You've got to let me in on this," I said.

She stared at me, and while the only thing I could imagine her doing was considering how to respond, I wasn't sure that's what was happening. Rather, Linda seemed to be not thinking at all—seemed instead to be dazed, as though having received a ruthless blow.

"Linda?" This roused her to attention. She hesitated a moment and then bounded out of her chair and past me. I followed down the corridor. She wasn't running and I didn't believe I was chasing. But her brisk walk became more frantic as she approached the door to the stairwell, like a diver miscalculating her depth and now thrashing in panic back up to the surface. I got in behind her, before the heavy metal door closed.

She slid down onto the stairs leading from the building's roof. I backed up against the wall across from her, giving Linda space. She made herself small, squeezing her legs together and leaning forward. She chewed furiously on her lip, which she tried to cover with her fingertips, as though she were merely chewing on a nail–doing something unremarkable, instead of this.

"What has happened?"

"Oh," she said, fighting to hold in the tears. "Well."

The scene frightened me–paralyzed me, in a way, kept me from knowing even what to ask. I couldn't imagine what could hurt Linda any longer. Mine was a complete failure of imagination.

"I wish you hadn't come up to my desk," she said, her voice greatly troubled. "I was sure I was going to make it through the day."

"You've got to tell me what's happened."

"I don't know," she said, beginning to cry. "It's just so . . . it's just dumb and I can't believe…" As she lost control the tears came faster, and her voice rose into great heaving sobs so that when I sat beside her, and draped her in my arms, the story was spooled out through thick emotion, fragments that suddenly came together with one word.

"Oh no," I said. "Oh, Linda."

PAUL KILGORE

She would tell me later it was cathartic, her breakdown. She would talk of it as a good thing. But it frightened me, the most uncontrollable weeping I had heard from her, or from anyone.

§

Gone. One unthinking moment she would always regret. Until that moment, two evenings earlier, Linda had comforted herself with a vague sense that some inherent justice, or mercy, was protecting her. She could not have named it, but a presence had prevented her from facing each day alone. That was all she could have expected, and maybe it was enough.

These are some of the things Linda said to me.

"What is the worst thing," she asked, "ever to have happened to you?" We were, as was nearly always the case, the only two in the restaurant.

"Divorcing Amy. Marrying Amy, I mean. You see the problem."

"What did that do to you?"

"You tell me. What you see is what you get."

"What I mean is, how did you view reality after that?"

"I took a dimmer view of it, it's fair to say."

"But people get divorced all the time. You knew that."

I shrugged.

"It didn't take Sheryl's death for me to know that people die. And that sometimes they die young, and horribly, getting mangled. I'd seen that on the news. And I even knew that sometimes people like Sheryl, utterly blameless, the *best* type of people, die horrible, violent deaths. I knew that. So why should it have taken Sheryl's death to change me? I *knew* such a thing could happen."

174

"And now you think differently about reality."

"It's always been right in front of my face."

"I don't know. Reality's a funny thing, Linda. I mean, if it's even a *thing*."

"If it's not a thing, nothing is. Isn't that almost its definition? It's the *only* thing."

"I could ask ten people to tell me what reality is. And when I'd heard all ten I'd know a hell of a lot about *them*. I wouldn't know one bit more about reality."

"Here's what *I* think reality is. It's like being an ant. If you smash an anthill, they all run around frantically in circles, looking for the anthill. They're looking for what they know, but it's not there anymore. It doesn't exist. And all day long, and at night in bed, I think about everything that has happened, and revisit all our troubles, and it's just like the ants. There's not a single thing I can do about any of it. The world has moved on."

She was talking about not only Sheryl, but all the cascading consequences. Her mother, whose crutch was anger; her father, whose was silence. She was talking about the answering machine at the house on Observation Hill and her sister's voice, the last breathing, living Sheryl; she was talking about her own instinctual carelessness. *Gone.*

This is another thing Linda said:

"Maybe the silliest idea I've had is to write Sheryl's biography. Even though I don't know anything about writing biographies and no one would want to read it."

"It would be a way to honor her," I said.

"I'm starting to know the way you think, Tom. What you really mean is that it would be a way to give meaning to something that's meaningless."

To prolong the finite. I didn't deny it. Instead I reached across the table and took Linda's hands in mine.

She said this, too: "I've been having a lot of dreams lately, and this morning it occurred to me that waking up in the middle of a dream is in some ways like when I learned that Sheryl had been killed. For the first few moments I'm trying to resolve conflicts from the dream, and make sense of it. You know? Trying to think it through to completion, I guess. But what I don't realize, not in those first few moments, is that it's just a dream, it's false. That's so much like how it was when I heard about Sheryl. When I got Mom's call at work that morning I was still thinking and acting as though something could be done, as though it was an emergency. When the fact of the matter was that the whole world, the Sheryl world, had already been lost. I could think all I wanted and try to make sense of it, but it was like that dream. Already vanished, and nothing anyone can do could have brought it back."

Linda had told me she no longer had a fear of dying, but this was and wasn't true. She refused to drive down the hill Sheryl had driven (though she would drive *up*), figuring out alternative routes. On some days she refused to drive at all. One evening she took the bus out to a clothing store at the mall. On her return—while everyone on the bus, Linda said, was occupied in conversation, or reading, or listening to their Walkmans, and while Linda was simply watching the world go by—the bus began to glide. "Not a single person on that bus noticed it before I did," Linda told me. "It felt like that moment when a plane lifts off the runway. Then we started to drift, wobble a little bit, and I could see people looking up. Stopping their conversations. Then somebody screamed. We seemed to be going faster and faster."

"Black ice." I had seen the story on the local news that morning. "You never know. When I drove home last night the streets seemed fine."

"I was near the back of the bus—it was one of those two-part accordion busses. We were swaying pretty good from side to side. We jumped the curb and smashed into a bench, then knocked over a little pole. The bus stopped, tipped up real uneven. Then everyone got off. Thank God it wasn't very cold. They had another bus for us in about ten minutes or so, no more than that.

"But here's the funny thing, Tom. At no time did I feel the slightest fear. I knew immediately what was happening. I just thought it was my turn. I know how the world works now, and if Sheryl can take it, well I can take it too. The bus crashed and my only reaction was that the whole thing was… interesting."

And then we rose from our booth at Peking and I drove her home, this being one of those days she didn't bother with the Mazda. I pulled up to the curb at the base of her long stairway. Instead of bounding out she leaned back in her seat, eyes straight ahead, and said, "Do you know what I've been thinking about lately? I've been imagining everything that will happen in the next fifty years. Basically over the course of my life."

"Pretty hard to imagine," I said, mainly to put myself on record as not having forgotten about Sheryl, the futility—the mistake—of assuming even one day, much less a life.

"Not really. I mean, maybe one day I'll have a family. But even if I don't, well, Karen got married once and I'd be surprised if she didn't again, someday. So I've been imagining nephews and nieces, born and then growing up, graduating and then off to college. Who knows what they might be. Probably jobs that haven't been invented yet. And *they'll* get married and have their own kids. Mom and Dad will pass, the house will get sold–I mean, you're right, who can *imagine* what the world will be like in forty or fifty years? And when that time comes, when I think of Sheryl I'll think of this young girl, in her twenties, which will seem like a baby to me at seventy. And I'll think of her living in this little house, which will be torn down, and driving a car–will there even be cars then? This world we're living in now will be gone. So many things will have changed, new presidents and wars and God knows what else." Now Linda turned toward me with a look of wonder on her face. "Sheryl wouldn't fit in–do you know what I mean? I'd be living in a different world than she had ever known. New generations of family. She wouldn't comprehend any of it. She'd turn around and leave. I can't stop thinking about this. If, *if* I would ever see Sheryl someday, *if,* would we even have anything to say to one another?"

Linda told me all this without a tear; with hardly any emotion. I slid toward her and put an arm around. "Way too much thinking," I said.

"I know."

"Way too much." I pulled myself as close as bucket seats, not to mention winter clothing, would allow. Her lips were cold–the short drive from Superior Street had scarcely allowed time for the car to warm–but the sensation was pleasant. How could the intimacy not have been pleasant? This was a good night kiss of the high school variety, but there's no denying the excitement of voices giving way to quiet, to breath, the impressive palette of communication having nothing to do with talking. If there wasn't enthusiasm on Linda's part there certainly wasn't resistance. Replaying the kiss later that night–did I do anything but replay the kiss?–it came to me that the Linda being kissed might not have been too different from the Linda riding the careening city bus. Knowing how the world works now. We held each other even more tightly following the kiss, fitting together very nicely, no words exchanged. Then I slowly turned my face and kissed her once more. She began to withdraw.

"Linda?"

"I'm sorry, Tom. This is nice. But I don't want–I'm not ready for it."

The words hit me as a reprimand. *Of course* she wasn't ready. Through all our evenings of talk I had been conscious of the fact that there was a part of her sorrow I couldn't understand and an even larger part–all of it, really–I couldn't share. Sorrow, I had often thought, is not something capable of being unburdened. It had been Linda's sister who had died, not mine. The thought had also occurred to me that if through some cosmic trickery I were able to see the living Sheryl but one minute, my sympathy for Linda would then be immediately replaced by grief. In just a few moments, as Linda used her hands to pull back her hair and then snap her jacket collar against the cold, I built up my behavior into a monstrous obtuseness. We were, after all, at the base of her sister's own house.

"God, Linda. I'm so sorry."

"No, no."

"Not thinking at all –"

"Tom, don't." She had turned away from me and was beginning to pull on her knit mittens, the ones she had been wearing those nine weeks ago and since. I waited in silence for her to tell me where our conversation would go, but only after opening the door did Linda turn back to face me.

"Thank you for tonight. Again. Thank you for all these evenings. I'll see you in the morning." She pulled herself out of the car joylessly, one more hard thing in a life of hard things. I leaned up toward the passenger window and watched her climb the stairs, watched the house lights come on, and then I put the Civic in gear and drove away.

§

I spent the night in restlessness, half asleep and half back in the car, Linda leaving. Our status quo was like a coin on edge, and my clumsiness had dictated the way it would fall. But upon arriving at work in the morning I was immediately chased down by a smiling Linda—a different woman, really, happier than I had seen her in two months. "I received a call last night," she said. "It was Sheryl's friend Erik. My friend, too. He's known all the Brekkes for years. He's just the best."

Since coming back to town I had become aware of a sort of under-population, a parallel community. These were people spread between college and their early thirties, single or beginning married life or having a first child. They had nothing to do with the Duluth of my memory, retirees mowing their lawns and writing letters to the editor that complained about potholes or the power bill. The men were bearded and shaggy-haired, the women rosy-cheeked and attractive in their high health. Indestructible. All were boot-wearing, moving often in groups, though not joiners, green but otherwise apolitical—or, I should say, political in a way that didn't involve anything like herd behavior. They had views, certainly. But their center of gravity was the outdoors: the strenuous outdoors of skiing down frozen waterfalls and climbing toward ledges. (One evening, during a terrific snowstorm, Linda and I saw a couple enter Peking wearing snowshoes, baby in the front pack.) They read about the same adventures to which they were devoted, taken to extremes: Jack London was a favorite, and they all knew about the Franklin expedition. Big dogs were their companions. They favored guitars and fiddles and mandolins. I picked all of this up through observation, overheard conversations, fliers in the record store, and what passed for an underground newspaper. From Linda, also.

Erik Mattila, I soon learned, was of this population. He had been in Sheryl's class (a younger brother, Peter, had been in Linda's). There had been three Mattila boys, sons of an orthopedic surgeon who was a colleague of Ed Brekke's. The Brekke and Mattila children grew up together. Now Erik sold skis and kayaks for a downtown retailer. "He wants to have a get-together for Sheryl," Linda said. The idea animated her. "Not a service, but sort of a commemoration. If you could even call it that. Tom, I'd like you to come with me."

As I learned more I shared the observation that I hadn't imagined Sheryl to have had a lot of friends, and not of the sort Linda was describing. "I don't know that she *did* have a lot of friends," Linda responded. "She was a friendly *person*, but she liked to keep to herself. I know that she and Erik stayed good friends, Erik and Miriam, and he probably introduced her to his group."

Erik and his girlfriend lived in a cabin tucked far into the interior that spread north from Duluth. The event to which Linda had been invited–what to call it: a service? a remembrance? or just a reason to congregate?–was set for a Friday night. The pattern that had been visited upon northern Minnesota all winter was given one last play: a snowstorm, this time running from Wednesday into Thursday, followed by ferocious northern winds and a plunging thermometer. Even in Duluth it was startling to see such temperatures in late February. On the appointed morning Linda, maneuvering a plastic container into the lunchroom refrigerator, looked concerned. "Did you hear what the windchill will be tonight?" she said. "Should we be worried about that?"

"The Civic laughs at danger." The anxiety on Linda's face was a fair indication of how important the evening was to her.

"It'll be okay to drive out-of-town after dark?"

"I'll get the car as warm as a living room."

When work ended I drove home and changed into long underwear and corduroy trousers, draping my upper body with an enormous wool sweater. I warmed myself with a bowl of soup and then threw a blanket, mukluks, and a small shovel into the trunk of the car. Linda was waiting in a recently-acquired parka when I arrived.

We worked our way up Woodland Avenue, past the college and the big houses constructed in the halcyon teens and twenties. The winding road took us through a hollow where lights mounted over a hockey rink fended off the shadows falling from the bluff. We were amazed by the perseverance of boys risking frostbite on such a night. Even inside the car we could hear in the dell's echo the knife-on-knife of skate blades nicking ice, the rebound of pucks knocking boards like knuckles rapping a door. "I like that," Linda said, meaning the thud of wood; the sound of home.

"Do you know which one that is?" I asked, leaning forward to look out from under the car's ceiling. Above us was a majestic heavenly body of the purest white, nary a twinkle, fixed as a god.

"Jupiter," Linda said with enthusiasm. "It's been a won-derful winter for Jupiter." Which I had heard mentioned, I now remembered; my father had made just that remark in the past week. "It makes me think," Linda continued, "that the North would be a degree off without it."

"As in temperature? Tonight?"

"Mhm."

"A degree which way, Linda? Would we be colder? Or is all that white light actually making things more arctic?"

"Well, that's the question, isn't it?"

The neighborhoods ended and we were now truly into the North, beyond America's last city, swallowed by the boreal forest that rolled on for as far as trees grew. It was breathtakingly beautiful, more so because of the flirtation with danger. "Such a long winter," I said. There was a point to the banality. I was thinking of the drive north from the law school in Minneapolis, one night being an echo of the other. But only the ferocity outside the car had been the same.

"Don't you feel," Linda asked, "as though we're the last two on Earth?" And indeed what surrounded us were dark pine tops and a field of stars overhead; otherwise, emptiness. Now and then the wind threw a sheet of snow down from the high branches. We would be blinded for an instant, but then the straight road would reappear. Occasionally the wall of black spruce thinned and sprawling before us was a swamp whose boundaries could not be seen.

Linda had a sheet with directions she had written out. She flipped the overhead light on once we turned from the county road and onto a narrower, winding track. By now we were half an hour or more out of town and, judging from the loops in the roadway, navigating through an area of small lakes. A plow had pushed high banks of snow along each shoulder—we were essentially driving through a tunnel. Linda asked me to slow the car. Soon we came upon a small red sign with a fire number matching that on Linda's paper. I eased the car into the narrow driveway. "Don't lose heart now, Erik told me. It's a long road in." Linda switched off the overhead and in silence we advanced as far as our headlights; then again; then again.

A last turn brought us to a low cabin obscured by a blazing porch light. With a blade mounted to his truck Erik had cleared snow from an area just large enough for the Civic and the five trucks that had preceded us. I switched off the key; last-minute winter clothing adjustments made, Linda and I hustled through the cold and wind to the cabin door.

Erik and Miriam greeted us as we entered. Both were immediately likeable, Erik for the ease with which he was Erik, Miriam for a smile that had found a way to accommodate both enchantress and mother. I tried to display myself by making a crack about having arrived at the Finland Station; Erik immediately responded with a memorably creditable *zdravstvuyte!* Both he and Miriam gave Linda enthusiastic hugs and then did the same for me. I had been wondering about the reception we might receive, the spectrum of my imagination running from somber to sentimental. I hadn't expected joyous.

The cabin was not large. There were two rooms, starting with the Miriam-christened Great Hall, where beyond Erik and Miriam I surveyed a group of maybe half a dozen friends. The walls were pine-planked but mostly covered with bear skins and mounted skis and snowshoes from an earlier era. Long underwear and heavy clothes hung on pegs near the door. In the center of the room a wood-burning stove stood on a small, elevated brick base. Its stack rose to and out the open ceiling. Surrounding the stove were three worn, quilt-covered couches, all inviting and undoubtedly pregnant with stories from their nomadic college years. In the back of the room a step-up platform had been built to serve as a kitchen. Crowded to the back of the platform were a refrigerator and stove-top oven, between them a sink and mounted pump. Erik watched me appraise the surroundings and immediately escorted me to the Adequate Hall ("but Really Great sometimes," Miriam said naughtily), partitioned from the kitchen by dark drapery hung on a rod. A dresser and mirror were cowering in the Adequate Hall's corner, the room being ruled by a queen-sized bed heavy with quilts and pillows. I asked how many trips had been necessary to cart all the bedding, and as if to highlight the question's irrelevance a gust of wind gave a violent rattle to the room's small window, peeking out between snowdrifts.

Besides Erik and Miriam there were, it turned out, seven others—a pair of couples, two unattached lumberjacks, and a woman who had taken it upon herself to feed the fire. As we began our tour Linda looked somewhat anxiously from face to face after failing to recognize the first of the couples, but she brightened as the others became familiar. None were shy with their greetings—Linda, she of the billowing bale of bovine fodder, was now Dorothy at her Munchkinland coming-out party. She enjoyed the attention—especially enjoyed the admiration her greenstone necklace was receiving. "And to think," Erik crowed, "that when I first saw her she was"— finger and thumb an inch apart—"*this* big."

"And you —" Linda said; but she was too caught up in the moment's pleasure to be bothered with finishing her thought.

"You've got to identify your date," the woman named Nancy said.

"*Tom*," Linda blurted out. "Tom Johnson, who has been the finest of friends since the accident."

"Tell us about yourself, Tom."

"I will. I will tell you everything. There's a lot of night left."

Erik and Miriam had beer, of course, and they also had whiskey. At first I stayed at Linda's side, but soon she was in a corner talking to a Sarah and I was near the stove with a Mark. I was taken with the setting–the warm cabin, obviously, but in addition the greater setting, uncountable acres of pine, balsam, and birch, nothing between us and the top of the world. "Do we dare go outside?" I suggested. "I can't imagine a clearer sky."

Erik joined us. "There's a sauna beyond the privy."

"Operative?"

"Not tonight. I'd be collecting bodies in the morning."

"But you and Miriam use it?"

"Oh, yeah. We'd charge out and into the beaver pond before it froze over."

"You hear those stories."

Erik nodded. "When you come out of the water you feel strong enough to uproot a tree."

I liked Erik. I had the idea to say something silly, tell him he was the sort of man I would feel comfortable buying a kayak from on a handshake. But I didn't want the conversation to stray from the North. I was that enthralled.

"Here's a personal question," I said to Erik. "Mark's probably wondering, too. If you and Miriam have a family one day, what happens to the cabin?"

"I don't know," Erik said. "What *should* happen to it?"

"Would you stay?"

"It's not something I think about. But why wouldn't –"

He looked across the room. "Miriam," he called in a voice designed for all to hear.

"Yes," she returned, drawing the word out to effect a tolerant and vaguely mocking obedience. Erik's sauna pal; I imagined the pink skin. She was among a group of four that now included Linda.

"Let's say we have a kid."

"Now?"

"Tom is wondering if we shouldn't move in that case."

"Tom?" she said, her voice rising in faux indignation. "Linda, where did you *find* him?"

"On a bus!"

"Let's say you and Tom had a kid on that bus."

"We'd move in that case!" Linda cried above the laughter. With a beaming smile she looked from face to face, saving mine for last.

"This," I said to Erik and Mark with a gesture meant to take in not just the cabin and not just the evening, but the world in which both resided, "brings to mind the great Russian novels." The whiskey was opening me up; that was part of it, but only part.

"Absolutely," Mark said. "Not to diminish the Icelandic sagas."

"Grieg," said Erik. "And," he added, lowering his voice with the majesty of stagecraft, "Johan Julius Christian"—the dramatic pause—"*Sibelius*."

Now we were joined by Joel and Nancy. "Tell all, Tom Johnson," Nancy blurted. "You said you would."

"Let the interview begin."

"Were you born in Duluth?"

"I've always thought so."

"Where did you go to school?"

187

"An essay question," I said, teasingly rolling out high school, college, seminary, and law school.

"Goodness but you're educated."

"I saw two of four to completion. The first two."

"Where are you working?" Joel asked.

"Boyer, Johnson & Salmi. The law firm. I'm a law clerk."

"What does a law clerk do?"

"A law clerk clerks," said Linda, who had wandered over with Miriam to take in the exhibition. "That's what you were about to say, wasn't it, Tom?"

"It's for lawyers who will never be lawyers," I said. "Who had the perseverance to finish one-sixth of law school, roughly speaking. Excuse me: *not* finish one-sixth."

"Can failed seminarians clerk, too?" said Mark. "Sort of an apprentice deity?"

"That's the boy I know," said Linda.

"I'm also a failed musician. It's annoying that people overlook that." In a camera's shutter speed I considered, then rejected, the idea of mentioning Amy, my most accomplished failure.

"Because it's an impossibility," Erik said. "Music isn't something you succeed or fail at."

"Is there a future in failing?" said Nancy.

"Damn right there is. Look"—spreading my arms—"where it's taken me."

Now it was Miriam's turn: "Sheryl's little sister must be asked where she found such a darling."

"On the bus," someone reminded her.

"But we work together," said Linda. "Though I got there first."

"Boyer, Johnson…"

"Are you the same Johnson?"

"My father and I sometimes differ on that."

"Nice, Linda," said Miriam. "Impressive. You've brought us the heir to your law firm."

"Not mine to inherit," I said.

"He'll end up in New York, wait and see. And it's not *my* law firm," Linda said, laughing at the idea. "In the history of the firm I'll be just a blip."

"But what a lovely blip," I said. New York: interesting that she saw me as someone likely to return to school, get back on track; dismaying that she was, after everything, so capable of misreading me.

"Not a lifer?" Erik asked Linda.

"Depends on how long my life is." As the words blossomed and faded—the wonderful music of her voice—Linda began to wobble from the sentiment before righting herself. "We need to make Sheryl a part of all this."

"Indeed we do," Erik agreed forcefully. The room quieted as though we had all been rebuked for the fickleness of attention, the imperative of pushing ahead. We found places on the couches—Linda and I side by side, our hips mapping one another—and Erik took it upon himself to remain on his feet. Standing near the wood stove he put on a serious face and began. "Being one of the Mattila boys, and therefore in love with the Brekke girls—"

"Vice versa —"

"—I am well-qualified to share a quite bawdy story about Sheryl."

"My sister," Linda warned.

"And about Linda as well."

Linda looked around with a nervous smile and shrank back into the deep couch.

"This occurred at the Mattila cabin down in Wisconsin, where the Brekkes were visiting for the day. Do you think it was the Fourth, Linda?"

"I don't remember this," she said guardedly.

"And we all went in for a swim. Well, Peter and I and Sheryl and Linda. Who knows where Joe and Karen were. Out of the house by then. The four of us began civilly but naturally a world war water fight ensued. And then Linda crawled up onto Peter's shoulders, way up into the sky, and declared a war of chicken on me and her sister."

"Oh, God," Linda said, mortified. "I remember this. Erik, you wouldn't."

"So it was the hyperactive Mattila brothers and the fair but scantily-clothed Brekke sisters. Mix and match."

"*Erik!*" But a locomotive would not have been able to pull the smile from her face.

"I told Sheryl to jump on and she turned about as white as her sister is now. And there arose in the land a great clamor, three teenagers yelling at Sheryl Brekke at top volume to climb onto my shoulders, swing her bare legs around my neck, and let the battle royal begin. And I recall that little sister Linda was the most vociferous of us all—'Come on, Sheryl, be a sport! You're ruining everything! Don't be a fud-dy-duddy! Don't be a stick in the mud!'"

Linda's face was bowed into her spread fingers.

"Being boys we weren't supposed to notice that Sheryl was shooting daggers at her sister and mouthing one big silent *NO* after another, trying to get her dense little Linda to understand."

"'Weren't supposed to notice,'" Miriam scoffed. "You were oblivious schoolboys! No *way* did you notice!"

"Poor Sheryl," Linda moaned.

"So there she was, trying to explain to an utterly *clueless* sister –"

"I *was* clueless!"

"–until finally a light bulb went on over my head and I told Peter that chicken was kid's stuff."

"What a noble guy," said Miriam.

"Peter didn't know."

"Peter didn't know," Linda agreed, hands on each side of her head, Munch-like. "If I didn't know, Peter couldn't possibly have known."

"So in an act of chivalry I plowed into Peter, knocking both him and Linda over."

"Saving the day," someone cheered from one of the other couches.

"But the best part was little skinny Linda –"

"Bad memory! I was fourteen!"

"–rising up from the water, doused as a drowned rodent, and aiming the most annoyed of looks at her sister and screaming"–here Erik's voice rose a couple of octaves–"'*Grow up!*'"

With that the laughter that had been building reached a crescendo. It was an odd story, in a way, more about Linda than Sheryl. But did it matter? Linda's face was back in her hands. I had rarely seen her so happy.

Richard was next. He had gone to school with Sheryl and recounted a couple of instances of skipping with her to get ice cream. But there wasn't more to the stories than that, and truancy was at the outer reaches of Sheryl Brekke's lawlessness–Richard had no other material to use. His story did, however, trigger a memory for Sarah, who had also gone to school with Sheryl and Richard. This story was more interesting, since it did revolve around an actual transgression: on the night before graduation a large group of seniors snuck into the school at midnight, and they were able to do so because during the day Sheryl had inexplicably covered a piece of masking tape over the latch bolt of a fire door at the back of the building. A rare case of bowing to peer pressure. But what Sheryl had imagined as a handful of girls soaping the window of the principal's office turned into a gang of two dozen, some of whom she barely knew, intent on mass desecration. Sheryl watched in horror as the bulletin boards came down, until one of the boys pulled a fire hose out of its box and threw it onto the floor of the chemistry lab. "You, you... *hoodlums!*" she screamed–Sarah was appropriately theatrical–"Show some respect for our school!"

Kersten, the woman who had taken control of the woodpile, now stepped forward. She was a nurse frequently assigned to Sheryl's shift. "Sheryl," she said, and immediately began to tear up, and then laugh at herself. "Oh, Sheryl. Why did you have to do that?" The room quieted and Kersten, who apparently hadn't prepared for this moment, cocked an eye at the ceiling and bit her tongue. "Okay," she said presently, composing herself. "So last summer a lot of the girls went kayaking to the sea caves." Everyone in the cabin had likely made this trip. It was pleasant to be reminded of the steps descending to the broad sand beach, the clear South Shore waters at midsummer, and the crossing to the point and the caves. Our memories filled in the sucking and murmur of water meeting sandstone, the orange of the rock and reflected green of the water. But Kersten's story didn't go anywhere–Sheryl, in her telling, had been on the trip but hadn't said or done anything. There was a charm to this, the recollections of a grieving friend who really had nothing to tell except that Sheryl had *been there*, on that Saturday and night after night on the hospital floor. Expected, familiar, *there*; and now, missed.

Others took turns until Linda finally rose. "I can't add anything to what you lovely people have been saying," she began, and in that one sentence–on the word *lovely*, actually–she went from smiles to the contortions of emotion. "I mean," she sniffled, "she was just my *sister*." But Linda did have words to add–not tales of adventure or punch lines, but a little about ice skating, and cooking, and stories about being sisters. Performance wasn't the point. The more mundane the memory, the quieter we all became. There was the time the girls were late for school. Long holiday drives to see grandparents. Arguing over clothes. "Oh, I don't know," Linda concluded sweetly, wiping a tear. "She would have so wanted to be here tonight. Except that she didn't like things like this."

As midnight neared the evening, which had never lagged, drew to a close. A long transition period began: the sorting and layering of coats, the lacing of boots, the adjustments of gloves and hats. Matti and Richard stalked out to warm their trucks and then returned with exclamations and pounding feet. Through the evening the wind had remained persistent; the tracks from our vehicles to the door were now drifted over. A storm of information had been exchanged over the past few hours; a storm of fellow feeling. We each believed one another to be ancient friends: when Mark lamented that Linda and I had ventured out on such a night in something so insubstantial as the Civic, Nancy chimed in that I should have appropriated my father's Lincoln—when during the evening had I mentioned that detail? "It's going to be a bear, though," Richard said. "I think we all need to caravan it back to town."

Linda and I were the last to leave; Miriam shooed us away from what could have been an elaborate departing statement. Hand in hand Linda and I sprinted across the plowed yard, which was now animated by four sets of headlights and the roar of engines over the wind. We tumbled into the tomb-cold car. Adrenaline from the danger and a dozen or more swirling conversations caused Linda to cry out effusively, "I *love* all these people! Every single one of them!"

"They love you back, Linda."

"I'm nostalgic for tonight," she chattered, "and it's not even over."

It was at that moment that the car key, which I had jammed into the ignition and turned with urgency, broke cleanly into two pieces. One piece, small as a nickel, I held between bare fingers and thumb. The remainder was locked deep in the crevasse of the ignition.

"Damn," I howled, more from the cold than the familiar bane of derailed anticipation. "Well, it's over now."

Linda looked across quizzically. I held the fragment up for display. "A little metal key is no match for forty-below windchills."

But such was her mood that she laughed. "Do you have a copy?"

"Back home. It wouldn't do us any good if I had it here. Half the key is still in the ignition." I was already trying without avail to grasp in my fingertips the runty edge of the embedded key. After a few moments it became apparent that the car–dark and silent but for the wind's reprimands–was no place to puzzle out a solution. We made a run back to the cabin door. Matti, seeing that something was up, followed us in.

Erik and Miriam's immediate solution was for us to stay the night. Which wouldn't have accomplished anything: in the morning the spare key would still be back at home, the broken key would still be in the ignition, and the car battery would almost certainly be dead. Matti offered to bring us back to town; his truck (where Kersten was waiting) was already warm. For a few minutes we all went back and forth, the compelling logic of Matti's offer warring with the aversion Linda and I had to leaving. But since Minneapolis I was, I fancied, beginning to see the value of sensible ideas. I had been living a routine now for a couple of months, holding down my undeserved job and living quite conservatively whether with Linda or alone. And nothing was more conservative than the responsibility I felt to somehow act as Linda's counterweight—to negate, for one thing, horoscopes and color wheels and unified theories of jewelry. More: I was daring to think a purpose had been served in not completing the examination, in busing out to buy shirts at the mall.

We were half an hour into Saturday when Matti's truck began snaking down the long and narrow driveway. Linda and I sat in the back, and while it took a few minutes for thoughts of the practical to pass—locksmiths and auto mechanics—pass they did. I leaned my head back and took in the starkness, black punctuated with the brilliance of the cold, glorious universe.

"Kersten," Linda said slowly. Kersten was up front with Matti. "Did my sister ever say anything to you about a boyfriend?"

There was no immediate answer. "I don't think so," she then said. "I guess with Sheryl I would remember something like that. She didn't share personal information much."

"There were things at her house that made it seem like someone else, a guy, might have entered her life. A Christmas present was one."

"Oh, I think that could have been true. You could tell, even without her saying anything. She was pretty happy."

Linda leaned forward gratefully, protecting herself against disappointment by challenging Kersten: "Sheryl wasn't an unhappy person generally. She was steady."

"This was happiness beyond steady. You can tell, Linda. You know what I mean–smiling when she thought no one was around, a little humming. Just always in a good mood. That was a little bit of a new thing for her the last month or two. Not so businesslike."

Linda leaned back, taking this as confirmation. Matti and I remained silent. "But she didn't say anything?"

"That wasn't Sheryl. Not with us, anyway."

"I know. But no name? Even a guess?"

Again Kersten thought before responding. "No."

"Oh," Linda said, a guarded frustration. "The thought that someone may be out there. Wouldn't we have heard from him?"

"There could be a million reasons," I said, but this aroused no reply. We were well down the county road now, black trees silhouetted beneath the unfurled stars. The truck's heater had warmed me into a slight drowsiness made all the more pleasing by the window's cold against my cheek.

"But isn't that a comforting thought?" Kersten said after minutes had passed. "That there is someone out there? Someone who Sheryl might have been in love with, and who loved her back?" And then, in typical Minnesota retreating fashion: "I mean, that's nice."

Linda seemed to think so, too. She let out a sigh and leaned into my shoulder. Nestled in. And with my shallow pan ears and jack-o'-lantern eyes I took in the world, that one place and moment, fully. Among the unending hopelessness I had fed on back in the Chicago days was this: having never seen heaven,

196

how, upon arrival, will we know it? I needn't have searched so far for such conundrums. How are we, so woefully insufficient, to recognize *this* existence, this seesaw of habit and desire, all the things we decide to call *life*? We take galaxies of galaxies and draw them down to our size, a counting number. We invent patterns. I glanced down at Linda, the part of her not so close that it wasn't exposed to me, and when I momentarily shut my eyes she was still there, a wired memory looking like a cartoon character X-rayed by electrocution. To my senses she no longer existed, except in memory. Could memory be existence? I thought of sitting with Linda in my parked car at the foot of Sheryl's house, and Linda's speculations about the course of her lifetime. A half-century or more, an incredible accumulation of years. With presumption I imagined for myself a life extending too long to remember even this evening. But if memory is outlived, what purpose can there be but affinity; magnetism, as it were? A coalescence of the dying while we are briefly alive. A name for meaning.

Linda, as though asleep, gave a deep sigh. With great familiarity she placed her hand on my leg, spreading her fingers. We watched the stars; we watched in quiet. And what is it we live for? Is it anything but this?

§

Events then began to move quickly. Last things never seem last at the time.

I did not in fact have a spare key at home. I had questioned whether a spare existed even while telling Linda otherwise. Erik and Miriam lived like Hudson Bay Company adventurers, and in Linda's glow I couldn't bring myself to admit an incompetence. But on Saturday morning Linda swung by to deliver me to a bald, mustachioed locksmith, sort of a Gay Nineties, Stage Manager soda jerk, whose phone-booth-sized shop was far from the shores of a mall parking lot. He inspected the broken key, sizing it up without expression, then referred to a catalogue that was thick enough to allow me to imagine an individual entry for each car in the country. Two shiny keys were cut; I gifted Linda the broken fragment as a token of etc., etc.; and then we set off for Erik and Miriam's dacha, the sky now graying and the journey a subdued prose, meager in comparison to the previous night's poetry. Erik had used a needle-nose pliers to clear the ignition. Jumper cables were produced and the Civic was soon back among the living.

Sunday was quiet; they all were. Mark Nielsen, who had participated in our Nordic-Slav rhapsody at the Mattila cabin, stopped by to drop off a tattered copy of *Grettir's Saga*. I was deep into the lore, cold and rock, virility and death by clubbing, when my mother roused me from my bedroom to take a call from Ted Salmi.

Over the years my father had devoted so much time to his practice–it was his garden, while my mother and I were the well-worn path he trod to get there–that it took me weeks at the firm to accept that it was Ted Salmi's firm, no one else's. Ted had his railroad company, and his power company, and dozens of other business clients; he had the whole of northeastern Minnesota's economy, it seemed. He was smart, and there was charm in his eccentricities, but his indispensable characteristic was perpetual-motion energy. Never did it flag. I had seen him charge out of the office at day's end with the same step-jump that had propelled him there twelve hours earlier. One of Ted's clients was the Greater North Superior Resort Association, a confederation of resort owners that stretched across the Minnesota Arrowhead and into Ontario. A lawyer from Thunder Bay handled the Canadian resorts, Ted the American. As the daylight began its climb toward equilibrium, when cabin fever was well-positioned to drive everyone mad, the resorts conducted a trade show to drum up business and generally push back against the tedium. Ted and Michael McCann, the lawyer from Ontario, used the opportunity to take stock of their clients' legal needs. The show had been scheduled for the coming week in a Thunder Bay exhibition hall. Ted wanted me to join him. The idea was that we would leave the office at noon on Tuesday and ride up the shore in Ted's Cadillac, over the Onion River and Manitou, the Flute Reed and Devil Track, crossing the international border and arriving at the Port Arthur Hotel for dinner. For three days we would mingle with the resort owners and Ted would amass a long list of assignments–listing agreements, purchase agreements, contracts for deed, easements, zoning applications. This all required a gopher: my role. There would be a grand luncheon on Friday and Ted and I would be back in Duluth by the weekend.

Monday was frantic in preparation, but arcing over it all was a sense that time had begun to move again: not just the brilliant sunrises and encroachment of afternoon light into early evening, but the slow building of a new life. The ferocious weekend weather slipped eastward and southerly winds were expected for a sustained number of days. I told Linda that I wanted to do something for her. She gave me a sideways look–a smile, I imagined–and I explained that after a week in Canada I would return with great tales that could be shared over a real dinner, a dress and a tie, a bottle of wine. The sort of thing that could be done with irony and yet enjoyed in perfect sincerity. A meal that wasn't egg rolls or Mongolian beef.

The anticipated dinner was a constant presence. Through the week I saw each episode with Linda's eyes—saw myself, rather, re-creating events for Linda, savoring the reaction. Ted told me on the long drive up the shore, climbing toward the top of the lake, that I was asked along because even though Lanny had made it clear that law wasn't in my future, he, Ted, sure as hell couldn't import Nicole or Toni into Canada, and Maggie would likely disrupt diplomatic relations between two peace-loving nations. I let Ted's words settle into my memory, a gift for Linda.

In his big car Ted kept a large burlap bag, filled with tennis balls, at his knee. The winter had driven herds of deer down the hill, and when one poked its way across the pavement in front of us Ted would roll down a window and give it his best shot, a bright yellow ball skittering across the road to Ted's *kirottu holmo!* I laughed helplessly and thrilled at eliciting the same laugh from Linda.

Ted regaled me. His wife, he said, was a raging hypochondriac. Ted's voice had little nuance; one timbre, one volume. "If the doctor asked her whether she'd noticed her elbow turning orange and levitating, she'd be thrilled at the new idea." This all came with an irrepressible smile, Ted's eyes darting from me to the road to an approaching deer. "And it's the damnedest thing, Tom. A new ailment appears and all the others are immediately forgotten. Disappeared. I ask her where they go. 'Where does what go?' 'That bad hip you had last week, or that smell of warm apple pie you thought was coming from behind your ear!' 'What?' she'll say. 'Ted, what are you talking about?' You'd think the thing that was going to do her in last week wasn't even worth remembering! I tell her, 'Vi, there's something bigger going on here than your symptoms.' Hell, I don't even think they *are* symptoms! But without symptoms, where is she? I tell her, 'Vi, maybe you don't even exist!'" By now Ted would be slowing the car, reaching for the burlap bag.

And I would be seeing the reaction on Linda's face.

For three days I took notes, photocopied documents, softened the resort owners for Ted. Lines of winter-weary fishermen filed past the exhibits, but they were no more captivated than I with photographs of twenty-pound northerns and Nipigon sunsets. I collected brochures, weighed one fishing camp against another. Ted told me it would be interesting to mark resorts on a map, and like a boy in Miss Peterman's first grade classroom I sat down with a box of colored pencils and a protruding tongue. All of it for Linda.

The whole cavalcade was a roaring success, story upon story, twenty new files to open, legal work to last well into the summer. Ted slapped the back of every man at Friday's farewell luncheon and we retraced the long journey home, arriving at the office shortly before six o'clock. I had made eight o'clock reservations for my dinner with Linda. I dropped a box of files on my desk, one foot turned for the elevator, when I saw Kay Knapp's handwriting. *Linda will call you at home at 8 tonight (Friday).* A single yellow sheet from a legal pad, draped over the seat of my chair.

(Friday) was the first ominous sign. The note had been written earlier in the week. And why not by Linda?

At 8. The precision was not innate to Linda.

I drove home. It never occurred to me to drive to Observation Hill or Park Point. I unpacked and threw clothes into the washing machine. I scanned three days' newspapers, the news stories already irredeemably pointless. My parents were preparing for a late dinner with friends; now and then they emerged from their bedroom in various stages of dress to ask about Thunder Bay. This was the bitterest of black humor: waiting like a high school boy for the phone to ring and hoping for no interference from parents. I could have called Linda, of course–I had her number, though since I saw her daily I couldn't recall having ever dialed it. But I didn't call. The note had made me fearful, and I waited.

Eight o'clock came and went. My imagination was in full gallop, and riding it was dread. When Linda's call finally came relief trumped eagerness: I waited until the cusp of the third ring (the thought that the call might be from someone other than Linda never crossed my mind) before picking up the receiver. The clock said twenty-five past eight.

"Tom?"

"Linda. Linda."

"Oh, it got later than I had planned. I'm *exhausted*." Her voice was distant.

"Where are you calling from?"

"I'm not sure where, actually. I was supposed to be in Rapid City, but I didn't make it quite that far. But I got past Kadoka, I remember that."

"What are you doing in South Dakota?" As though words were what this was about, not disorientation, relief, trepidation–a general morass of uncertainty. I tried to hear my voice as Linda would hear it.

"Tom, a lot has happened this week. It's been–the week seems like a month, so much has happened."

Rather than reply I waited.

"It's pretty big news, actually." To this point Linda's voice had been matter-of-fact, but now it began to rise in excitement. "Karen called Tuesday night and wants me to come live with her."

"You're driving to California?" That was the moment that stayed with me, of course. All that followed would be merely data. Nothing would be capable of reversal.

"I can get there by Sunday night, maybe Monday. Probably Monday. But I can't be later than that. It's really exciting, Tom. Karen got a couple of jobs for me teaching community classes, one in ceramics, which will take some on-the-job training, but one in jewelry. She said it's very low-key, very *California*"–my heart went cold with her giggle–"and I was sure I wouldn't do it, but the more I thought– and then there's being with Karen. She said she can cover my expenses at first, but the big thing is she won't be alone by herself out there. The more I thought about it, it just seems right."

This all offended me–how could it not have? I would eventually be shamed to recall that I was hearing thoughtlessness, even selfishness, in Linda's voice. I was stuck on the pettiest of objections: for an entire week I had been anticipating this evening.

"How long will you stay?" I asked.

"I don't know. We'll see. There's been a lot to think about, packing and making arrangements so fast."

"Yes," I laughed, careless to keep out the bitterness.

At this Linda's voice became quieter, more studied, possibly defensive. "I wish I could have waited for you, but everything begins the middle of next week. It was such bad luck for you to be gone in Canada."

"How are your parents on this?"

The question seemed to strike her as inconsequential. "Oh. Well. Anywhere else probably would have made them unhappy. But Karen and I will be together. They haven't said much."

"And your job here–just, *done?*"

"Sandy was really understanding about it. Everyone was." She paused. I imagined she was deciding which course she wanted the conversation to take. Though the truth is that I could only guess at what she was thinking; could only guess at what was really happening. When Linda spoke again her voice was circumspect once more. "I wish you'd been in the office this week, Tom."

"It's all abruptness, Linda. I feel like I'll need to absorb all this before I even know what I should be saying."

"It *is* abrupt," she agreed.

"Had this ever been an idea before? I got the impression your family wasn't hearing much from Karen."

"No, it came out of the blue," she said, the excitement once again rising in her voice.

"Linda, can I tell you this makes me sad? Can you see, Linda, how this could be crushing to me?" *Crushing*: did I realize that this was a thing that would never be said unless one were in the final moments of having the opportunity to say it? I was helpless, of course, powerless before the anxious twitchings of a beautiful bird looking from the branch toward the dark, swallowing forest.

"Crushing to you," she repeated, cautious in the presence of such an exotic idea. "Well–well, it shouldn't be." Linda said this without malice, which was possibly the most wounding of all. The thought that destruction might be the consequence of her decision, and that the thing being destroyed might possess value, seemed to be a revelation.

I had no response, because responding would have required asserting that what was paramount was something other than Linda reuniting with her sister, or finding a way to move beyond Sheryl's death. I loathed my selfishness, but that selfishness was my means of survival. I was the sinking man, clawing my rescuer, frantic to drown us both. This is all too melodramatic–I realized that even as I struggled through Linda's call. Of course I would survive. But survive for what?

The idea that her decision might cause me harm seemed to frighten Linda. It was not an idea she was willing to entertain. "Anyway," she said, mustering the energy to inject an attempted cheer into her voice, "we'll see what happens when I arrive. I still have a lot of miles ahead."

"Will you call me then?"

"Yes, we should talk later." Her little rally had ended. "I can't believe how tired I am. It would be better to talk another day."

And the black humor prevailed, my parents at that moment emerging from their bedroom, dressed for the evening. But if they hadn't–what, anyway, would I have said?

The weekend was the true echo, the true bookend, so like the weekend when I had arrived home eleven Fridays earlier. Emptiness had, I knew, the potential to devour me. I examined those eleven weeks, each turn and pivot, and furiously wrote page after page as a means of capture, knowing all the while that such a feverish attempt to preserve for the sake of edification–the idea that I could fill a notebook and then find in it the truth that had been always hovering before me–was the conceit of a life whose entire trajectory had been for the purpose of disciplining me to know better. No call arrived Saturday evening. No call arrived on Sunday.

Monday brought a new kind of emptiness. I passed one time by Linda's deserted desk and thereafter stayed clear of her side of the office. In fact I found excuses to work in the law library at the county courthouse, a place where no well-meaning, curious, or cautiously voyeuristic secretary could inquire about Linda. Sandy seemed to harbor no ill feelings as a result of Linda's sudden departure. By Tuesday she had brought back the same feather-duster-headed temp, confident enough now to waste nary a second thought on whether six or seven would bring her to the top floor.

And the days passed slowly, one slab of week dropping heavily onto the others.

I came back from the county library on a Monday afternoon near the end of March to find a note from Kay Knapp on my desk. *See me about Linda.*

"She called a couple of hours ago," Kay said in a brisk, well-ordered voice. Kay was pacing toward the day's-end mailroom deadline.

"Out of the blue."

"We talked for a few minutes. Everything's fine. It's the same old Linda. She said she needed to talk to Sandy about some paperwork. She was going to have you transfer her."

Bravely I asked whether I had been Linda's suggestion or Kay's.

"Nope, hers. I knew you were at the courthouse." Kay pulled herself away from the task at hand, the incorporation of a riot of handwritten revisions into an agreement. Teasing chaos into order. "Here's the number she left," Kay said, handing me ten figures on a sheet of yellow paper.

"But things are good?"

Kay raised her eyes upward, a little inventory. "Weather's good, she and her sister are happy to be together, life's treating them well. She sounded alright, Tom. Let her tell you herself."

I imagined Linda receiving my call, the backwards pull of my voice. It was a redemption of sorts, this idea of letting her be. A new survival aid, something I dared think of as heroism. There was more to it, obviously, the less flattering aspects including pride, stubbornness, even abnegation. The non-negotiable vow to never again accept a second chance. I kept the sheet Kay gave me, tucking it safely inside my desk, preserving the idea of the call. But it was a call I was never to make.

A SKYFULL
OF ANGELS

The joke is that I purchased my wife. This is a joke Bobbi encourages. "Life is the process by which the unimaginable becomes imaginable," she says. Of course she must have heard this from me, and it shocked me the first time she said it.

Sixty miles north of Duluth–to Erik Mattila's cabin, roughly, and then the same distance further–brings you to what is still one of the most remote areas of the state. Virtually no human presence existed before loggers established a mill near the end of the nineteenth century. A small settlement followed, accessed only by the ore trains running between the Mesabi Range and Lake Superior. No road reached this settlement, and internal roads were simply woodland trails. Liquor was the medium of exchange. An old section hand's diary–I came to collect such things avidly–tells of repainting the hotel to cover the streaks of urine stilting down from the second-floor windows.

In 1907 a miners' strike in Hibbing failed spectacularly; it was, after all, 1907. The instigating Finns, quickly blacklisted, scattered to the woods, arriving just as the lumber boom was pivoting to bust. Small farmsteads were slashed from the forest, footholds for a life that was idyllically horrendous. It was not unusual to see settlers carrying their possessions while wading through the swamps, a bedspring balanced on the head and a chair beneath each arm. There were bedbugs and lice. Starvation taunted. Disease was rampant–in one case four young brothers all succumbed to diphtheria in a span of months. One heroic woman, married at fourteen, gave birth to fourteen children. The deer her husband shot were supplemented by foodstuffs purchased at winter's start and then carried in a large pack the two miles from general store to homestead. Buried deep in the pack would have been pounds of Red Star Coffee, hammer and sickle prominently displayed on the can's label. Not everyone in the settlement was a communist; socialism, imported from home, was in fact the ideology of choice.

Young women who arrived to teach school were greeted by parents puzzled with the English language. (The children soon left their parents far behind, but language is a stubborn thing. The recorded minutes of the town council meetings didn't make the switch from Finnish until the Eisenhower years.) Teaching in so remote a territory was unspeakably difficult—most teachers left before the end of the school year and more than one took her own life. Suicide was common among the population generally, often the child of alcohol and desolation. Stories of hardship abounded. The small pulp loggers began their winter days a mere three or four hours after midnight. They carried Mauser pistols as a defense against wolves. One young couple, placing somewhat more emphasis on poorer than richer, spent their first summer of married life sleeping in the shaft of a disabled threshing machine. Eccentricity helped. One fellow shaved and cut his hair once each year upon spying the first returning robin. Another enjoyed drinking shaving lotion. Soon enough the snow would fall and it was back to the camps. Imaginatively-named camps, to my ear. One was *Lahde Korpi*: Spring in the Wilderness. Another was *Paa Kallo*: Head Skull. Paa Kallo, gone by the time radios and then electricity arrived—again, with Eisenhower—had been located not far from Dead Wolf Lake.

The weeks following Linda's departure were desperately pointless. Work became a slog, but also a reprieve, the alternative being sequestration at home, picking my way through Halldor Laxness or relying on the easy comfort of music. I found loneliness to be frighteningly seductive–so sly, in fact, that I manufactured reasons to visit city hall and force myself into a misadventure with Lisa Szczury, the short, sorry affair crashing in precisely the way any objective observer would have predicted.

Spring in fact did arrive–unevenly, of course. There was still a wintry feel as May approached: black water in the swamps, snow remnants banked up against the ledge rock.

"This is your lucky day," Ted Salmi said to me. But I didn't want it to be my lucky day–such was my state of mind.

He took me into his office, closed the door, and there I learned that Jerry Palomaki, whom Ted and I had met at Thunder Bay, was looking for someone to buy Dead Wolf Lake Resort. *Resort* was pushing it: Palomaki had ten small whitewashed cabins, numbered in Finnish, and a handful of docks, canoes, fishing boats, and fire pits. The cabins had been built soon after the War by the returning son of one of the area's pioneers. After twenty years Palomaki had bought the property, proceeding to give it a quarter-century of his life. "It's a young man's game," he told Ted–or at least that's the way Ted framed his conversation with me, introducing the idea of a wider world, a different life. Dead Wolf Lake wasn't a brochure-style resort lake. It was swampy on three sides and half the lake was littered with boulders and deadheads that were the product of a mill, now dilapidated, at a far corner of the lake. This geography prohibited water sports–nearly prohibited, in fact, motors. Dead Wolf's primary virtue was its wildness. The entire shoreline was national forest; Palomaki's resort was the only development on the lake. Seasons were short, as was true for all northern resorts. The cabins were opened by early May, when the fishing season commenced, and closed by mid-October. In his early years Palomaki stayed the winter, working on repairs, but as his children grew he and his wife were more apt to move to an East Range apartment, relocation being the only real option besides homeschooling. There were four children, a girl and three younger boys. In Jerry Palomaki's conception of things one of his sons would have been the logical candidate to partner with him and eventually take over Dead Wolf Lake Resort. But all three boys, even the impressively-named Rex, grew to hate the place. They weren't into isolation; were more interested, instead, in twentieth-century life. The course of events became clear. Running a resort was a young man's game. Thunder Bay convinced Palomaki that he wasn't up to the work that would be needed to keep the resort viable. So one brilliant spring day, as the receding winter revealed flaking paint and soft windowsills, rotting life jackets and sagging mattresses, Jerry Palomaki picked up the telephone and called Ted Salmi.

"Of course you'll do this," Ted said to me. He wasn't talking about legal work necessary to facilitate the sale; *I* was the sale. "If I were thirty years younger *I'd* do it." Palomaki had pulled strings with a man named Petko Pejovich, a frequent resort guest who happened to be a mine manager, and secured a mechanic's job in Hibbing. And Mrs. Palomaki was a teacher—bottom line, Palomaki didn't need a big downpayment and would accede to a reasonable cash flow. A little bank financing would make the purchase more comfortable. "Nothing against Jerry," Ted said. "But you'll be buying low. In five years you'll be the sweat equity tycoon of northern Minnesota."

Buying Dead Wolf Lake Resort was something an adult might do. Was I ready? This question so consumed me that I didn't consider those that followed: despite Ted Salmi's soft-pedaling, where, precisely, would the money come from? And: without ever having given it a single moment's consideration, what made me think that come summer people would actually write me checks to spend a week in a cabin little bigger than an ice-fishing house? And: what qualifications did I have, anyway, to fix a punctured screen? split a cord of wood? advise when and where to catch northern? maintain a double-entry accounting ledger? run a resort? And: what precedent had there been in my life for avoiding failure?

I saw myself as weak. This weakness was the thing that made my decision. Ted Salmi, relentless in his crusade to plant me on the shores of Dead Wolf Lake, told me after a week that I had dithered long enough. "I'm going to call your desk at eight tomorrow morning," he said, "and you're going to give me your answer." I agonized until midnight, actually making pro and con lists like a schoolboy weighing whether to spend his hundreds in savings on a third-hand car. Then I dreamed through the same exercise another six hours–dreamed in anguish; quite a lot of anguish–before summoning the courage to drive in to work and, at ten minutes to eight, dial the extension of Ted Salmi's office, sixty feet away. I praised him lavishly. I argued impressively on behalf of my due diligence and soul searching. And when I told him I could not in clear conscience attempt to uphold and sustain the good reputation of Dead Wolf Lake Resort, Ted responded with nothing more than a simple, "I see." Ten minutes later my phone rang. "It's eight o'clock," Ted announced brightly. "Isn't this the time we agreed on for your decision to buy Palomaki's place?" And I said yes.

The numbers wouldn't add up, obviously. Even with all of Ted's machinations there was no way a twenty-seven-year-old ne'er-do-well could afford to buy a resort, even a resort on Dead Wolf Lake. By the time I discovered this I had been infected with Ted's enthusiasm. His *imperative*. I saw the purchase as not so much a new beginning as an ending. A way to put behind me years of missteps, to close the casket. Even clerking at the law firm, a task I had grown to enjoy and be grateful for, had lost its attraction. It was surprisingly easy to ask my parents for the loan needed to bridge the gap, and with exasperation but pride I marveled at my father's wisdom in turning me down. When he opined that this venture, given the nature of the property, the future of rustic small-scale resorts, and the problematic nature of the buyer, had little likelihood of success—well, who could question his judgment? My mother, seduced by sentiment, objected. They fell into a Cold War stalemate. An anxious week dragged on and then the one thing I hadn't fully appreciated—Palomaki's ardency to sell and be done with it—came to my rescue. He, too, wanted to close a casket. At Ted's behest Jerry Palomaki lowered the price in exchange for a promise that Cabin 10— *Kymmenen*—would be available to him or his family for two weeks each year, into perpetuity. It was, I assumed, a sort of revenge on Rex.

I moved into Palomaki's crackerbox home on Dead Wolf Lake shortly before the end of June. It was audacious, of course—not, granted, like young nineteenth-century men leaving Europe for the New World, never to return, or abandoning their farms for the Klondike, but audacious nonetheless. The goal being success, I accepted that the move from my parents' house to the woods was to be the last move before the nursing home. Only upon walking the shoreline for the first time as an owner—I had inspected the property three times before the closing, and shadowed Palomaki for a week—did I understand the gravity of my decision. The risk seemed to endanger not me, but the resort. I had failed before, each time moving on and picking something else to try my hand at. But there might not be another chance for Dead Wolf Lake Resort. I had a quarter-century of Palomaki's toil to safeguard; more broadly, half a century of the resort's survival; more broadly still, human existence in this part of the world, on this lake. Dead Wolf Lake looked no different to me than it would have looked to the miners pushed out of Hibbing in 1907. Much was riding on my success. Palomaki was at least as interested in success as I, and the resort he handed over was generously booked through the end of the summer. Many of the families had been returning for years; they knew where the plunger was kept, even if I didn't. To some I was a source of well-intentioned merriment, the boy king of Dead Wolf Lake. All were unfailingly helpful—they, too, were invested in the resort's survival.

This was a period of hard work—long hours, though most of them pleasurable—and unwanted introspection. Common sense told me to focus on the task at hand, to not try and fit pieces together. But common sense, in my rationalization, was the refuge of the slow-witted. I was consumed with the standoff between anticipation and boredom: the essential struggle, as I saw it, of life. Even on my best days—sun and a west wind, birds in riot, the methodical completion of projects and benevolence of guests—even on such days, if I had been told while falling off to sleep that the day had been a dream, and that I was about to wake and begin that day—that good day—and live it precisely over again, the idea would have been intolerable. Having dreamt the day, I would have lost interest. The anticipation could never have been recovered. In that respect it was better to be kept in the dark about life: who did Basil treat more mercifully, the ninety-nine he blinded or the hundredth he left with one eye? But it's true that when tedium threatened I was often rescued by the sheer particularity of my new life. The sight of tamarack waving in the wind like stalks of weeds in a river's current. The approach of muffled thunder late on a humid afternoon, mimicking the sound of a duffel being thrown to the back of a dark closet.

Days were long in a way that only a young man could sustain. My companionable pessimism was controlled, so hopeful was I that with a force of will I could outrun failure. As I've said, I've been blessed with a tendency toward mental health.

The most consequential decision of that first year was what to do with winter. I decided to stay. There was no end to the improvements that could be made, but courage, not industriousness, was the bronze serpent I held high. Dead Wolf Lake was isolated even in summer, tucked deep inside the boreal forest. The nearest residence was seven miles away. The steely elongated clouds that preceded autumn began to arrive late in August, and with them a shiver of something approaching fright. Abandonment arrived suddenly with the close of Labor Day weekend, which was followed by four consecutive days without a single guest. Then arrived Sean Sullivan and Julie Sullivan, a power couple from Detroit. Lord knows how they had heard of the resort, but the glee in their voices indicated they had found what they were apparently looking for. "How many men would you estimate, white men, have ever set eyes on this lake?" Sean Sullivan asked before answering his own question: "It can't be more than a handful." The next morning a fierce wind blew from the northwest: puffs of clouds, here and there, raced across the sky and the trees were in full roar. The lake, shallow and raked with obstructions, but with a long open lane aligned perfectly with the wind, surged high upon the beach. With great confidence, great proprietorship, Sean convinced me to outfit one of the fourteen-foot aluminum boats so that he and Julie could explore. They bobbed away from the dock–great smiles, great presumption–and out of sight. All morning long worry hung over me like a descending fog. I sharpened the mower blade, taking breaks to walk down to the lake. I tended to the laundry, again breaking to look hopefully for the returning Sullivans. Why had I let them go? I was young. I had wanted to be helpful. I was–and this was the heart of the matter–so unimpressed with my judgment that I was willing to defer to recklessness. The water was jumping as though brought to boil. From the resort Dead Wolf Lake, dotted with postage stamp islands and gnarled with bays, was concealing. But by noon it became clear that the Sullivans' twenty-horse motor had been no match for the gale. The boat had flipped and they had been drowned. My imagination ran with the thought. It had not been the lake that had killed the Sullivans. Windstorms arose every fall without causing people to die. It had been my folly–the idea that I was capable of stepping into Palomaki's shoes. The presence of death surrounded me: only hours earlier a man and woman had been at my side, full of life. The give-and-take of conversation. The singularity of human bodies: Sean's maple eyes, the shining contour of Julie's long neck. The jumble of past, present, and anticipation–anticipation of small things even, small things *especially*, like what time dinner should be eaten that night. This line of thought had no endpoint. The horror of death was in the simple arithmetic: we had woken to three people at the resort;

by nightfall there would be one. No, I chastised myself, arithmetic had nothing to do with it, for the Sullivans, like all people, were worlds unto themselves. A team of biographers, giving themselves tirelessly to the effort, would never grasp the entirety of all that was them. That's what had been lost.

With finely-honed nonchalance Sean and Julie, prepossessing in their Grosse Pointe north woods slacks and flannel, strolled into camp at midafternoon. They poked around here and there before thinking to report to me that I could find their boat a mile and a half up the shoreline, where they had been forced to beach it before walking back.

Maybe the essential struggle was not between anticipation and boredom; maybe the reefs I had been navigating for so many years were those of anxiety and purposelessness. I can't clearly recollect how this all came to a head. I became, oddly enough, a better student of human nature now that I had banished myself to a place no person lived. Sean Sullivan was a case in point. He was a leader, running a business and toying with the idea of making a try for Congress. But what was leadership? He had a large stature; a head the size of an anvil; a deep voice; a Hemingway beard and thick lips that broke naturally, as if by gravity, into a big toothy smile–how could a man born with such anatomy *not* be charismatic, *not* be a leader? The next summer there arrived a guest who actually *had* run for Congress, and won. He too was a wonderful physical specimen: tall, long-legged. He was comfortable with himself–that was how he was described to me. Serene. But while watching him it occurred to me that the congressman seemed serene only because his long legs forced him to walk slower than those around him, so as not to outpace them. They had to double-step to keep up; they were excitable.

The congressman and the Sullivans were, as guests, aberrations. Dead Wolf Lake Resort was a working class destination. We (*we*: already my identity was merging with that of the resort) received plumbers from Pengilly, electricians from Eveleth, teachers from the Twin Cities, retired folk from Duluth. A pastor from Wisconsin liked to come. I immediately, instinctively, distrusted and disliked him. He would look past me, thinking of the next thing. He smiled falsely, conditioned as he was to keeping everything on schedule. He was not in the moment–that was the crux of the matter. For some reason I found this to be infuriating. So in learning about human nature I was, unavoidably, learning about myself. For my guests, what was the attraction of Dead Wolf Lake Resort? Well, most fished; I had boats and canoes for them. Most, when you got right down to it, enjoyed having a place of retreat from the world. The resort had a radio but no television; more than one teenage boy was incredulous at having no means of watching the All-Star Game. As the years progressed and computers became available, the resort had no computer. Once or twice a week I drove into Hoyt Lakes to collect mail.

Human nature. Early on–the second summer, possibly; I was generally flying a bit higher that summer, flush with the glory of having found my way, day by day and then week by week, through a solitary winter–two old army buddies rented Kaski for a couple of weeks. They were mostly at each other's throats: all those years had not convinced them of their incompatibility. The role of mediator fell to me–I was young, but running a resort afforded one respect. On a pleasant high summer evening the three of us sat around a fire in silence for most of an hour. Then Alvin, who was generally snarly to Pete's obstinacy, rose and without a word left for the cabin.

"That's a bitter man," I said quietly. "Well," Pete replied after a long silence, "I've known him since boot camp, the war and everything after, and I can tell you he has reason to be bitter." But that comes with being human, doesn't it? Everyone on Earth has reason to be bitter. Some succumb to the temptation and some don't. I remember the epiphany yet.

There was so much time to think. I was rarely idle, but activity didn't medicate the mind. Distractions did not distract. I puzzled over most of the riddles—puzzled over *the* riddle, I should say, taking a holistic approach to existence. Happiness was always the terminus. Happiness was the litmus test, the goal. But why? Faith, hope, charity: why did it come down to *happiness*, a word with synonyms but no real definition? Maybe, like God, happiness's freedom from definition was what made it the root, the One Thing. But happiness *can't* be the point, I told myself. There was a tremendous emptiness in admitting it was. Life seemed an unending series of tensions and release. One necessarily resolved into the other: equilibrium (and why equilibrium?) was the natural law at work here. Movement from quiescence to tension was no less an imperative than movement from tension to resolution. In this view unvarying happiness was just as destructive as unrelieved suffering.

But all this puzzling got me nowhere. Happiness was the light to which I sought to return. And what, at root, *was* happiness? Happiness was the absence of loneliness.

Jerry Palomaki, after selling the resort, received my monthly payments and never returned to Dead Wolf Lake again. But his daughter did. Bobbi was by then a few years out of college. She lived in Montana, guiding families on raft trips during summer and working the ski patrol in winter. The down season was September, after the schools were back in session but well before the first snowfall. This was when she took advantage of her family's two-week claim on Cabin 10. That first year Bobbi arrived with a girlfriend the day the Sullivans departed. Only a few months had passed since the sale, and my first (and wrong) impression was of a quiet, slightly mournful young woman. The resort had been her home. The man lugging around outboard motors and greeting new arrivals had been her father. I was grateful for her standoffishness, being somewhat intimidated by the watchful eye of a Palomaki. *That's* not where the canoe paddles go, *we* kept the grass shorter than that—the objections would have been taken as personal. At the same time her presence was not wholly unwelcome. I enjoyed her company, even from a distance—her wiry hair, more white than blonde; the way she moved, fluid as would be expected of an athlete; the sunny disposition and easy laugh that appeared now and then, defeating any impulse toward mournfulness. The two women took to their canoe with a vengeance. I often saw them across the lake, Bobbi with an extended arm, pointing out where her brother had let the big fish get away or where the moose and her calf had crashed through the brush. Bobbi's two weeks passed and she left to visit her folks for a few days before returning to Montana. I forgot about Bobbi Palomaki. The next year her stay was altogether different. She had, I discovered much later, intended to bring along a boyfriend, but at the last moment he had flung out of her orbit. Bobbi's visit coincided with the first of the autumn rains—low clouds, omnipresent gray, fallen rain unabsorbed by the leaves and grass—and Bobbi kept to her cabin.

By the third summer all nostalgia for an Edenic girlhood had seemingly been lost. This visit was different—she came alone, unlike the first year, and she came early, arriving in

May, before the trees had greened. I had been living on Dead Wolf Lake nearly two years. By now there was a familiarity between us. We seemed, those first few days, to be seeking one another out. I appreciated Bobbi's refusal to instruct me. I was beginning to make changes to the resort; she didn't seem to mind. We started to tell each other our stories, a process that we knew could not be quickly accomplished. Her last evening we sat late around a fire and then I dreamed a dream of her. In this dream Bobbi was an unnamed acquaintance from school, one I hadn't seen in years or known particularly well or much liked, truth be told. But my dream was a wonderful gift to this woman (who, besides not sharing Bobbi's history, did not look like her–but nevertheless *was* her): I gave her a charm and energy that had not been hers, a brilliance no one had seen from this girl. I gave both of us a world thick with vegetation, fluttering birds colored the red and yellow of flowers, water tumbling cleanly over stone. We were in Quito, though it was not Quito. Most surprisingly, I gave us a generous affinity for one another. Among ribbons of morning sunshine, gardens suspended from fluted ruins, we were charged to delirium with an unexplained joy that carried me far beyond waking. What, I wondered as I fixed myself breakfast, had been the source of such audacity, this outrageous escape into exultation? It was a world without parts I had dreamt, perfectly formed for just this once. A visitation. Life often makes me happy, I thought, it's true. But not like that. Not like that.

I thought of Jerry Palomaki and imagined him as a father-in-law.

Of course there was more to the story than that. It isn't a simple story; no true story ever is. Bobbi returned in June to again see the resort. To see me. She was bringing her life in

Montana to an end. A host of things happened, little things, intricate things. Two lives changed. It is a full story, a complex story; but it's not this story.

We were married that September, telling no one but the judge in advance. The judge was actually Mark Soleski, who eighteen months earlier had been appointed by the governor to the bench. He had a full docket set to begin at nine o'clock, so we were under strict instructions to arrive at the courthouse by eight-fifteen. But overnight a windstorm took out the electricity; we overslept, and even a heroically reckless drive could not get us to Duluth until five minutes to nine. Mark conducted the ceremony in two minutes and fifty-four seconds—four seconds longer, this old guitarist observed, than "Day Tripper," though four seconds shorter than "Tomorrow Never Knows."

§

And the years seeped from one to the other. A century rolled into the next. Bobbi and I became adept at running a resort—not destined to make much money, but not destined, either, to fail. Our guests developed warm feelings for us and we for them. Their children became, in a sense, our children. Christmas cards were exchanged. The long arms of progress stretched even to Dead Wolf Lake: never a paved road, but eventually a satellite internet connection. For a few years we dreamed of empire, hiring some college girls from Duluth to do housekeeping and office work. When they moved on, finding replacements proved difficult. This was true for many resorts, and the government got involved with a program that brought Eastern Europeans over to see the Natural Wonders of America. All of Minnesota was in

PAUL KILGORE

the Chicago District; the worker assigned to us was Marjanna, from Poznan. Day after day she stood behind the desk, sullenly taking reservations and checking in the arriving families. Finally I pulled her aside—Bobbi wouldn't talk to her, so incomprehensible did she find Marjanna's behavior—and asked what was wrong. "This is not what I imagined to be the Chicago District," she said, fighting back tears. "There is nothing but watching trees and the lake to do."

Dead Wolf Lake Resort became a member in good standing of the Greater North Superior Resort Association. I became aware of the acceleration in lakeshore property values. Many resorts were being subdivided to create lots available for purchase by longtime guests. For the Nelsons from Fargo or the Andersons from Eau Claire, no price was too high to avoid the risk of losing the cabin that had been theirs, two weeks each summer, for nearly a generation. Bobbi and I resisted: we were still young, not yet into our mid-forties, and life away from the lake was hard to imagine. But eventually we consented to an appraisal, the results of which shocked us. It made us quarrelsome, troubled. We dithered on for another year or two and then the national real estate market collapsed. Our million-dollar resort once again became ten Finnish huts on Dead Wolf Lake. The irony was not lost on me. The man who had never stuck out anything had waited too long.

I went to my twenty-five-year reunion, Bobbi staying behind for the guests. It was a shock, being thrown from Dead Wolf Lake into the swarm of school acquaintances a quarter of a century removed. I took it on faith that Amy would not attend, and in this I was rewarded. "Do you remember what you said on that bus!" gasped a woman whose name I was unable to recall. I looked at her quizzically, but of course I remembered, the entire world, as it existed that March evening

226

decades earlier, flooding back. We were on an ecumenical youth ski outing. Amy, with her advantage of indifference, was befriending John something-or-other while I was moodily alone and observant, the ski resort's high lights casting shadows into the trees, songs of lost love drifting from the mounted speakers, the night sky and winding runs gorgeous beyond measure. I was discovering that there could be joy in suffering. On the bus home a young pastor conducted a Bible study about the passion while Amy sat to the rear with John, leaving me behind. How I had anticipated that weekend; how quickly everything had slipped away. "Since when," I had objected petulantly, grievously–this is what my old classmate remembered–"are there three days between three o'clock Friday and dawn on Sunday!"

Some had heard I had become a pastor; nope. Others, a lawyer–wrong again, I had to tell them. Those who knew of my marriage to Amy were gracious enough to keep silent. That I now ran a resort was of great interest. Only one or two knew of Dead Wolf, and then the isolation of my life became itself a subject of interest. Todd Straught had heard of a hermit in the vicinity; his story, immediately suspect, grew in implausibility–the hermit, happening upon an outsider's game camera, had ordered away for a Bigfoot costume, and in mid-dance before the camera had been shot dead by a hunter. "No," I said, smiling but hating each of them, "that's not what it's like at all."

The women were dismaying–the prettiest and kindest and best of them now struggling with bad marriages or alcohol, the most wayward now repentant and rigidly intolerant, crediting Christ for their well-distributed bigotries. This all shocked me, since the guests Bobbi and I had been receiving over the years struck us as largely open-hearted, daring us to wonder if mankind hadn't made an evolutionary step forward. But in the midst of my funk appeared Nan Fredrickson, a delightful surprise, a girl I had completely forgotten, and for ten minutes only the two of us existed, so enthused at rediscovery that Susie Jelen told us to hold still for a photograph. Nan crouched ever so slightly and in the sun of her smile I glanced down to see her flat shoes. In the flicker of a second Nan saw my discovery. A chill seemed to pass through the room. This was rather late in the evening, and shortly afterwards Joey Scoggins pulled off with aplomb the very stunt he had first performed at a Halloween party so many years earlier, sneaking outside and then staring into the darkened room, his face pressed hideously against the window pane. The first person who saw the white flesh and terrifying leer screamed and then, taking notice, all of us screamed, one after the other. "Oh my *God!*" a woman cried. We all laughed at the horror: a window is for looking out, not in. How long had we been watched? How long had we been known?

§

For three or four years of my youth my parents actually owned a cabin on a lake not many miles west of Dead Wolf. Those were my formative years, so most every detail of our visits was destined to never be erased. One July day, events at the resort well in hand, I took a kayak to this lake and paddled along the north shoreline, cabin after cabin, until I came to the small log structure of memory. I floated a dozen yards offshore. There was once, above the sink, a big box of a radio from which Arthur Godfrey, in his decline, would speak. I would read from the davenport across the kitchen, sunlight streaming over the cold lake and through the window pane. There had been a scent to the wood. There had been a hum to the refrigerator. There had been a pattern on the chocolate curtain preserving the modesty of the back bedroom. How was it possible that I so clearly remembered such things?

I could have tossed my paddle and hit the circle of stones around the fire pit. We never saw an airplane from that shore, but at night often tracked satellites. Could those stones be the same stones? Why wouldn't they be?

The neighboring cabin through the woods had collapsed in upon itself. The next cabin down, I learned upon inquiry, had seen owner following owner over the years. What I was looking for wasn't really there. Time will do that, I've learned. It will swallow entire worlds out of existence. You never see it but it's something you notice long after it happens. My imagination opened expansively: I saw the cabin as a place like heaven or hell, one you can't fly or bore into, or float, not a place at all, but nonetheless with me for a few more years still.

There was a radio show Bobbi and I enjoyed. It was a jazz program, beginning late on Sunday night and therefore a reward for the week. We would sit on the couch and simply listen; very occasionally we would dance. Those evenings were quiet, eddies tucked alongside the unrelenting push of work (even at Dead Wolf Lake) and, really, of life. Sidney Bechet and Thelonious Monk drifted in, old music from clubs in Harlem or New Orleans, laughter in the background, chiming glasses, doors opened to sidewalks washed in rain, the *whoosh* of black water troubled by cabs, headlights bobbing with dour resignation. We listened to that show for years, never thinking that time or place mattered. This flowering of imagination had made its way through half a century and more to our tight little home in the northern forest. The world, even from here, would always be ours. All manner of reasons led to tweaks in the show's format, little

229

diseases meant to prepare us for the death of cancellation. We actually laughed at the show's replacement, a panel of celebrities outwitting one another. The young parents who visit the resort mention the new show often, in fact. It isn't new to them, though it is their discovery. It was that easy for the world to move from one generation to another.

§

Over the years an odd divergence has occurred. Bobbi and I, as you would expect of a couple working side by side, have become virtuosic at reading one another. The resort, too, has become familiar–predictable, even–in its patterns: the ebb and flow of guests and tasks, the dependability of seasons. But at the same time life has proven itself confounding. So often the things I have hoped for have come to pass without making me happier. And just as often the things I have dreaded have occurred, only to reveal themselves, slowly, as advantages. I've lost confidence in knowing what to pursue and what to fear. In this there is a kind of serenity.

At times the resort will be too much–claustrophobic in the closeness of things, the unavailability of escape. There are always chores to do and people to watch you do them. My mood will sour–our guests, strangely enough, come from everywhere, and the tongue must be held when a Bob-Evans-eating, NASCAR-worshipping, pistol-polishing stars-and-bars enthusiast grows despondent over May snowflakes and asks accusingly, "How can you *live* like this, fella?"–my mood will sour, as I say, and I will in fact grant myself an escape. There can be business reasons to visit Duluth: plumbing supplies, resort association meetings, a query to the accountant.

Usually I spider in on the back roads, but occasionally I'll swing far west and hook into the last leg of the interstate, just for the grandeur of the unbroken horizontals of land, water, and sky that open themselves as I descend Thompson Hill. In doing this I will sometimes recall that dark, cold drive from so many years earlier, returning from law school to a future that, it can now be said, overmatched my imagination. As I approach the hill's crest I pass Pine Hill Church, which will ever be etched in my mind as it appeared to me that long ago December midnight, its modest cross glowing above the steeple. Now the church is almost completely obscured by a grove of resplendent pines—a new arrival would have no idea that a church even exists.

Has the city changed? Last winter I sat in a Canal Park coffee shop and, after scanning a hopelessly thin newspaper, pondered just how one might go about evaluating change. The freeway sweeping down into town still feels like a draw-bridge above the moat of post-industrial West Duluth. The snow-crowned birch near the college still seem a wonder unlikely to be replicated, in exactly that beauty, elsewhere in the world. Every place has its particulars, of course, its basement breweries or summertime winter jackets. Its end-less string of dueling letters to the editor, screaming for and against the plausibility of God. Its fundraisers designed to finance a lark—a summer devoted to reaching Hudson Bay by canoe, perhaps, or hiking the lake's circumference, the cure for cancer being the means, not the end. Everything comes back to the lake. One recent November a fierce storm pulled from the depths, and deposited on shore, a timber crib the size of a modest house; to this day no one knows what pre-cisely it is or who built it, or when, or why. This is a mystery, albeit a small one. I have never heard anyone comment on the fortuitousness of foggy Duluth sitting on Superior's *north* shore—possessing a southern exposure it was built, you might say, for sun. The town's gaze is toward the rest of the world, seeking approval so it can deny the effort. Perhaps a northern exposure would have turned all of us into wild animals.

But perhaps not. Many days the lake is still enough to be a mirror. When God looks down—I'm disappointed, Bobbi teases, that the Chamber hasn't coined this—He sees Himself.

It is strange how durable everything not human can be. I once lived in this town, as did my parents, the Norgaards, the Tiedlows—all of us lived here, and our lives were so full! There was so much joy, so much distress, so much hope! Today there is no reason to believe any of that existed. The houses still stand, the Bridge, even Boyer, Johnson & Salmi. But not Boyer, Johnson, or Salmi. Entire worlds have been reduced to names.

These musings ran their course and I returned to the coffee shop's counter, jamming a hand deep beneath my long coat for a few dollars. "Who is it standing in front of me," a voice said, "a puppeteer, or a priest?"

And in this way I discovered that Maggie Metaxas was still Maggie Metaxas, even as she neared seventy years of age: pique had preserved her. Maggie looked great, actually, and even consented to join me at the table for ten minutes before heading across the street and back to work. Yes, she was still at the law firm. She had outlasted them all: Sandy, now retired and living in the Twin Cities, close to grandchildren; Ted Salmi, ancient now but apparently active in Fort Lauderdale; and, of course, my father. Maggie spoke kindly of my parents. "Bertie wasn't much, when you got right down to it. But your father, you know, he and Ted, they were the giants. There's no one like them today. There was no other law firm in town like ours. Believe me, others were different. Clients calling a hundred times a day, bitching and moaning about every little thing, fighting every undercharged bill. Ethics complaints flying. Plowing in ten thousand dollars of time to collect fifteen hundred dollars on a file. We've never had any of that shit. Men like Ted and your father, they were the reason." Which meant that not only Maggie benefitted, but so did a whole generation of lawyers and staff, and another generation today. I thanked Maggie for her gracious words and left genuinely touched. Chastened, even.

But ultimately days away from the resort have a tendency to gnaw. Nostalgia and speculation are not my allies. It's true: one of the reasons the resort has suited me is its controlled environment, distractions stripped away. In the early years I was not disciplined enough to disinvite intrusions, but that is rarely the case now. I don't allow myself to believe that the resort is a garrison, that nothing can reach me. But there's no denying the advantages. The routine is, more often than not, enjoyable. No task is too mundane. I re-roof the buildings and I bail rainwater from boats. I analyze next year's pricing and I vacuum the cabins. Earlier this year I was vacuuming Cabin 8 when I discovered a children's book left between the couch cushions. It was a library book, its long, hard cover protected by plastic. The cover was a pleasant swirl of abstract blues and yellows that drew the eye to a peanut-shaped– key-shaped, on closer inspection–character. The title was *The Broken Key*. The author and illustrator was Linda Brekke.

The Keys lived in Keyland. You would, too, if you were a Key. These were the book's first sentences, accompanied by a merry, charming drawing, splashed in color, of six smiling keys. They were depicted primitively, being unclothed and not obviously male or female, though one appeared to be a leader, likely a parent. They were more akin to space creatures than keys, but made human by facial expressions that were decidedly *not* primitive–that had, indeed, been drawn with such skill that the characters seemed to jump off the page. Four Keys looked to be identical to one another. One was larger than the rest, and one–the most vulnerable and irresistible of all the Keys–was smaller. *All year long they had waited for the Biggest Surprise Ever. Baby Key most of all.*

I turned to the back of the book to see Linda's smiling face. She was Linda–an approaching-middle-age Linda, but in every important respect the same woman I had known twenty-six years earlier. She had a different cut to her hair, pulled back a bit more consciously, and gray was beginning to make an appearance. Her face had matured. But Linda's smile was so inviting, so *guileless*–it was the smile of a children's author, after all–that I was overwhelmed by the sense of reunion. Involuntarily I spoke her name. "Linda Brekke," the bio below her photograph said, "is an author, artist, and lover of all things California. She is the creator of ImagineNationCreation, an interdisciplinary arts curriculum for the independent child. On most days Linda can be found scribbling in her notebook, capturing her corner of the world in picture and story."

"What is the Surprise?" said Baby Key. Mama Key only smiled. For a number of pages the Keys journeyed over hill and dale, suffering harmless misadventures along the way. Finally they arrived at a large castle with an enormous wooden door. High up the door a lock was prominently displayed. It was shaped like a tunnel, as though the Keys were gerbils and the lock a chute through which they would scamper. With a terrific leap Mama Key bounded headfirst into that lock and executed a high-spirited twist, causing

the door to swing open. Mama Key plopped back down to the ground and led her troop in to their Biggest Surprise Ever. But Baby Key was too slow, unable to keep up. The door slammed in the face of Baby Key: locked out. Now Baby Key spent a couple of pages gathering up the courage, the gumption, before springing with all of his or her might and sailing into the lock. But next a new challenge arose. Baby Key wasn't strong enough to turn in the lock, and after three valiant tries Baby Key incredibly, horrifically, fell to the ground, greatly damaged. A broken Key. Linda had placed a masterful tear at the corner of Baby Key's eye. *"I'll never see my Surprise,"* Baby Key said. *"Ever. And I'll never again see the other Keys. Ever."* By now the sky and in fact the entire page had darkened—surrounding Baby Key in a most imaginative fecundity were shadowy leaves and trees and all manner of sinister vegetation. I was appalled.

"You see us now," a voice said. *Baby Key looked around. She didn't see anyone.* On this page Linda reproduced the previous page's landscape, except that in the trees and shrubbery were hints of human—well, Key—features. A pair of eyes here, a smile there. *"If you imagine us, Baby Key, you will see us."* And on the next page this became apparent. Baby Key was indeed among the rest of the Keys. They didn't emerge from the landscape; they *were* the landscape. Expressions of sympathy and compassion came into focus. Some of the family hovered near Baby Key. Others floated above *like a Skyfull of Angels*. And, like an angel herself—for by now I had no doubt that Baby Key (whether Linda understood this or not) was Linda—the smallest Key began to gravitate toward the others. *Now Baby Key understood what was the Biggest Surprise Ever. It had never been inside the castle door. It had been inside every Key. The Biggest Surprise Ever was that the Keys would never*

be alone. They would always be together, helping one another and loving one another. Even when Baby Key couldn't see them. Especially when Baby Key couldn't see them.

This children's book, then, was about death, which struck me as pretty nervy, pretty outrageous. Did Linda know what her book was about? Of course she did. I only need look at the title page telling me that *The Broken Key* had been published by something Linda had decided to name Three Sisters Press.

Despite its subject the story had managed to avoid being plodding or preachy–Linda had accomplished this mainly by the playfulness of her drawings. The Keys were earnest but also of good humor. They had been drawn for the young readers but also for their parents: *very good*, I could imagine a mother thinking as she read the book to her child. *I didn't think you'd pull* that *off*. In all this the book was utterly lacking in condescension or pretense. The story was goofy, it was true. But goofy in precisely the way that Linda was goofy. The match was perfect.

No guests would be occupying Cabin 8 that evening, so I left Linda's book on the table by the window and returned to it twice more that day. The story was delightful, I decided– there were details to come back for, cleverness and whimsy and gravity and heart. Later in the day, though, I began to doubt my judgment. *Was* the book, in fact, delightful? That Keys–keys–were the best way to tell such a story seemed less than obvious. But I was no expert, having no children myself and having not read a children's book since the last century. I *wanted* the book to endear itself to me, of course. The existence of such a book, of *this* book, told *this* way, spoke well of me, did it not? I spent the afternoon reliving the February evening at Erik and Miriam's cabin, recalling how prodigious that long-ago winter had been. The snapped key in the ignition: it was flattering to believe that nothing short of fate, possibly design, could explain how such a trivial snip of time could lie dormant for years and then blossom into significance. The disintegration of a shaving of metal: that's all it had been. That disintegration had been its own ignition, firing Linda's imagination so many years later, leading to the creation of a world, Keys and the Biggest Surprise Ever and *You see us now*. Of course I felt a pride at being present at the creation. Maybe, I allowed myself to imagine, my presence had been part of what gave the moment such apparent significance. I was living, that summer afternoon, between the ears. Linda could have written about anything. The thing she had chosen included me. Were there other books? I began to think less about Linda writing *The Broken Key* and more about Linda in a general sense. I mean the Linda from that distant winter–the only Linda I knew–but also, as the day progressed, the Linda who, while I moved about the place I had chosen to live my life, was herself moving about, blinking and breathing, an aggregation of years spent in the place she had chosen to live *her* life. I was working and sleeping, planning and fretting, sliding between joy and solace and simple unconscious existence; and Linda Brekke, somewhere else, but in my time, was doing the same. Bobbi commented that evening about my silence, and in bed I lay a long while without sleep. I, too, could construct a world. Linda was still in California–her book had said so. She seemed not to have family; none had been mentioned. Long ago Linda had told me she would always think of herself as an artist. She had been right. I remembered the night we had ventured down from her parents' house and onto the beach. That would be the sort of thing she would enjoy in

California, too. I thought of Erik Mattila's cabin and tried
to imagine the friends Linda had now. I began to imagine
speaking with Linda. This was not new.

Over the years I had occasionally thought of her, of
course. At first I made a determined effort to *not* think
of Linda—refusing to cut her loose, I realized, could only
damage me. Leaving B, J & S helped, but the solitude of
Dead Wolf was the fire to the law firm's frying pan. There
came a time when it felt safe to recall the winter we had
spent together. Not recalling was not an option, I suppose,
those months being so charged with a fight for survival, me
battling the demons of consecutive debacles and Linda the
catastrophe of loss. Certainly the turbulence of that time
must explain why someone I had known but eleven weeks
should be—well, hovering over me like a Key. We had not
even been lovers, properly speaking, though perhaps this
was a reason my memories of Linda were so difficult to
dismiss. My fondness for her wasn't sexual; or, I should say,
extended beyond the sexual: a happy marriage had not been
conditioned on recasting those months with Linda or challenging their significance. Some memories were persistent.
Her ice cream cone on the bus—the casual indifference to
opinion was what attracted me, surely. The lunar cold of
Park Point Beach. The day Linda had moved into her sister's
house, January's thaw both mocking and seducing us. The
night at the cabin, obviously—*Bad memory! I was fourteen!*—
and the ride home. How often I had lamented the inexo-
rable progress of that return. How often I had lamented
that we had ever arrived.

But what I mostly remembered was talk. All the probing,
all the fearlessness and sympathy at Peking—even after the
passage of so much time I recalled our conversations with

an almost Ussher-like precision. At some point in the past few years a resumption of that winter-long conversation had seemed the most natural thing in the world, as though one of us were returning to the table.

"You were saying…"

"Only that we overrate life because it's all we know. I was saying that if a comet hit the Earth and killed everyone—you were teasing me for adding in dinosaurs—it wouldn't really be so bad. No one would be left behind."

"I remember you saying that, Linda. And I thought at the time that there was something to it. But that's not what I think anymore." Which gave me permission to talk about the idea of *anymore*, to talk about my parents and regret, to talk about all that had happened, much of it internal, over two decades and more. "You have to fight against death in any form. Fight for the most basic of all desires, remaining alive. Early on, Linda, this couple came up to the resort from Detroit. The Sullivans…"

Many times I had imagined showing Dead Wolf Lake to Linda. This was, I am convinced, something more than the male weakness for sentimentality, something more than covetousness. Certainly she would come, were I to ask. And how, after the miracle of happening upon Linda's book, could I not ask? I imagined a long, slow dinner, Linda and Bobbi and I enjoying the enduring northern summer evening. "I couldn't believe this perfect stranger was obsessing over me and my ice cream cone," Linda would say, and Bobbi, accustomed to my foibles, would laugh with her, unthreatened by friendship, and the three of us would watch the lake from the screen porch, happy to be alive, happy to have survived, silently thankful for life.

This was no longer the world of our youth. Finding Linda, even from Dead Wolf Lake, would not be difficult. It was a few minutes after midnight when I crept into the office and switched on the computer. *Linda Brekke California author*, I told it. *Linda Brekke Obituary*, it said in reply.

§

Three weeks passed—a period too short to lap the disbelief, but long enough, paradoxically, to make Linda's death seem an inevitability, something that should have been predicted. Which was foolishness, the way anticipating any death—entertaining the *thought* of any death, though death be the one certainty—is foolishness. Life can't be lived without that blinder and, anyway, the gods' plotting is nothing if not crude and amateurish—who has the courage to engage it? Late in the afternoon a weathered pickup bounced to the end of Dead Wolf Road and turned into the resort's grassy driveway. "You'll see me Tuesday," Karen Brekke had said over the telephone. Maybe I should have been offended by the generality, the indifference to such obligations as I may have had that day. But I took no offense. Working my way through the chores—not listlessly, or at least not unusually so, given the color of those three weeks—I fiercely suppressed any anticipation. Finding *The Broken Key* had been the culmination of my gathering worldview, my conviction that everything is in disguise, the wrong things hoped for and the wrong things feared. It is a torment to remember the hope with which I turned the pages of that book. How long were the odds that Linda's book should have found its way to that cabin; longer still that the book should have been left behind. And, now, for what?

The years had not been especially kind to Karen. By my memory she was three years older than I; she would be pushing into her late fifties. The sun, or the years, or life, had done a number on her face, cementing in place the grooves and general spoilage. A basal cell nick here and there. A wind-and-sky tightness beneath the eyes. She wore her hair long, probably the length she had liked as a schoolgirl and stuck with. Karen's hair was frizzled and of independent mind, a light, colorless gauze. Her bare arms were fleshy, her bosom large. She wore north woods jewelry, informal and pleasing. Her faded sundress, patterned with wildflowers, fell long.

"Good Lord," she said quietly, as though deserving an explanation. "Who is it you're hiding from out here?"

"That's our calling card. We're for the family that finds Canada crowded."

"Nice." With one arm she gave me a perfunctory hug. "You were right in telling me to listen carefully to your directions. I suppose once you found your way here it was impossible to ever find your way out."

I led Karen to a small, round table inside a screen porch and to the chair meant for her sister. Bobbi had asked that morning what I wanted her role to be. "Let's just the three of us visit," I had said. After a moment's thought she had shaken her head, shrugging off the idea. She was now at the property's far corners, painting trim at cabins 9 and 10. Summer was coming to an end, and with it the fullness of our season. The resort was quiet.

Karen and I made small talk as I poured ice tea into two glasses. A coolish humidity hung in the air. Karen was measuring me, trying to determine how much effort to expend, how much emotional capital should be loosed. All that she knew of me she had learned from Linda, which had given me at least enough of an advantage to persuade Karen to drive north from Duluth for the afternoon. "It worked out well," I said, "that I found you before you headed back West." What I had actually found was her answering machine in California; a house-sitting friend had forwarded the message to Duluth, where Karen had been spending the month of August for the past several years.

"At first I started coming out here to visit old friends," Karen said. "Now I seem to spend more time with new ones, people I didn't know a few years ago. We have a good time. I listened to your message and decided to take you up." There was a warning of superiority in her voice, the type that is born in combativeness and ultimately self-doubt.

"Thank God you're still *Brekke*, and still around Santa Rosa. I was lucky to have found you."

Karen paused a moment to let this pass, her marital history, I was slow in recalling, being complicated. "There's not a single Brekke left in Duluth. Both of my parents are gone. Both of my sisters are gone." She looked down blankly. "It's shitty," she said in explanation.

I nodded. Linda's obituary had been a testament to abandonment, Karen the sole survivor of a family of five. "I met your parents a few times."

"Sheryl's accident killed them. Dr. Ed never recovered. He lost interest in medicine. He went into a semi-retirement and then just retired. He lost interest in everything, really. My mom was a little stronger. But they never even had a funeral for Sheryl—just kept putting it off, and finally accepted that they couldn't face it."

"I suppose Linda shipping out didn't help," I said, closely watching Karen, the force behind Linda's move, for reaction.

"No, but it didn't make any difference, either. Just like me moving back wouldn't have made a difference. Mom wanted me to come home. But Minnesota wasn't home to me, not by then."

"Did your folks stay in Duluth?"

"No. They left pretty quickly, actually. Five years after Sheryl? Maybe not even that. They moved to Santa Fe. Cancer got both of them, Dr. Ed first."

"I could see your father in Santa Fe. Roping the doggies."

Karen shrugged. All of this had happened so long ago; this was old news.

"My parents left, too," I said. "It was Gulf Shores for them. My father liked the water. They lived a while down there. My father also died first. The man always dies first."

"Once they get past middle age, maybe. Anatomy asks more of women."

"Yes," I said. How could I have said otherwise?

Karen held the sweating glass of tea in her lap, grasping it with chubby hands. She scanned the lake. The afternoon was still, no sway to the tamarack across the bay and no chop on the water. A large crow declared its presence and in the heavy air the primitive call had an immediacy to it. "This is nice," Karen said. She turned to me. "Linda talked about you, especially at first, when she came out. Later, too, though it got complicated. Tell me again how you knew her. From school?"

"Not from school. I was '80, she was '84, I think. And different schools, anyway. I met her on a city bus."

A small smile. "Oh, yes. And it was right at the time of Sheryl's accident."

"Days before. The very same week. That was the umbrella over our whole time together. We spent many hours in each other's company, though it didn't last very long."

"There was no way she could stay in Duluth. Leaving Minnesota was the best thing she ever did."

"Well, perhaps she did better things. But yes. I won't argue the point."

"She was a great sister. Little Linda. We lived together for three years and then she bought the house next door."

"I'm sorry," I said. I was beginning to see the enormity of Karen's loss.

"Having this discussion is very strange. I'm guessing you think of yourself as having some sort of claim on Linda. Something more than just old school friends."

"We weren't school friends."

"That's what I mean. You're Minnesota polite but I can tell you're feisty about this. You *do* think of yourself as having a claim."

"That's not the way I would say it." I felt no tension in talking to Karen. I was gratified by her forthrightness, there being no other way I would have cared to talk about Linda or her death. "But it's true that I think of her more often than I do any other person from those years. We were on the razor's edge. Her turmoil was greater, obviously, but at the time I was at sea myself."

"Were you pursuing her?"

I smiled at the phrasing. A strange and silly tinge of guilt. "I suppose I was, but that's not the way I would say *that*, either. We were single and in our twenties and saw each other every day. At some point there's no difference between pursuing and living."

Karen laughed at this. "Good answer. I do remember that occasionally Linda would talk about feeling guilty over you. Leaving you behind."

"We were both working at my father's law firm and I was asked to help out in Canada for a week. That's how it happened. When I got back"–I turned my palms upward, pausing for Karen to hear the *poof*–"she was gone. I never saw her again." On those final words my voice, to my vast surprise–a quarter-century had passed–rippled, the emotion sneaking up on me.

"Well," Karen said matter-of-factly, "that's the other thing that makes this discussion strange. You just saw her obituary a few weeks ago, right? To you she just died. But to me Linda's been dead four years. I've had time to get past it–begin getting past it."

I nodded, stalled by the complexity, the largeness.

"And I recall the part about Canada, now that you mention it."

"It was twenty-six years ago and things were very different. But I've thought about our parting now and then over the years. I could never truly believe there wasn't a way she could have found me up in Thunder Bay, could have called to tell me she would be leaving."

"Of course she could have. Thus the guilt."

"Why didn't she?"

"I'm not saying it was a conscious decision not to call. But sometimes things happen the only way they can happen."

"That's true."

We sat in silence. Linda was feeling baggy to me, a jumble of the person I knew (as distorted, I readily admit, by memory), the person I had over the years imagined her to mature into, and the person her sister was now beginning, very slowly, to selectively disclose. And that jumble included the person described in her obituary (written by

Karen? another?), which by now I had, through repetition, committed to memory. *Linda Kay Brekke, 46. Artist, author, teacher.* The obituary hadn't mentioned *The Broken Key*—hadn't, in fact, mentioned any specific achievement. The focus had instead been on personal qualities: *She will be remembered*, one line had said, *for her laughter, her warmth, and her ability to see the world through the eyes of a child.* And then an unattributed quote: *"In any soul, I am still that small child who did not care about anything else but the beautiful color of a rainbow." Linda*, the obituary had continued, *was preceded in death...* A sad procession of names, followed by identification of Karen, the sole survivor. No mention of marriage, a spouse or ex-spouse, a companion, a child. Linda would have wanted gifts to be given for the benefit of Redwood Animal Placement.

"Did I tell you how I came upon Linda's obituary?" I asked. "How I thought, I mean, to look for her?"

"That was a long message you left on my recorder," Karen said with a smirk that straddled the boundary between admiration and disdain. "What *didn't* you tell me?"

"Did Linda write a lot of books?"

"She waited too long to begin another. Five years went by and then came the mammogram. *The Broken Key* was her first and only."

"Was it successful?" I eventually said. "It's not something I would have expected, to come upon it in the woods outside Hoyt Lakes, Minnesota..."

Karen allowed herself a smile of pride, quickly swallowed. "It was a big hit with our friends, the arts community along the coast. But that only meant she sold a few hundred books. Then some months went by and Linda got her big break. *Library Journal* had a blurb on it. 'A fable with heart for an age of indifference,' was the tag line. 'A fable with heart.' After that recommendation, every library in America bought the book, it seemed."

I smiled sadly. "I would have liked to have shared in that."

"It wasn't a great book."

"I think it is."

"No New York publisher would have put it out. But it was *Linda*." Karen's smile broadened. "Those drawings."

"Keys."

She shook her head. "Keys, yeah. Why keys? That didn't add anything to the story. A *broken* key. But it was important to her."

"I know about that."

"So do I," Karen said, cutting me off to save herself from having to hear the story. "Linda and I talked about the book a lot, its conception, everything. Some of it made no sense. It wasn't logical."

Logical; the word had, over the years, lost some of its shine. "It was Linda," I said quickly, asserting myself. "As you said."

"But what does it matter now? The bad news just overwhelmed everything."

"It must have been very difficult for you," I said, not wanting to hear, yet, how difficult it had been for Linda.

"I acted badly, naturally. I wasn't up to it." Karen looked at me keenly, deliberately. "First I told her it was nothing. A false result. 'Come see me when you have real news.' She would come over in the evening of a day when I knew she had had an appointment, and I wouldn't let her speak. I'd take charge of the conversation, point it in every direction except cancer. She got the message: Karen's not a person to discuss this with." Her eyes glistened. "A terrible way to treat a baby sister, and a terrible way to treat *myself*. It was absolutely brutal, and all self-inflicted. She shut me out of the medical news and so I suffered even *more* anxiety. I was always fearing what I wasn't being told."

"She shut you out out of spite?"

"Linda? Of course not. Out of *kindness*. She didn't want her older sister to worry. There was no one to blame for that but me. Finally I told her what I should have said from the start: 'I want to hear everything. Spare me no detail.'"

"That must have been an improvement."

"For Linda, probably. For me, I guess. But it's cancer. The one thing I learned was to never forget bad news. Remember it first thing in the morning and be damn sure it's the last thing you think of at night." Her voice was gathering force. "Because bad news doesn't like being forgotten. When it comes back after an absence it hits harder than the first time."

"Linda didn't go to her appointments alone, did she?" The question was not asked dispassionately.

"Don't judge. I went with her, eventually. It would have helped everyone if I had left my brain at home. My mouth, certainly. Eyes, ears… Because Linda just needed the presence. That was enough. I would silently pray as we sat in those little rooms, waiting for the doctor to come in with his x-ray or test results. *Pray*–me who hadn't prayed since twelve. As though the test was the thing that was killing Linda." The tear that had been gathering now dropped, running a tumbling fall down Karen's cheek. The tear stole her attention, annoyed her. She waved at me dismissively. *What are we talking about this for?* Karen said as much, looking me in the eye and asking, "What is it you wanted out of this meeting?"

"Mainly someone I could talk with about Linda." Which wasn't a lie, exactly, though insulting to Karen, whether she knew it or not. I had little doubt she knew it.

"Well, she was my kid sister."

"She looked up to you."

Karen considered this before letting it go, as though fashioning a response would require too much effort. "The age gap was pretty big those years when I was at home. Seven year gap. I mean, she was eleven when I left for college."

"The thing I liked about Linda," I volunteered, "was the very thing that meant we'd never have a future. I enjoyed having someone to care for. I never thought about it in those terms, but there it is. She was too much a free spirit for that. Too independent."

"That comes with being at the corners, oldest or youngest. Her sister"–Karen laughed gently–"was not a 'free spirit.' Not Sheryl."

"A little quirky, though. There were some good Sheryl and Linda stories." I liked the way the conversation was turning, the reminder of how pleasurable it was to think of the Brekke girls, both the idea of it and the particularities.

"A brother would have given us some balance. I'll concede that."

"Linda and Sheryl would sometimes cook together…"

Karen laughed again. I had given her permission to open up a memory. But she said nothing–the memory was hers, not to be shared.

"What is it *you* wanted out of this meeting?"

She gave me a look of curiosity. "There's nothing you could give me. I mean, that's just a fact."

"But you came."

"Linda would have wanted me to."

I didn't reply, instead giving silence its chance to restore equilibrium. Giving both of us space. The air was so fragrant, so textured, that nature threatened to overthrow the disorder Karen Brekke and I were sowing–the sky and water and earth were a challenge to our self-importance.

"Here's a memory," Karen said. "Linda and I were in the hospital cafeteria. By then it was our place, it was that familiar. And I said, just to have something to say, 'Do you know what I hated about Dad?' 'Dr. Ed?' Linda said. She was shocked. That was the name we used for all purposes–Dr. Ed. If we were poking fun it was Dr. Ed. If we were standing up for him, Dr. Ed. 'The reason he was so wise,' I told Linda, 'or so fearsome–it's all the same–is that he understood all is vanity. I hate that about doctors in general.' This was at a time when Linda was seeing lots of doctors. I told her, 'They know the cut of your underclothes–"Oh, so this is how she imagines herself, this is what she thinks will work." They hear the patient ask what it would take to remove a birthmark. They hear the patient say she thinks one ear looks higher than the other, or something smells funny–"here, sniff it." You can't stand up to someone once all the pretense is gone!' I was becoming silly, but I meant it. And just as I was saying all this a doctor who had come in and run through the line, one of the docs Linda knew, walked over to the window, tray in hand, and looked over the parking lot for a good minute before finding a table and sitting down. He had been looking with pride, like a boy. 'Those spots just outside the window are reserved for the doctors' cars,' Linda said. 'So we know things about them, too.'"

I laughed a laugh that couldn't be sustained. "How long was she sick? Did you say?"

"Two years."

"So the days weren't uniformly dreadful. There were respites? Laughter?"

"Oh, sure. Like I said, that's part of what made it so cruel–the bad news hit harder each time it returned. 'A life of constant sorrow'–that's a laugh. It'd be easier if it *was*. It's suffering, relief, suffering, relief, just a battering. And the persistent anxiety. I swear, Linda was better at handling it than I was. Sometimes in the evening I'd stop over and ask her how the day had gone. 'Good," she would say. Always with a smile. 'I got some painting done,' or some pottery, something–she'd kept herself busy. But she would admit the worry could never be pushed out of her mind. It's nature, really, is what it is. Nature doesn't let you forget a threat until you've dealt with it, even if you're incapable of dealing with it.

"And there's one more thing. As long as you want to know." Did I want to know? Karen was warming to me, satisfied with my fortitude. "During the scariest parts the only way to see Linda was as elevated. Idealized. And then immediately after a scare had passed I would become irritated with her. She was so–you know, *Linda-ish*. Absent-minded. Floating in space, seeing the best in everything. It was irritating. It took me awhile, but eventually I realized why I was being so short with my sister, who was, after all, dying of cancer. It was because she could never measure up to the idealized Linda, the person whose hand I held while the scans were being put up to the light. *No one* could have lived up to that. Fear puts you in a rarefied air, and when you're back down to Earth people become so muddled again, useless and, what's worse, intolerant of the uselessness. I'm talking about myself. Those who are afraid they'll die become resentful of those who are actually dying. *Already* dying, I should say. No one ever talks about *that*." Karen's face glowed with exertion.

"Was her death hard?" I asked, because I couldn't know Linda without knowing that.

"Was it hard?" Karen repeated. "Here's the deal," she said, scowling. "People who are dying want to hear two things."

"Hope."

"That's one. Something to cling to. And the other is this: For once in my life, I want to be told the truth. The hard, honest truth, no matter what it is or where it leads. No bullshit."

"No time left for anything else."

"And the two are irreconcilable. Give me hope, but give me the truth." Karen looked down. "Yes, Linda's death was hard." She then stood up, one knee cracking. She approached the screen and stood with her back to me; watching the lake, I assumed; composing herself. All this talk of Linda had the effect of bringing Linda alive again. At her parents' home on that first evening, I had told her of going to South America and she had laughed. Half my lifetime had passed since I had heard that laugh. Linda's laugh had been hearty, full of personality. Where, I wondered, was that laugh now? If it existed nowhere in the universe–which seemed an impossibility, for reasons of physics; the universe, being everything, doesn't lend itself to addition or subtraction–if it existed no more, why had it ever existed? What had been its purpose? Had its purpose, its sole purpose, been to serve as a gift, I so new to Linda and yet she willingly opening herself to me? The thought was immensely appealing, not least because it struck me as true. The pleasure I had felt that night I felt now, if only momentarily. Linda was giving that pleasure, and here her sister and I were speaking as though she no longer existed.

"Is there a difference between memory and experience?" I posed to Bobbi. "Tell me, is there really a difference?" But that was later. Now Karen Brekke was turning toward me.

"Two things convinced me to come out here and meet with you," she said, "because I didn't want to come. I knew that what would happen is exactly what *is* happening. Everything flooding back. But when I told Linda she needed to come to California, that I could line some things up for her, once she arrived she told me about you."

"I wonder what it was she said. I can't imagine, really, given the circumstances."

Karen approached her chair and sat down. "Now how could I remember something like that, so long ago? I do recall thinking that the relationship was somewhat ambiguous. It didn't strike me as a relationship that I needed to pay attention to. I mean, she did leave. So I forgot about it. But as the years went by your name would come up now and then."

"*The Broken Key*."

"That's exactly right. Naturally I asked where the whole idea came from, and she told me about this evening in the middle of a snowstorm or something, and she was with this Tom Johnson who I had heard about before, and way in the middle of the night as you tried to get back to town it was so cold that the car key snapped in half."

"It did."

"Like I said, the idea of *keys* didn't seem essential to the book. Couldn't they just as easily have been rabbits or turnips or just nameless blobs? But the key motif"–Karen smirked, a little sister, even at forty, still being a little sister–"was important to her. Because after that key broke, all your friends stepped up and rescued you. Kept you from freezing to death?"

"It wasn't that dramatic. But yes, they stepped up. Linda wasn't exaggerating the night. I think of it still."

"So obviously this Tom Johnson meant even more to Linda than she had told me. Or maybe she told me, in her way, and I just didn't get it. I asked her about you. You both worked at that law firm Linda had gotten her job at. You spent a lot of time together and it was that period when Sheryl died. I guess I knew that from before."

"I was there the day your parents helped Linda move into Sheryl's house."

"I'd forgotten that Linda did that, if I ever knew. There's a lot of family stuff you don't know when you live half a country away. Without having heard it from Linda, your name, when you called, would have meant nothing. So obviously I wasn't going to ignore you." Karen gave a wry smile. "Unless I could justify it to myself, I mean. Like I said, I didn't want to go through this."

"The second reason?"

"Yes. The second reason. It was the voice message you left. If you had said, 'I'm Tom Johnson, I knew Linda, what happened, let's get together,' that would have been the easiest thing in the world to ignore. It's fucking unbelievable how often grieving people have to fend off the *curious*."

"I *was* curious," I protested, not wanting to leave Karen with illusions. "Not primarily curious, but I'd be misleading you –"

"Curiosity wasn't the reason. I could hear that in your voice. Three minutes that left me damn near tears. So much sadness. I get suspicious when someone opens up like that. I've been married twice." She cocked an eye. "I was prepared to erase you. But if after, what, twenty years, you felt so strongly about Linda–I couldn't ignore that."

Now I was the one to stand, to stretch my legs, to quell the agitation. "Why didn't she ever call me?" I said, ignoring the fact that she *had* called. "It's gratifying to know I wasn't forgotten. I don't know why I should care, but I do. If I meant that much to her, or if that evening did, it would have been the easiest thing in the world for her to find me. At some point over twenty-six years. I found *you*."

Karen stared at me and said nothing.

"I can understand why she left. I was never going to be as important to Linda as your sister's death. I never expected to be, or wanted to be. And how could I blame her for deciding to move in with you? Your folks were traumatized. They weren't going to be able to provide any support. A change was actually the very thing Linda needed. And she was twenty-three. How could I second-guess her jumping into a car and driving to California? At that age I jumped into a plane and flew to Ecuador. We're all permitted our flights of fancy. So I understand all that. I understood it at the time. I didn't like it, but I understood it. What I *can't* understand is why she stayed hidden."

"Why didn't you contact *her?*"

"It wasn't my place."

Karen looked at the table, mumbling a laugh at the hopelessness of me. But surely I was on solid ground. Sheryl had just been killed—of course I would have deferred to Linda's wishes. And by the time it became apparent that I would not be hearing from Linda, not in any meaningful way, what was there to do but push her from my mind? After that came the resort, marriage, one year upon another, the unconstrained momentum life deploys against the preservation of human bonds, of simple friendship.

"So," I said. "It's as straightforward as that? I suppose it is. We just *didn't*."

Karen looked at me again, deliberating. "Linda told me once about a dream she had. She dreamed you had been killed."

"Linda dreamed I had been killed," I repeated slowly.

"This was a few years before she wrote the book. I didn't really recall who you were, since I hadn't heard much about you after those first few weeks when she arrived. But she told me she had this friend back in Duluth, Tom Johnson, and she dreamt he had been killed. She was pretty shaken. I told her it was entirely natural–I'd been having similar dreams myself. Friends of ours had, also. It was that fall when death was on the whole country's mind."

"She dreamt I'd been in the towers?"

"She never said that. Just that you had been killed. I told her she should just call you up. Obviously you never connected."

"Never," I said. "I mean, I'd been long gone from Duluth by then. So had my parents. There weren't any of us left in town. I was up here at Dead Wolf Lake. She could have called the law firm–someone there probably would have remembered."

"She did do that. I remember her telling me she called for one or two friends she had worked with. But by then it had been, what, a dozen years since Linda had left? No one she had been close with worked there anymore. And she told me you weren't the sort of person to hang around Duluth, which as it turns out, you weren't."

"Well, no. But Dead Wolf Lake is pretty much the polar opposite of Lower Manhattan." I said this desperately, as though a chance were slipping away, though I was fully aware that Linda had been dead four years.

"But I remember her saying that New York was where you had probably been. She never said you were still at daddy's practice in Duluth. Linda was convinced you had gone back to law school and were working for a big firm out East."

"That's just–reckless," I protested. And with the smallest charge of panic–with bitterness, even–I recalled, of all the Lindas, the Linda of the color wheel, the Linda who was respectful of astrology.

"You know," Karen said, standing up for the family name, "Linda's dream *could* have been true. It wasn't *unreasonable. I* remember looking it up. There were three Tom Johnsons who died that day."

I knew that. Everyone had scanned the lists, if only to find their own surnames. "Didn't you remind Linda how common a name it is? Even outside of Minnesota?"

"I don't remember ever talking with her about it. Maybe she never knew. But if I took the trouble to see if you were on the list, she must have."

"You never asked her?"

"No."

"You never said, 'Linda–'"

"It wasn't my concern. It wasn't that important. It only seems important now. Who knows what was going on inside Linda's head? I mean, we can't ask her now, alright? A few years later she began working up *The Broken Key,* and that was when she started talking more about who you were. Who you had been. I mean, do you want me to apologize for Linda? Or for myself?"

I didn't want any apology at all, obviously. But oh, the lost–the lost opportunities, I was about to say, before realizing more acutely than at any other moment of my life the utter inadequacy of language. Because Linda had believed me dead and I had believed her alive. Alive while I was paddling to my parents' old cabin, alive while I was giving away an evening at my school reunion. The one thing that prodded me to seek out Linda, her book, had been in the world seven years before she died. I had never seen it. I had never known her devotion to that evening among the angels, and to whatever contribution I had made to that memory. I had never known she was dying. Something so unremarkable as happening upon Linda's book—not now, but earlier—would have had such consequences. I had spoken with Linda so many times over the past few years; had spoken to her, it was now apparent, after she had departed the world: after she—Linda, the husky laugh, the glorious mouth, the colors and jewelry and Baby Key—no longer existed. I felt at that moment—again, the inadequacy of language—I felt the thin line between being part of this world and not. The dead are with us. I felt a sensation I hadn't felt since that bitter cold December morning when Linda learned of her sister's death: when a soul passes from this world to whatever is beyond, it is not an airtight passage. Something of the eternal leaks into our world. I began to feel an enormous sympathy for Karen—began to feel that comforting her was reason enough to exist, the only adequate response to helplessness.

"Did Linda ever marry?" I asked.

Karen looked at me steadily, studying my face. "No," she finally said, and then, as if to bring an unspoken conversation to its end, gave a slight toss to her head. "And anyway, wouldn't marriage require something like passion? In some ways Linda was too childlike for passion. She was too happy for passion." Which sounded like something an older sister—an older sister like Karen, at any rate—might say.

"Linda had a good life, you understand," Karen said. Rising, she must have known that was all I had really wanted to hear. One true fact outlined against the mystery. It is enough, I have sometimes believed—I believed it that moment—to simply acknowledge the mystery, acknowledgement being its own form of honor.

When Karen had left, when Dead Wolf Lake once again became mine and Bobbi's, I took Bobbi's hand and we walked down to the lakeshore. The clouds, striking in their red and violet, bubbled down. A band of thin blue cushioned the horizon, and these two colors—red near the shore, blue in the distance—were mirrored in the lake's surface. The trees were black in silhouette. It was as remarkable an evening as we had seen in our shared lifetime. All of this, calmed by the amniotic consolation of still water, amounted to a heavy persuasion toward immutability; more, toward comprehension. The skyfull of angels could be approached, their radiant eyes and ours wed in understanding. At dock's end I held Bobbi's hand, drawn to—worshipful of, really—the great untruth.